The Intelligence Man

Barry Swan

Valley Press

First published in 1999
by Valley Press
236 Tokyngton Ave, Wembley,
Middlesex HA9 6HJ

Typeset in Horley Old Style by LaserScript Ltd,
Mitcham, Surrey
Cover design by Linda Blakemore
Printed and bound in Ireland by Colour Books Ltd, Dublin

ISBN 0 9530768 2 2

TO THE FOLK OF JAMAN
especially one or two

contents

chapter
one

As the decrepit Air Economy Three Four descended over the lush tropical landscape, the tree tops rushing up like the waves of some green ocean, Gerry felt a painful tightness in his stomach. He had, when the plane occasionally ceased its bumping, groaning and creaking, been tasting freedom up in those blue, wide spaces. The paradisial calm of the deep dark air suggested to his consciousness an eternal, blissful forgetfulness, like a prayer or the after-effect of some exotic drug. The anarchic clouds floating like happy, dimly perceived thoughts and the pleasant sensation of quiet movement were a sort of gratuitous haven from his personal problems and indeed his hateful, cynical profession. But ... here was reality again ... racing up to meet him at a speed of approximately two hundred miles per hour. One hand went to his brow, the other hastily to his pocket for his cigarettes ....

Darn, there was the no-smoking sign, just when he needed a smoke most.

Morbid thoughts. A cold sweat on the palms and forehead, a temporary blockage in the throat. He bent down, put his head between his knees and lit up a cigarette anyway.

He had always felt he suffered a cruel punishment from the gods, condemned to that occupation which appeared banal to most people (he was 'officially' a teacher and specialist in economic statistics), but which had its own moral perplexities, its secret bodily dangers that were not obvious to ordinary

1

people. For this, like the other apparently harmless occupations of some unusual people, was not what it appeared to be.

His heavy grey suit, his carefully combed hairstyle, the pen in his top pocket, all gave the picture of a mid-stream executive, or else a certain sort of low grade academic. It would have taken an immense leap of the imagination for anyone to believe that here was a dedicated officer of the world's most efficient intelligence corps, about to land on a potential hotspot in a suit entirely inappropriate to the climate.

A few hours before Gerry had glanced at the female, blonde passenger seated beside him. He should, by then, have learnt her name at least. Intelligence officers were expected to take an interest in everything, and everyone, around them. But ... he wasn't really much good when it came to people, especially when it came to analyzing their characters. It seemed his mind always worked in broad, abstract sweeps. Many times in the past he would cover up this lack of attention to detail by concocting fictional events and false names for people, even non-existent people, in the reports he sent in to CIA headquarters in Langley, Virginia. He reckoned it didn't made much difference to the use or value of these dossiers to the authorities anyway.

He also calculated that his strategic 'mistakes' got him out of more trouble than they ever got him into, despite some painful embarrassments. But that was all water under the bridge, in any case!

Ineptitude, cowardice, laziness, a spiritual lethargy that somehow worsened the more demanding the job he was given to do. That was him. He felt now he was caught between the devil and the deep blue sea, and literally, as he looked out of the window down to the dizzying, sickening watery mass below.

He had once quipped to 'the boss' (they had another name for him) on being sent on yet another distant assignment (were they hoping his plane would crash, sooner or later?), that he didn't suffer from a fear of flying, just a fear of landing too hard! The boss of course hadn't laughed. Neither perhaps would the lady beside him, should he dare repeat the quip, for she hadn't shown any interest in him during the flight, or any wish for the slightest conversation or even a 'hello'.

They were out over the South China Sea, heading irreversibly for Jaman, before he had attempted to break the ice.

The low steady hum of the engines had been giving him an unusually prolonged feeling of false security until he remembered what a fellow had told him about a reputed structural flaw in these particular planes (one of the disadvantages of being in his job was that you invariably got to know just a little bit too much about everything). Apparently, it was the way the three engines had been rather haphazardly balanced around the aircraft, one sitting precariously on the tail, leading to a centre of gravity fault (certain identifying facts here necessarily have to be altered to comply with the libel laws). He had studied this particular aged plane carefully from the departure lounge, watching it taxi in and he had a slight suspicion (he eventually put his unease down to imagination) that the tail engine was slightly loose. The particular problem of balance was overcome at take-off point in a surprisingly crude manoeuvre with a sudden frantic sounding acceleration, the aim of which was to counteract the centrifugal pressure. Then there was that awful cranking noise the engines made as height was thankfully gained, which the pilot always made a joke of and an apology for at each take-off stage of the journey. Landings at staging points along the route were equally noisy and unstable. Most people, of course, knew nothing about what really went on in supposedly safe modern airliners, much less this obviously aged and ill-maintained version. Once, in his Mexican days, he had spotted that the flight cabin was empty of human beings as they hurtled down on autopilot the descent to

Merida airport in the Yucatan. He had found the crew playing cards at the back of the plane. Now he had to fly Air Economy, in this suspect plane, for low profile, to what was a former British colony (the worst sort of place for a non-cricket obsessed American), this 'Paradise Isle' which was his latest destination.

Perhaps it was nerves which made him open the conversation in a surprisingly aggressive, yet peculiarly introspective way:

"People think," he said in a voice that was adamant, yet almost tearful, "that it's trouble with the wife that keeps me away from home. Our reputed cold relationship is a very good cover, in fact . . . ."

He stopped speaking. He realised that he was on the point of giving away the secret of his real occupation. He had noticed this devil-may-care attitude in himself lately. It was either an intuitive, super-sophisticated ploy, or else just his 'nerves' coming back. This was something he had begun to suspect was indeed happening.

"It is also . . . true . . . in a way," he found himself admitting, self-consciously.

He remembered their last farewell. Meanwhile the lady passenger was doing her very best not to show the slightest interest in his 'confessions', yawning and flicking over the pages of the magazine 'Hollywood Romance'.

"Oh, so you're off again, are you? Well, Gerald, don't try to pretend to me that it is all for some high ideal or altruistic motive. I am well aware of how you like to spend your evenings in seedy, hideaway bars."

She never called him Gerry. That was too . . . familiar. She was all 'dressed-up' as usual. How he hated her gaudy, bouffant hair style with those copper tints, her purple dress, her red shoes, her penetrating voice. She appeared to him as a harridan. Perhaps that was actually why he, a masochist, had married her. He loved to hate her. Her attempts to control his life were a joke.

"Some one around here has to make a living," he replied with a shrug of the shoulders.

"Living? What you bring in doesn't pay for the cat food. Everybody in Washington earns more than you do, even the garbage collectors. I never stop wondering what you really get up to when you are away. It's always a mystery to me why you have to take these assignments abroad in any case."

"I happen to know that you are delighted when I leave home. Anyway, I have important, secret missions to carry out which I cannot talk about."

She didn't cry, or laugh, or rant then, just gave out a sharp whistle which was midway between a sneer and a curse.

"You and your missions. I don't know where you ever got these so-called 'ideals'. Most people grow out of that infantile nonsense before they reach adulthood. To me it's just a cover for something else, probably something deeply unpleasant."

The plane flew on, the engines still sounding fairly quiet and with no sign of smoke anywhere. In her heart the lady passenger loathed this man, this whining spoilt male. One always meets them in late-night bars or on long airline flights, cribbing about the woman back home, ungrateful for their undeserved blessings.

"How I came to marry her is another story. It was an arranged marriage – would you believe it – in this day and age?"

"It's a wonder that she has stood beside you all these years, what with your chauvinistic attitudes."

"Well, as a matter of fact I have taken a course in Equal Opportunities. I took the *original* course! There aren't many left around from that. She is only too glad to see the back of me. She has them in for bridge parties all the time. Cigarette ash and spilt drinks all over the carpets. I can hear them now, laughing at the poor fool who pays all the bills. I blame her dad. He it was who got me into it. He was a big noise in The Firm. Not that she knew, or knows, anything about it. It's the story of my life . . . ."

"Tell me," asked the lady, completely unimpressed so far by what Gerry insisted on telling her, "did you ever once buy her a bunch of nice flowers or give her a passionate kiss or warm embrace as you came in the door?"

She looked at Gerry's craggy if unherculean features, seeing little potential for the faintest bit of romance in that peasant body and melancholic, some would say suppressed, countenance. His eyes had a perplexed, though soulful look; perhaps they were even dreamlike.

"That would be going beyond the call of duty," he said mysteriously and seriously.

"What kind of a relationship is that?"

She was somehow shocked, even if she didn't care.

"It's all because of her dad, General Baxter. Have you ever heard of him?," he said quietly.

She did not reply.

Simply to change the conversation the lady, who also was American, advanced the information that she was on a photography modelling assignment to the island; and her mention of photography made Gerry feel immediately uneasy. It was an involuntary reaction. Photographs had been the bane of his life and career. For one thing they never seemed to capture anything other than the dramatically maladroit, uneasy side of him; and they had also featured in a malign fashion at significant, crucial, and sensitive moments in his affairs. His wedding day had been the worst embarrassment of all, with his best friend Jim snapping away; especially as he was intelligence gathering at the time and his new wife was not even present. Then there was that final, apocalyptic incident in Taran with a camera that had changed all their lives. To him the subject was summed up in one word:

... *danger.*

The sea below was blue or perhaps a shade of marine green, shining and very, very close.

"Photography, eh?," he had gulped as though she had said something subversive or ominous.

"Not a bad career really, I suppose, even if my heart is more in acting," said the lady, opening up a little now;

"as long as one keeps the figure in shape and knows how to maintain just that right pose, at all times, you can get many lucrative offers. Once I was modelling avante garde in a country down in South America whose name I can't remember, but it was near Brazil. The dictator La Mancha was very pleased with me; you could see from the way he grinned behind those big dark glasses and clapped and shouted at my performances. I have big plans for the cinema. I am having a screen test when I get back to LA for a big movie. With Antonio Umbria. Have you heard of him?"

"Is that the one they call The Godfather?"

"Yes. He made 'The Godmother'. 2 and 3 were made by his brothers, or some of his cousins, I can't remember. Great movies."

"I'm impressed. I haven't met many film stars. Do you think you'll get a part? From all appearances you've got what it . . . takes . . . ."

"I'm not dependent on all that, really. I've got other interests. At the moment we're doing a . . . lovely tourist brochure out here for the government. Palm trees swaying in the breeze, blue, sunny mountains, white sandy beaches, all that. I also make a hobby of collecting tropical seashells and other things. I have a big trunk in baggage that is completely empty. I will take all my new specimens and anything else I pick up back in that."

She put down her magazine and for the first time actually looked at Gerry.

The man still irritated her. She thought he was boring, with his intense, nervous talk . . . Weird really. She'd have to find a way to stop this conversation; there was still a long flight ahead of them.

He, for his part, looked at her closely, her flashy, blonde hair, the streak of light that shot from her bright blue eyes. Suddenly he realised he was about to fall into a trap that had seen the downfall of many a lesser agent and, more ominously, represented a grievous strategic failing, for which long ago he had received, from his masters, intense de-sensitisation to resist. He caught himself in the nick of time, just as he was starting to think '*isn't she a beautiful woman . . . ?*'

"Hell. I must be starting to lose my touch; this would never have happened before. Blackmail ... the lure of Venus ... perhaps it is possible I could be a victim after all? And what an ignominious ending that would be after all the adventures I've been through!"

40 year-old Gerry McArthur was just thinking these thoughts silently to himself.

His mind slowly drifted back to those rigorous training sessions. Then, one had lived from one moment to the next, second to second. He had even started to tell her about it when the voice of his lady companion came angrily into his day-dreaming consciousness:

"D'ya mind if I coincintrate on moi magzeen naw? It's impoitant that I read up on moi woik," she had uttered in a New York accent and if Gerry hadn't been so preoccupied with remembering his younger days he might have noticed how she had either slipped unconsciously back into her native accent or, alternatively, was putting on this funny accent in an exaggerated way as some kind of ruse.

Or perhaps Gerry did notice.

He continued to reflect, dimly. Lately, in-service training had become more sophisticated; recent marathons had aimed at removing all sexual, social, racial and religious prejudices in officers and even in the hearts and minds of lowly agents in the field. These modern courses, too, had been thorough, even ruthless and successful in their own fashion (despite wisecracks by those impervious to any idea of progress that the only 'brainwashing' involved was the opportunity to get out of the mind-numbing, boring humdrum of the office for a while). His attitude to the remote countries and native peoples he invariably visited in his role as 'Mr Fix-it' had greatly altered from his early days, especially since his stint in murderous, war-torn Taran. But even these contemporary 'indoctrination workshops' had been nothing compared to the training courses that had prevailed in the 60's ... those secretive, dark, perhaps illegal proselytizing sessions that no one 'in authority' knew anything about.

"Of course not," he replied absent-mindedly; "I was thinking about how much I have changed as a person. In my twenties I knew it all! Now I go on a seminar and, bam, I'm a new person. I know that's why they keep me in this job. They think that I'm malleable. They like somebody they think they can manipulate. I go along with the game."

She was deep into her reading and wasn't listening.

"What ... I've been thinking aloud!," he suddenly thought to himself; "just nerves, not carelessness, I hope."

He wiped the perspiration off his brow. He found himself reflecting on the pioneering, specialised training in anti-seduction techniques he had received. They had learnt at last from the mistakes of the British; the airwaves were being used insidiously at that time, unknown even to responsible media folk, to spread subversion by means of pop music and other such trivia; even top American agents were heard humming these tunes. It had been essential to produce a new incorruptible agent (not just a Superman, a Superperson, he told himself now). The effects of this original course had stayed with him all his life, never once being tempted by all the seductive vices that came his way. (Except whiskey, the cynic might say, but his drinking he considered to be only a bulwark against other, worse temptation).

As the plane did a pulse jerking turn his mind went further back, as if reviewing his life history. He was a different man when they had first signed him up. It had all seemed to be an accident. Everything at that time seemed to happen by accident.

Including how he got to be in Taran. □

chapter
two

It was 1964 and he was cursed with brains. That was his big problem. If he could only have gone into some boring clerical job, or any sort of safe office work, he would have had a far happier life. In any case his top academic grades allied to certain inducements (mainly the freedom to lie in bed every morning and pass exams with the minimum of effort), forced him to prolong his time at college, pursuing as many courses as were available and dawdling in, amongst other things, various new Socio-Dynamic Theories of Society.

Of course the most important reason why he had opted for staying as long as he could in the Ivy League was because, as *they* saw it, the mental development of intellectual college youth came before any physical expenditure on the fields of Taran, one of those strange, paradoxical values of the times (one would have expected that intellectual upstarts should have been the first to be put in the firing line); but there were plenty of less well-developed minds to take their place.

There was just one curse word going the rounds at that time. The Draft.

So he was safe. For a while.

Later on, with imminent graduation on the horizon, a big question came to bother him: what would happen when he finished his studies? A new factor, urgency, had come into the equation and then he started to use his brains, perhaps for the first time in his life. He discovered a loophole in the regulations that many other draft dodgers had failed to notice, but which was pointed out to him one evening in a desperate conversation in the college library with a like-minded, fellow-student who had been doing a bit of research on the military, especially ways to stay out of it. It was permitted for *volunteers* to choose their own branch of the forces. The logical step then was to select one that was least likely to send people plodding stupidly over minefields in the hot, swampy bush; one that would use its inherent common sense (and brains) to keep out of trouble. One that probably would not even go near the front line in Taran, operating, as always, from a safe distance. There was the answer standing before him as clear as daylight, or so he thought. INTELLIGENCE.

So he walked in along with a right collection of oddballs.

Meanwhile the war dragged on.

How he had initially enjoyed those laid-back lectures on espionage, counter-espionage, clandestine operations, textbook drilling (these were explanations of amazing theories on square-bashing, but they never actually had to practice any of it), methods of Military Intelligence Operations with ancillary courses on the 'Company' at Home And Abroad, advanced eavesdropping gadgetry, dirty tricks, personal survival tactics and some peculiar anti-interrogation techniques (very useful later). All this was very fine as long as it was just theory; the lectures on different marching drills, for instance, illustrated on the blackboard with chalk squiggles and geometrical lines were particularly stimulating. The first moment of anxiety came with their 'practicals'. One day an M16 rifle was officiously handed to him, an unwilling recipient (it was later to become his favourite bigger gun, it being the lightest of its type), loaded with live rounds. Much mockery ensued when he asked the Nazi-admiring, sadistic Sergeant Kruger if he would ever be expected to have to use it. Sergeant Kruger was their chief instructor in these practicals, and he was responsible for bringing forth in Gerry his very first awareness of a moral (even physical) weakness that made him question, deeply, his own suitability for any serious military work. It was called by some 'lacking in moral fibre' and in later years he asked himself whether his life, spent as it was 'on the dangerous edge of things' pursued by the malign enemies of mankind and attacked by a multiple of aggressive, destructive forces bent on destroying human civilization, as well as given hell by the lady who claimed to be his wife, was essentially his attempt to face up to this aspect of his character.

He had imagined Military Intelligence to be simply about maps of enemy positions, plans laid out on tables showing strategic movements, surveillance by means of high-flying aircraft and even satellites, chess-like war games, invasion strategy, etc. None of this *bloody* business.

"When the Lieutenant Colonel walks in that door, shoot him," Kruger had barked at McArthur, awakening him from a distant reverie.

"Should I really?," asked Gerry in some confusion, to the amusement of the others.

"Shoot the bastard, or else."

It was a question of his fear of Kruger's reprisals over a multitude of other fears, even that of not knowing what he was really meant to do. There had been no lesson or lecture about this, as far as he could remember anyway.

The door opened and weakly he fired at Lieut. Col. O'Hagan as the latter stumbled drunkenly into the room. Gerry was surprised at the bloody mess his seemingly 'lightweight' weapon had made of the officer. It was an incident he quickly put out of his mind for most of the rest of his life.

The next day they were being forced to practice on warm, living if camouflaged targets with rifle blades, K-bar knives and even primitive bamboo spears. When there ensued a period of temporary adolescent angst along with extreme nervous tension, an unwillingness to face people and especially one's immediate acquaintances or colleagues and unconscious confusion over psycho-sexual matters (emotional immunity programs had just commenced) he sometimes thought that anything might be better, even bleeding painfully to death on a battlefield, than remaining where he was. Later on, amazingly, he would look back on those days with some nostalgia.

And still the war dragged on.

To his dismay he found that his presumed colleagues in avoidance but now infinitely more adept, enthusiastic military connoisseurs were all pushing for HRE (high risk and exposure) assignments behind enemy lines in that far-off tropical land, so he took himself pale, trembling and empty inside from that stubbornly clinging, enervating feeling of inadequacy, to his commanding officer to request a transfer. He remembered, now, how he had stood there, a raw faced, freckled, red haired youth, looking distinctly unsoldierly. One would have said that it was a brilliant job of acting if he had set out with the deliberate intention to convince his superiors of his unsuitability. Indeed, he thought later, he was not even sure himself at the time how much he was exaggerating an undoubted 'indisposure' in order simply that he might be extricated from an unsatisfactory situation.

It was then that he first spoke about his personal problems, insisting that he felt he no longer made the grade.

"And where would you like to go, young man?," Col. Baxter had asked kindly.

"Anywhere."

This interview did not have the expected result. But, to console himself later, he worked out that the odds of at least mental survival would be better even in the unluckiest infantry unit than where he had previously been.

At least this was what he told himself.

A week later he found himself with the 'Lucky Seventh' landing noisily in an Air Force Globemaster at Wan-Go airport, Taran, June 1966. He felt he had somehow scored one over fate. Loaded down with M16, heavy jungle boots and survival pack (not consisting of favourite, familiar, technical gimmickry but crude digging gear and basic toiletries) he stepped out of the plane and stared for the first time at a foreign country. They had not told him that it would be very hot there. He had an instantaneous experience, not completely unpleasant, which he was to have again at regular intervals in his life, a feeling of total lethargy and disinterest. It was as if he realised, then, that no matter where he was, or what he was supposed to be doing, he would *never* be where he *really* should be or doing what he *should* be doing. He sensed that he would be at home nowhere in the world, and certainly not in the stifling air of a faraway land of palm trees and humble huts baking under a hot, steaming sky where the foreign humans seemed distant, incomprehensibly dressed and barely decipherable in the glare of the eye-cutting sun. And yet it was to be his fate, many times, to frequent these tropical lands on different occasions.

Only the bad language now of his fellow soldiers (to his sensitive ears a constant bugbear for the duration of that war) made his arrival appear to have some grounding in reality, if only that of familiar, unpleasant embarrassment.

A few weeks later when plodding on patrol – he was given the most exposed position, point duty – in the mangrove swamps near Can-Do in order to make known to the locals the security of the American presence in that area, he realised that the accident of his being there was part of a much larger accident. It came to him as he reflected on a letter which he had received that same week from his father in Boston.

"Dear son," he read, and after all the initial 'morale boosting' advice and assertions of paternal pride he came to the part that now entrapped his mind:

15

". . . and my old friend Col. Baxter too. We all thought a little groundwork with the men of the infantry, the salt of the earth, would stand you in good stead. I have no doubt that you will go on to greater things . . . overcome scruples . . . with the best of us . . . highest recommendations."

He now remembered all that talk as he was growing up about Wild Bill Donovan, the OSS, the Italian Mafia and his dad, as the claymore mine was set off by the foot of a man twenty steps behind sending them all to the earth in a cloud of shouts and swirling matter; later the only survivor, Gerry, was quite astonished to discover that the platoon had suffered a 95% casualty rate, if you worked it out mathematically.

"Your poor wife," she had muttered as the plane taxied across the tarmac and he had lit another French cigarette even before the No-Smoking sign had gone out; he took in the heavy, scented smoke in a sharp ecstasy of relief. The plane came to a standstill at the main building at Kingstown Airport, a glaringly white modern prefabricated structure of plastic and glass that probably belonged to at least the twenty-ninth century and seethed with swarms of locals hanging from roofs, windows, shouting and waving wildly at all the comings and goings. Gerry, perhaps to allay the monotony, always imagined airports as having the charisma of intergalactic staging posts, landing pads from, or launching pads to, much better or worse worlds, avenues to the possibility of exotic life, or perhaps slow, mental death.

"Yes, I agree, she has never had a fair deal. We have not been together for any longer than a three day stretch since we got married. And that was a long time ago, relatively speaking. I'm always getting sent overseas."

"Very convenient," said the lady.

Now that they were on the verge of parting both felt an obligation to separate on the best possible terms. He was talking too much, but did it really matter? There was something about her that attracted him; there was something deep in her eyes.

Also, although he couldn't put his finger on it, he found something odd about her.

She would soon be gone out of his life, in any case.

"What do you do, what brings you here?," she asked him.

"I'm an academic and government advisor. I've been sent . . . invited here to give some hints on how they might improve their economy and raise their standard of living. You know, make sure they learn how to regulate their financial affairs and uphold the democratic way of life. I expect I'll be here for a few years."

"How very interesting. They must be very glad you're coming, as it's a very economically underdeveloped country."

"I am a representative of that generation that was brought up on political idealism, intent only on doing good in the world. The agency I work for has no ulterior motives as regards military conquest, political ambitions, religious imperialism, dirty tricks or espionage," he said slowly and adamantly.

"That is so admirable. How different it is from the old days when we were always invading countries or poking our noses uninvited into other peoples' affairs, always for our own selfish motives. You know, you should write a long letter, a serious letter, to your wife and explain properly to her why you have come out here."

He felt that he had, somehow, made an impression on her.

"I will write her a long letter one day," he said in a world-weary voice.

He had already unfastened his seat belt and was getting his hand luggage from the overhead rack (he had already taken the precaution of checking that his gun, hidden in his inside pocket with all his pens, was still there) when he remembered he had not found out her name. He noticed that her accent had changed again, becoming somewhat more educated as they spoke; there was definitely something odd here and he was not hopeful of getting the truth from her.

"Are you from New York? I'd like to know your name in case one day you are the world's most famous film star and then I can say that I once met you."

As Josephine Jones, as she had previously been known to her old friends, prepared her face in her compact mirror to meet the rigours of a tropical climate she looked at Gerry again, for only the second time since the commencement of the flight, and suddenly she felt a slight inner sympathy for him. She thought he looked 'weather-beaten', even haggard. She felt that in a different situation she might even have bought him a cup of coffee.

"My professional name is Jean Blue. 'Bye now, have a nice time here. And be careful"

"Jean Blue," Gerry muttered to himself. □

chapter
three

The formulation of this mission was an odd affair. He tried now, as he stood in the baggage queue, to put sense into his life. At first it seemed to have simply come off the top of Dick Warner's head (his immediate superior), in response to a speech the new president of the United States of America had just made during his inauguration in front of the Capitol building, downtown Washington DC.

The president was dressed simply in jeans and T-shirt, breaking with tradition.

"I want none of the trumpery of dressing up of past times," he had said grandly, to which someone had whispered: "Well, I have heard rumours that in the old days he used to put on an evening suit and top hat and slink out to formal dinner parties in the dead of night."

'Fellow Americans, I am humble, keen to serve, etc. A new and better era has at last dawned in the world. Forget everything that I have ever said before. We, and our fellow citizens of what I now term The New First World, the Russians and Chinese, see it as our mutual duty to maintain order in what is, unfortunately, still an anarchic universe. There have only ever been two great systems in the world, our one and the other one. Once they were known as the Capitalist system and the Communist system. Before that it was the Christian system and the Infidel system. Originally it was the Roman system and the Barbarian system. And I do not stop at the boundaries of our present earth either. Let there be, in the whole universe, no more bloodshed, hatred or confusion over national-identity. Don't we all belong, now, brothers and sisters, to the *one great system*, the American, Russian and Chinese Conglomerate, and these three are Now Forever One! And remember, the only religion allowed is to be that of Peace and Friendship, into Infinity . . .!"

He had to pause to take his breath, for he had become carried away by his own enthusiasm. He had departed from tradition and written his own speech at the last minute.

"So what?," replied one of his party men in response to a query from a member of the public, standing in the crowd, concerning the new president's sanity; "when has enthusiasm *ever* been bad in global politics?"

Before the concerned citizen could reply the public address system boomed out again.

"Where now we still rely on those big, evil bombs and the technology of Armageddon to enforce our political ideals, let us instead, encourage peace by sending up colourful, more-massively-built-than-ever-before, peaceful balloons to carry, utilising the free energy of the upper atmosphere and at absolutely no financial cost to the taxpayer, the people of the world, the poor, hungry, the simple as well as the proud, the wealthy and clever, to wherever their hearts will take them. Where now our best scientific brains are set on developing such things as nasty death-rays, directing them from outer space at the innocent as well as the guilty, let them be encouraged to develop instead a more reliable, better breed of mule and ass to carry on the eternal, workaday tasks of ordinary mankind. It is indeed my objective to take away all the harmful weapons of destruction in the world and replace them with the tools of construction. Look at all that dangerous technology that's about, those lethal, technological Frankenstein Monsters which, despite harmless sounding brand names such as Theme Parks,

Virtual Reality Games, Personal Computers, are taking up so much of the attention of humanity and off the subject of solid hard work. Even children can now manipulate the most advanced computers! Not to mention pre-pubescents hacking into our sensitive national security. It is no wonder the world is going to pot and forgetting the roots of civilisation, such as how to talk to one another in front of an open fireplace hearth in the evenings. We must, indeed, restore the world to its *original state of innocence*".

"This was not in the speech I wrote for him," complained the chief presidential scriptwriter.

"The great thinkers now agree that everything that was believed in the past was really true," went on the president; "every belief is valid. There is no need for war anymore. Religion has always been the same as Atheism; Anarchy is the same as Conservatism, Protest the same as Apathy, Liberalism the same as Totalitarianism. Pity our forebears who wasted so much energy over their imagined differences! Today nobody should differ in thinking from those on the other side of the street, in the next country, or indeed on the other side of the universe (for there may be aliens out there, and I would like to be the first president to talk to them and convert them to the truth). Today, if there is to be conflict, it should be conflict between *similarities*, like in a football game between two equally matched teams. That is progress. Silly local conflicts, ever-lasting, petty boundary disputes, all that nonsense will be no more. After all, what is the *real* difference between us and the Canadians? Their objection to incorporation in a Greater North American family shows their immaturity, even childishness; so we will have to treat them as children from now on, if only for their own good. A document to the effect that time-wasting opposition is outlawed will be proposed by me soon, and hopefully will be passed by Congress. I am sorry I was not able to tell you this good news before polling day, but I thought that there are always some who see bad news where there is only good.

Note our new flag! The Red Star of the East, joined to our own Stars and Stripes, side by side, happy together at last! We live on Planet Home now, Spaceship Earth! The soil, air, water, the plants, the little creatures, these are our allies! We will soon see to the natural redundancy of all that is evil, for all time, for evil by its very nature is unnatural. Our grandchildren will inherit a perfect earth. I was saying only the other day to Comrade Alexandri ... why, isn't that a lovely fur coat ...".

Dick Warner had jumped in the air and banged his desk in CIA HQ at Langley with his fist at this point in the Inauguration (which continued for many more hours, with the president clearly enjoying himself immensely and apparently unable to stop talking).

"This is what we have been waiting for, for a long time! It's the best thing that has happened since the American Revolution. We must play our part here in the CIA and make sure that nothing stands in the way of our great new American President's plans."

Dick was detested by everyone in the office. There were various theories on how he had got his job as Deputy Director. Some said it was due solely to the paucity of his qualifications, for no boss likes someone second in charge who is better qualified than himself. On how he had kept it with each change of president there was another theory.

"Here we go again," Jack Beam, Operations Manager, snidely whispered to Gerry who, as the intellectual teaboy was up in the office giving a report on the brainwashing efficacy of certain economics courses run by the suspect Harvard School;

"with every new president Dick is immediately into devising ways to blackmail and manipulate him by holding him to the implications of his own policies, something which no president ever even remotely understands. The first president who cops on to Dick and announces that he really will carry out his policies will be the first to break Warner's grip on the Security Services."

Snaky Wallace, Chief Dirty Tricks Director, spoke next.

"Now we will have to put up with weeks of speeches from Warner extolling President Hooligan and the brilliant policies of this New Experimental Party (NEP) of his, just as we did when that crafty old Demagogue Party ex-President Rodrigues gave Dick the inspiration to send us all off on 'Self-Consciousness' courses, raising our consciousness with Peace Studies, Alternative Living, Holistic Values, Contemporary Moral Issues, Anti-Stereotyping and what-not, making some of us more sensitive to sexual harassment in the workplace than to foreign military subversion. Why, I could hardly walk down the street for weeks afterwards without passing someone of a different sex, colour or religion and thinking: here, too, is a fellow-human being, worthy of equal consideration and respect . . .".

Their minds now all turned to wondering what courses they would be sent on next.

Gerry listened quietly. He normally did not let his personal opinions or feelings become public knowledge, having learnt the danger of doing so all those years ago in his first encounter with the Intelligence Services. In any case his usually sensibly thought out academic views were not welcome with these people at the top of the security apparatus. But he felt obliged to make a comment here, as Evaluation Of Retraining courses was part of his brief, and he might be expected to show at least some enthusiasm for the prospect of new courses under Dick's ever-imaginative leadership.

There was danger too in silence, as he had learnt once when the suggestion was made of spiking with a T.I.D. (Truth Inducing Drug, a mild type of LSD which lowers the inhibition barrier just enough to make the person speak the truth without he/she being aware of any abnormality) the cocktails of some delegates at an important conference, and it went ahead against his private misgivings. When the American ambassador began blabbing his head off there were many repercussions and Gerry, as the fall guy, had told the Inquiry that he had indeed foreseen how the drug would affect people but had assumed that the truth could harm nobody. He received as his punishment soon afterwards, a posting to Switzerland to study the changing consumer habits of the populace there in relation to chocolate, an assignment deliberately chosen he believed in full knowledge of his dislike of heights as well as his peculiar antipathy to living in advanced, highly cultured societies. And whereas he could converse in many Asian, African and South American minority ethnic languages (the CIA had cultivated these tribal groups in the sixties to counteract left wing infiltration) he was pretty rusty on all major European languages.

"I can't think exactly what we will be expected to study, or re-learn now," said Gerry in a detached voice;

"but if Hooligan's policies are what he says they are then we are going to hear a lot more about the advantages of the Russian and Eastern ways of life and the benefits of sharing all our spiritual or holistic values with Moscow, Beijing and the East generally. I can see our top people going over for long stays in the wastes of Siberia, the Gobi, Tibet, places like that, while their crowd will take to sporting themselves in nice holiday spots like Rio, Monte Carlo, Las Vegas and so on, learning from the idle fraternity no doubt the details of some new, future ideological Rich Socialist Puritanism. At the same time, while some of us will be on workshops explaining the new political and technical co-operation to our allies in remote dachas in the coniferous forest and yurts on the Inner Mongolian plain, others of us will be busy debriefing all our agents around the world. Those agents who are working for us will be retrained to work for their old adversaries, while *their* officers and agents here will have to be reoriented to work for us. In the case of all double agents the matter will be even more complicated but I can already see ways around that. There will be plenty of 'identity crises' in this new world-set up which will prove tricky. Much of our people's energy and initiative will have to be directed at new targets. I foresee a great opening up of opportunities on other fronts, particularly the monitoring of development and technical projects in exciting Developing countries ...".

"Ugh," was the most common reaction to this.

"Do you mean to say that we will be no different from egg-headed, idealistic college graduates working for UNESCO agencies or even ... the Peace Corps?," demanded Spooks Schultz, Espionage Director for the Central American theatre.

Spooks had a particularly contempt for any idea of 'progress' or the 'good of humanity'. He was a firm believer in Evil and the Perversity of the Other Side. His agents had a reputation for always finding what they were looking for. As Cultural Liaison Officer of the Agency, Gerry had always found Spooks's department the easiest to deal with. Knowing the director's attitude to Latin America and its countries generally, he usually was able to prepare beforehand full reports and intelligence data which he himself was still waiting to receive. It was short-cuts such as these he had learnt over the years that left him with plenty of spare time, of course, for his private hobbies, such as meditating on the eternal perplexities of existence, whilst boozing.

"Well," said Gerry, "let's put it this way. Our former rather morbid preoccupation with Atomic bombs, chemical weapons and other ways of killing people; our obsession with power games and schemes to wrongfoot equally powerful adversaries may soon be a thing of the past like Religious wars, Inquisitions, Torture On The Rack or the Burning of Witches At the Stake. The way I see it now we will all be playing a far more sophisticated game in the future, a battle for the control of people's minds and souls, their conversion to Peace and Friendship. This will be far more demanding of our skills and courage. I can foresee a far higher death rate in the theatres of operation than we have ever suffered to date. More wars have been caused by the concepts of Peace and Friendship than War and Hate, I believe."

"I don't know if I like what I am hearing," said Spooks suspiciously; "I certainly don't understand it. Do you mean we are to be pacifists or something?"

"We are what the government tells us we are," butted in Dick suddenly, for he had come in and overheard the conversation at this point; "it is our patriotic duty to obey and carry out orders, not give them."

"Yes, sir," they all replied in unison.

"McArthur, can I see you for a moment? I need some advice about something," Warner asked in his most tense, officious voice; the changeover of a White House administration was always an anxious time for him.

Gerry was wary. He knew that, as an egg-head, he was the one who could never be fully trusted when illegal plans were afoot. Dick, for his part, never knew what went on in Gerry's mind when policy was being discussed. Gerry was the dark horse as far as Dick was concerned, someone to be put safely far away when sensitive decisions had to be made. McArthur had always been an unpopular, even despised member of staff; surprisingly for one supposed to be so important in the scheme of things; in fact it was more than unpopularity and contempt. He had become the bogey man, a scapegoat for all that had gone wrong with policy over the last twenty years (much of which came down to the decline of Pure Capitalism and Religious Orthodoxy in the West and their simultaneous rise in the East). Ever since the photograph incident in Taran, in fact, it seemed that McArthur had been present at every ensuing catastrophe. His continued employment at the Agency (The 'Firm', in the parlance), and immunity from 'elimination', was laid at the door of unknown political forces. He was always being given the strangest of tasks by Dick; to most it seemed that these assignments were constructed in a manner that exposed him to the minimum overt, but maximum covert, danger, not to mention the highest degree of boredom, the greatest potential killer in any operation. All of these assignments seemed to be informed by no particular logic, as though in fact they did come from the top of Dick's head. Still, they seemed to have at least some deeper philosophical significance, especially when they terminated in their usual way, guaranteed failure, imperceptible dissolution of the customary Working Party and apparent further retreat of Western dogma. However Gerry was usually happy to see things end this way, as it always gave him increased time to continue his lifelong task of trying to get through Marx's Das Capital, or relax in various out-of-the-way bars.

Dick's office was something else. The deputy director occupied in fact the official residence of the Director of Intelligence himself, the latter rarely being seen about the place. Gerry followed Warner down a long corridor, nodding knowingly to passing worried-looking fellow 'minions' and going through glass-like filaments of what looked like an oversized computer Visual Display Unit (VDU). It was in fact an experimental MSCA, Mutual Security Clearance Area, paid for out of certain nonaccountable CIA funds; Warner had a penchant for high spending (seldom officially approved) on the latest, technical wizardry.

Mutual Security Clearance: ever since it became known that the eastern powers had made a breakthrough in their ESP (extra sensory perception) experiments and were believed capable of breaking into the discussions and actual thoughts of top officialdom in the US, it had become imperative to introduce 'thought scramblers', 'brain synthesizers' and 'conversational dummies' into High Security Areas. Mutual Security meant that it was important not to be thinking about what the other fellow had on his mind.

"I reckon you want to talk to me about early retirement, or perhaps a long-overdue holiday?," said Gerry with a wink, showing that he too had mastered the art of conversational dummies, and killing two birds with one stone. By pretending to be indifferent about whatever irrelevant new assignment Dick might have decided to demote him to, it would show, at least, that he didn't give a damn about the job. At the same time any eavesdropper would think it was just a straightforward, periodic career appraisal.

Dick pulled a small brown envelope out of a drawer and handed it without comment to McArthur. This was not exactly where a nosy person would look for important messages. Gerry perused it unexcitedly. To say it was a quixotic message would be an extreme understatement.

It read:

"It's very boring here in the doldrums of headquarters. They are having a rum party in old Jaman. Your wife has been pestering us with phone calls, day and night. It seems you have been neglecting your duties, old boy! And she's always going on about what she terms your long-overdue advancement to head of department and when is it going to happen! The situation clearly calls for a holiday, a change of air. Another spell abroad away from all the tedium, pressure and inactivity that you are experiencing here. Nothing is more of an anti-climax than a change of presidency. You are obviously bored to the teeth and not much is expected to happen in Washington over the next four years while this jerk occupies the White House. Why not take yourself off to Jaman and write another of your detailed economic reports for us on, say, the coconut trade? I am sure, between you and me, that no difficult relatives will insist on accompanying you down there, what with the

heat, tropical storms, mosquitoes and all that! By the way, please try and ensure that your reports are more down-to-earth this time. No more self-indulgent theorising, please.'

This could only be a coded message, to thwart more easily-read thought processes. Either that, or the height of patronising cheek to someone who had been in the subterfuge business for donkey's years.

A major initiative is underway? Perhaps it *was* for real. You never could tell. The first principle of I.T. (Intelligence Work) is: never let them know if it's a rehearsal or the real thing.

But much still did not make sense.

'Rum party' – a euphemism for ... a revolution, a political assassination, a major incursion of illegal contraband? The usual activities.

The 'coconut trade'. Another dummy? Or late strategically important commodity in the contemporary Porridge Inc. (American Foods Giant) era of increasing world food shortages? Strange how this precious tropical product had been down-graded by the major foods and advertising firms, always being portrayed as a poor man's fare or even as an object of fun or contempt; and, insidiously, attacked by some supposed 'bug' (Lethal Yellowing was the official term) over recent decades which now meant it was facing global extinction. Was this really a 'natural' phenomenon? In an age when vegetable oil was at a premium, coconuts were just one in a whole list of natural products which were facing extinction in an increasingly technological and artificial food scenario.

Perhaps.

But much still did not make sense.

Especially as Dick was now expected to espouse 'Good Neighbour' policies in line with the supposed foreign policies of the new Hooligan administration. However it was clear that he was acting *before* any new orders had come through from Washington. He probably just wanted to get another little inoffensive country in his grip in order later to be able to use it as a bargaining counter with the president at their first meeting.

Why Jaman?

Well, it was a place where Dick Warner had once notoriously gone on holiday and been ripped off both by his hotel which had blatantly billed him, an official government representative, the full rate on his luxury suite and phone calls, as well as by a cabby who took the longest route back to the hotel. And what was more, and even worse, he had lost all the 'secret Jaman fund' in the casino. He had always vowed to get revenge. And what better feeling of revenge than being able to have the very country one hates, its president, prime minister and cabinet, in the palm of one's hand?

Gerry's role? Most likely to implement some blueprint and to report on progress. Also, to interpret any failures and embarrassments as paradoxical successes for their political masters. As the Agency's chief Culture Jumper (the agent who insinuates himself or herself into another culture so thoroughly that he/she is able to see and analyse everything from inside that culture) he might also be expected to report back on how the Jamanese saw everything.

Clearly the matter of coconuts, one of the island's staple products, was to be a key feature in the picture.

This time there had been no mention of secret photography, no pulling out from a lower drawer of some old photograph. He had always suspected that the time-honoured tactic of presenting at briefings sensitive prints from secret surveillance of him on his missions, was done mainly in order to remind him of the disconcerting denouement in Taran and his inadvertent role in the disastrous outcome of the war. This had occurred via public exposure on television of some sensitive photographs which had been the product of freelance photography of an amateurish nature, and which had never been meant to be seen by any member of the public, much less by the Washington crowd. Ever since, his employers had never lost the opportunity to show him 'random' exposures of himself in dubious locales, or display before him pictures, from the most abstruse of spying positions, of his shady, apparently banal daily activities. Lately high-tech but incomprehensible satellite pictures had appeared showing, for example, complex agricultural patterns with his good self leading some students in observation field work right bang in the middle. It was all done simply to embarrass him, he was convinced.

He would have to decode the rest in the privacy of a bar, his brain protected from outside ESP snooping by lashings of whiskey. □

four

Mary McArthur would, as usual, be putting a brave face on the latest departure of her husband overseas. Her late-night card games, the partying, drinking, the sarcastic comments about her 'other half' as well as bitter asides on life in general were meant only to conceal the sad emotions of a gentle person. Her's was a lonely life, the spouse of a man who was very seldom around, a man whose life was, in reality, sacrificed to a higher cause, the unspoken servant of two powerful national institutions, viz the CIA and that body which controlled every aspect of American mental life through complex influences emanating from its academic echelons, namely Harvard University.

None would have imagined the self-sacrifice, the idealism that were in fact a part of that marriage. 'Divorce him' her friends had advised her many times and they had assumed it was a rigid Catholicism that had prevented this outcome, though who could assume from Gerry's characteristic devil-may-care bravado and carefree, agnostic talk that he was a stickler for any religious belief? Or perhaps it was the overpowering influence of Col. Baxter himself, even if now deceased, that kept them together, if only at least out of filial loyalty on the part of Mary.

The truth was stranger.

The hapless wife had already been informed, by the Church, that her marriage was null and void, due to non-consummation.

When she had brought up the matter with him in the early days he had said, 'you know the reason, Mary, that bomb at Can-Do . . .', and she had accepted, with much pity for him, their sad predicament, but she sometimes secretly wondered about it, as he had never mentioned in correspondence before their marriage any permanent physical damage. She never told anybody, other than her spiritual advisor, of her secret sorrow and compassion, her indeed heroic loyalty. Even Gerry did not seem to be the slightest bit aware of this generosity and forbearance.

His attitude to her was, to say the least, paradoxical. In public, indeed even in the company of complete strangers, he was off-hand about her, often being grossly crude. However in her presence he would instantly change, being usually obsequiously polite and even altruistic; he would bring her rare and unusual presents from remote corners of the globe (it was symptomatic of the situation that he had never even noticed that these were nowhere to be seen around the house, for she found his taste somewhat uncouth). To her he still appeared to be infused with an undirected, immature idealism and strange eccentricity, always enthusing naively over some novel politico-economic idea or plan to change the world; indeed it seemed to her as if, subconsciously, his whole life was devoted to bringing about some spectacular, impossible achievement that would obliterate the embarrassing memory of the past, of Taran in particular as well as his other career debacles.

Such was all that she was able to make of the pithy, abstruse and ambiguous comments and statements he made about what he called his secret work whenever he graced their home for a few short days. So she continued to portray the image of one who scorned her husband, partaking with false enthusiasm in the hectic social world around her, keeping to herself her regret and pity, even her loyalty for an apparently incurably straying husband.

President Hooligan, ex-psychology student, ex-businessman, ex-journalist, ex-farmer, ex-'man-about-town' and ex-disciple of the previous President Rodrigues had, despite his genius and experience, a roaring headache at the end of his first week in the White House. Electioneering had made it all seem so easy, the criticism of Rodrigues's policies of 'inner enlightenment' in favour of Hooligan's 'zone of outer reality'; his assertion of a new approach to politics and life by ignoring the 'human neurosis' and concentrating on 'the physical entity of the universe' as the only reality, had appealed to the newly-sophisticated American electorate, tired of the old shibboleths. How they had clapped and cheered him!

Now, nobody seemed interested in his ideas! What did he get instead? senators, congressmen, presidents, premiers wanting to 'discuss their views'. This morning President D'Alamo from Venezuela wanted military advice on how to invade two neighbouring 'anti-democratic' countries which 'belonged to him'. The problems of mankind and of history could be laid at the door of such subjective fantasies; didn't he realise that all countries, black and white, even Capitalist and Socialist, were friends now, he had shouted at the South American visitor, alarming the whole White House staff.

Everybody wanted to visit or speak to him! Hadn't they got other things to do? He wasn't elected to sit around chatting away to people all day. He had given strict instructions that every branch of government attune itself to technical and economic commonsense. Politics were to be abolished. The power of Reason, Technical Efficiency and Practicality in the management of resources were to be encouraged everywhere, all over the world. To encourage the new era of calm and sound management he had decided to issue all future White House statements by internet and would not be appearing in Congress or public much again. Six days a week were now put aside for attending to family or personal matters, including as much time as possible relaxing on the golf course (a sure certainty to gain the respect of the public); and only his phoneline to the two comrades in the East would remain as his sole communication with the outside world. He was continually having deep, long conversations with Comrade Alexandri these days about how to unite the world. Russia's possession of immense nuclear weaponry, now controlled by the secret Russian underground, made them a headache for the West and the Russians still a power to be reckoned with. He sought to allay Alexandri's neurotic anxieties about his personal image, which had led to the Russian leader's unnerving preoccupation with personal hygiene and the question of what was the most satisfactory mode of hairstyle to be seen sporting on the international stage, by talking to him gently about the joys of golf and the need to rediscover the Yin and the Yang. He must ring him up soon and talk more about that new 'World Equalisation Force'.

Hooligan smiled to himself and lifted his feet on to the Oval Office desk as he contemplated his policies with some self-satisfaction. He was, if he would admit it, surprised both by his electoral success and by the keenness with which the Eastern hemisphere appeared to have accepted all his ideas. A grain of worry suddenly knurled itself on his face. He knew that the Russians thought him a genius (whatever the Chinese might think; they were often quite sphinx-like with him), so why couldn't his own advisors see things that way? He sometimes thought that they had only supported him in order that the Party, and by inference themselves, might win the election. Did they really respect him as a president, as a man? It didn't matter really. He had realised for quite some time now that it was what the external person did, not what one's subjective consciousness or inner soul valued, that counted.

He had contacted Mr Warner at the CIA and told him to find the most brilliant economic and political brain in the country and send him, or her, on a tour of some of the Developing countries of the world to explain the meaning of the new economic policy of co-operation.

"I won't have to look far," Warner had enthusiastically replied and Hooligan had been heartened by the briskness of this response on the part of a notoriously difficult member of the Establishment.

He had heard them talk about Warner, how he had got the job because he had a dog which could speak Mandarin, and which Warner had brought along to the interview with President Niceman dressed bizarrely (for a dog) in a dark crepe suit. This unusual man had survived many changes of Administration. His fame for this achievement alone now ensured his continuance in office, and his biggest plus was the fact that he, alone, knew the identity of the CHIEF OF THE CIA. This was an anomalous situation, left over from the time when even president's couldn't be trusted with information.

Many were the legends surrounding Warner; one day he would invite the man up to the White House and learn more about him; maybe they might even become friends. The 'legends' could all be simply smokescreen of course. He, Hooligan, hadn't been born yesterday. In fact it was quite likely the CIA was rife with militaristic and psychopathic weirdos and Warner was probably at the top of the pack.

Hooligan took his feet abruptly off the desk and sat on the floor to begin his Third Zen Yoga Meditation of the day.

"The President wants me to send someone abroad to implement his new policy of persuading the world to behave rationally and intelligently, a very dangerous mission", said Dick Warner addressing one of his impromptu staff meetings. "Therefore we send our most useless, expendable person; the one we would all like to be rid of; you all know who that is. The one who is always finding fault with our plans and methods;

who never agrees with anything that is proposed by the salt-of-the-earth in this organisation; who always laughs whenever our plans periodically fail; the one who helped to lose us the war in Taran. McArthur. We all know he is protected here by the powers-that-be; but one day, hopefully, he will buy it, perhaps whilst flying in some rickety aircraft from one grotty airport to another, or whilst employing his irony against some unsuspecting foreign citizen. I'm glad to say he has already been briefed and has gone on his way happily believing he is on a goodwill mission for Hooligan to our new target country, Jaman. At least he will not be around for a while undermining staff morale with his craze for theorising and thinking."

A cheer of satisfaction went around the office, with everyone being careful not to appear disapproving of any of Warner's words.

"I have decided to prioritise that notoriously irrational country Jaman which, despite its global insignificance in terms of land size, is of great importance for it has a population ideally suited to be guinea pigs. People there are very self-opinionated, full of confidence in their own irrationality and assumed resistance to brainwashing techniques, just the way it should be if we are to get them to do things our way while, at the same time, allowing them to think that it is all their own work. They are also excitable and straightforward, rebel and riot at the drop of a hat and, quite disarmingly, they take questions of right and wrong seriously. They believe in Truth. They are a hungry people, hungry for the Promised Land, for leadership, for approval and, of course, hungry for food. Above all, they are proud of their little island and wear their flag and sing their anthem with enthusiasm. They will accept anything that they think will aggrandize their tiny country. They will take to the teaching of ol' computer brain McArthur as to the prophecies of a messiah! Our people have already paved the way telling them, off the record, that the man is a wayward genius, an eccentric Harvard scientist and a visionary economist all in one. His amazingly boring textbooks have been placed in all the libraries of Jaman by USAID. The word on his heavy drinking, his unusual marriage, his many debacles in diplomacy that always benefited the enemy has also been put out, all marks of a blessed person in their eyes. They will find his methods unusual and even spooky, never doing what is expected of a CIA officer (don't we well know it?); they will feel very privileged to have such a famous, or infamous, man in their midst. For at least a while. He is made of just the right mix for them, the 'eminence grise' who is also an ordinary, weak human being. They will feel free to laugh at him and his foibles. Yet their expectations of him will be infinite. It is not for nothing that he has for long been our chief 'culture jumper'! If he drops the ball you will hear the disappointment in every corner of Jaman. It will be like the death of a god. They will be quick to crucify him."

Dick Warner changed his tone now, to a more sinister intonation.

"It is our plan to use Jaman as the testing ground for something the lab boys have been working on for some time. The chief scientist has become a great proponent of genetic economics and sees this as the way forward for everyone, especially for downtrodden countries. It's another one of his strange enthusiasms which may prove very useful for our own purposes. It reminds me in some ways of his late mysterious Micro-dot technology which he, rather abstrusely I thought, tried to extend to a theory of All-Knowledge claiming that not only knowledge but reality itself was a mass of dots. That helped us to launch those experiments beaming micro-particles at financial centres in the great cities of the world, which had some interesting results but which we unfortunately had to 'stop' (of course we are still experimenting on other targets) when rates of interest began to go haywire in the money markets.

Now mention a backward Third World country to McArthur and he is off at the drop of a hat to reform the place. He is our last idealist, a bloody pinko underneath. He jumps at any chance to get away from the office and he has gone willingly down there to help to get the Jamanese, hopefully, to change their economic system to a new set-up that will alter forever the old jaded relationship between capital, land, labour and enterprise. You see, they have all become neglectful of the coconut in Jaman, considering it to be a colonial relic, claiming disease and 'low, unfair prices' as reasons for having to change over to other crops, most of which fortunately are still of much use to us in the First World, like marijuana, for instance, or even tobacco. But times have changed, the coconut is coming back, in a big way!

Now, the big news. Our recent genetic testing has produced a Supercoconut which is still hush hush. It is in fact an important new secret weapon. Few will realise at first the importance and value of this nut. It is still all gold, special steels, plutonium or exotic chemicals with most people! People have all gone off proper natural foods, healthy nutriments like the ordinary coconut. But food fads represent the movement of deeper forces. Soon he who controls the coconut, its natural juices, copra, fibre and by-products, will control the world! This, paradoxically, is why we are ensuring the destruction of all known species of common coconut around the world, and replacing them with our own, man-made specimen. You see what everybody will soon realise is that if you have these SuperFoods you do not need anything else; factories, schools, banks, machines, technology and non-American factories, for we will control any processing industry, become secondary to the natural elements. In fact all our worldly wealth comes from natural products if you just think about it. Believe it or not the coconut, in its infinite resourcefulness, contains all that we could ever possibly need. The human race can live off the coconut. That is why we have to stop all these countries, once they realise its potential, from exploiting and manipulating the power of the coconut, by removing it from their control. We must put in a substitute coconut over which we ourselves will have complete command. We long ago realised here in the CIA that before you can have military or political influence in a situation you have got to get in on the basic fact of life there, which is the food they eat. Political power lies in the barrel of a stomach!"

Dick always put on these high-powered, cocky shows whenever he felt insecure. Nobody was sure if all this talk was just a pretext for something else; or a cover-up of some sort.

"It will be a high-tech coconut. It is McArthur's official brief to propose the indispensability of native food and raw material products, something which he is fond of extolling in his pernicious 'Self Sufficiency in Developing Countries' book anyway. That book would have landed him on the scrap heap only some clever jerks in Harvard saw it as an avenue to mind-control in those illiterate countries. Hopefully we will, eventually, both by means of McArthur's education programme and propaganda using advertisements on the local radio and media, on billboards etc., introduce the concept of the Indispensable Coconut to the subconscious as well as the commercial consciousness of the Jamanese. The desire for its cultivation will become all-powerful among ordinary, easily impressed, media obsessed people, its planting taking over from every other facet of agricultural and economic activity. Eventually even people and human institutions will be taking second place to the coconut; in fact in the last resort the living space of humans, their farms and other uneconomic set-ups, will have to give way to the ever-growing coconut.

But of course it will not be the specimen as they know it.

Furthermore, should we meet any unforeseen obstacles, the new prototype will have to be introduced surreptitiously; and since we can't take a chance with a whole continent as yet, in case of unforeseen environmental problems which could work their way back to us, it has got to be a smallish, fertile island. Initially it will be mixed in with the pods of the normal banana. That will have to be done at night by specially trained squads of our Green Berets attired as banana pestacidists, who will be trained to plant them in the manner of high explosive mines or other military gadgets. It will be an overnight operation; we would have them off the island by dawn. McArthur will think he is simply involved in a normal humanitarian econo-agricultural project and will be promoting the coconut for all he's worth. He is the last person in the world to be entrusted with the military and political truth of our operations! It's nice that he's a teacher for it's so easy to set him up. Intelligence operators around the world could never get by without the likes of his sort!"

Warner pulled a cigar-shaped pen out of his top pocket, took one chew of the metal at one end and then used the instrument to point to a map of the Asian subcontinent on the window. What was strange was that the map sometimes appeared to be outside the window... or else it was a map behind glass behind which was a sky and landscape of very realistic quality, indistinguishable from the real thing.

He said nothing as he pointed at the position of Jaman and chewed silently as if on some strong tobacco. The staff stared at him silently; they wondered who gave Dick his ideas, what books he read. There had always been something artificial about the milieu of CIA headquarters. Even subdued, newly-appointed minor officials could see it all as a reflection of the personal fantasy Warner and those others who had been desk bound most of their lives (except for a few rare and always disastrous forays into the real world on missions to supposedly promote policy aims of the president, such as Dick's ill-fated visit to Jaman). It appeared as if it really was the case that the ambitions of the most powerful agency in the world were only private fantasies, a dream-like reverie whose ultimate nature was revealed in the decor of the high offices of the government departments responsible for implementing the same policies: rooms with bizarre art work portraying fabulous battles in faraway, mythical worlds, pictures of toylike technology from science fiction that would never see the reality of daylight except in comic book dramas; arrays of sporting paraphernalia and 'objects de conquest' as in some adult's Christmas toyland, the possessions of people who spent every night watching corny, Hollywood adventure movies.

"That is Jaman," said Warner suddenly, his voice croaking with some hidden emotion; "they will all finally be subject to the new coconut. It will be in the forefront of economic and social progress, overcoming the reactionary beliefs of mankind, with whole societies living and breathing in unison with its growing and harvesting, all celebrations taking place in the shade of the new magnificent specimen. But Jaman is only to be the start. In other countries, for example in the lands of the Citrus, the new Super Orange will be supreme. We hopefully will soon have gigantic Buffalo specimens destined to overshadow the high mountains in the interior of South America; huge types of fish to inhabit the rivers and lakes of Canada," (there was an inexplicable hatred for Canada in the CIA); "the oceans will have new breeds of whales, their breeding and growth controlled from here or the Pentagon by thermonuclear beams emanating from our secret satellites. We will control the world's food supply! The world will be our farm, the farm will have its workers and managers, its planners and shareholders, its inputs of massive amounts of fertilisers and the new energy of controlled radiation giving us immense quantities of food, drink and good health. Every available bit of land in the world will be used up; there will be no room for useless millions of human population as the new hi-tech superplants spread everywhere. Squatting and vagrancy will be a serious offence ..."

Dick was all puffed up, his face aglow.

The special signal for dispersal from a staff meeting, beloved of Langley cynics, was heard (it was an amplification of the sounds of a New York socialites' cocktail party with glass clinking and the background chatter of intellectual conversations), but Warner called out one last instruction just before they left the room.

"Don't forget the Fancy Dress party tonight. I expect to see you all there. I am coming in a Russian Field Marshall's uniform, Snakey is a Chinese comrade in khaki, and Spooks will be Fidel Castro. Any member of staff not present on time will no longer be considered to be a respectable member of our exclusive Mock Battles social club."

The hot air swarmed up through the legs of Gerry's suit as he stood outside the plane. It was true that there was a certain masochism in Gerry's attitude to clothes, ever since Taran, when he had to wear all that heavy gear. Even now he felt he was entering some surreal underworld laden with the weight of a hundred political and moral concerns as he descended from the plane. Like a warm, sticky soup the tropical liquid penetrated every nook and cranny of his skin and body. He felt aswim in an arena of glorious colour, of blue and white streaks, blurry red flowers and bobbing greenery everywhere like flashing fishes darting around some terrestrial coral reef. The pungent smell of the tropical flora, herbs and incense came from the earth and sky filling once again his nostrils and mind with that sense of nostalgia for a lost and beautiful paradise which had often haunted him in the past.

But there was also a fear of those unpleasant incidents that happened frequently in the Third World, and of unwelcome red tape. This combination created an uneasy stirring inside him, giving him a strong desire for a drink. It was probably like this when he had been born, he contemplated; it would be like this again when he had shed his skin and bone and stood on the threshold of eternity. For a moment he thought he might never smoke a cigarette again, so fresh did this blue-green world seem. Gerry, a natural contemplative, felt at that moment an urge to sit on the ground there and then and inhale all the scents and blossoms of that isle as an antidote to life's drabness, not to mention the tedious journey. It was something, after all, to have survived the journey. The problem with arriving at any destination, however, he thought to himself with unease, was that at some time in the future he would have to face the unpleasant and unnerving experience of another flight out again.

'Jean Blue' was making her way down in front of him with business-like determination. Perhaps he would see her again in the terminal lounge, most certainly in some movie in the future, if he ever got to watch one. He would certainly make a point of doing so if she happened to be starring in it!

It was always a disappointing, and lonely, fact that whenever he landed in a strange country there was never anybody there to greet him. All the other Agency officials made a point of arranging morale boosting receptions by minor officials, often being hailed in trite phrases like 'Hi ya doing pal', 'Bring any proper smokes with yuh?' or 'Great to see ya' which were in fact exceedingly difficult to decode messages put out in order to counteract eavesdropping on the tarmac. A terrific reception was always the privilege of the top brass, whizzed away to local luxury hotels to pursue their 'business deals' in style, or else to the embassy station where they would pretend to be technical or political experts on some controversial or interesting matter and bore everyone, including the eavesdroppers, with convoluted theorising on some aspect of military strategy, some new department of defence technical innovation or in-fighting amongst the Washington set. Then there would be their plans for the 'natives'. Come to think of it, with such high profiles and their flamboyant recreational activities it now occurred to him that they never made any attempt to hide their presence. Real, proper business people would conduct their affairs in more sober, less ostentatious fashion and certainly not attract attention to themselves with such antics. It was most unprofessional. His own habit of paying with his own personal cash for food and accommodation at least certainly gave him a welcome inconspicuousness.

He also envied them their inevitable social and professional success later in their careers. Some would go on to congress, even the presidency. Gerry was always finding himself on assignments where he had to go it alone. There would be no official recognition of his arrival in Kingstown; he would work for months, maybe years, without hearing a word from HQ or much even from the local office; he would eventually return home and have a quick debriefing with some minor clerk while all around him would be the evidence of the happy careers and numerous attainments of his contemporaries. His hard-work, his diligently written reports would be totally ignored; that is until the time came when some political disaster would happen just as he had forecast and there would be recriminations all around and he would receive inevitable censure for being a 'facilitator' or even an 'encourager' of the said event and for failing to prevent it by giving any forewarning or proper advice. Nobody ever actually read his reports, at least not until it was too late. There was the occasion when he had predicted the fall of America's 'only friend' in the Central Hemisphere, the Emperor of Azan. This man claimed divine lineage but was so unpopular that he had actually to make himself believe that he was an elected politician who was so close to the roots of his electorate that he had never had to hold an election at all. He based his democratic credentials on a famous proposed referendum, the first and only such electoral test ever to be held in Azan, solely on the question of whether he was immortal or not. McArthur had seen the end coming when he reproduced some accounts, universally known as 'old hat', of how the emperor had actually already left the country and handed his divine status over, temporarily, to the palace caretaker, a certain Mr Pat who was of course already well-known to the CIA as the only reliable car mechanic in Azan; but nobody at Langley or the Pentagon had believed him, or even read the report. Of course when it all came out he had to take the blame anyway.

It had been the same with other episodes and now, deja vu, nobody took the blindest bit of notice as he descended the steps. He felt like shouting:

"I'm *not* just another ex-patriate come here to show you how it's all done. I'm here to *conquer* your country just like Julius Caesar and make it a part of the largest empire the world has ever seen, known now as the World Hooligan Empire. My very academic appearance is misleading and is in fact the key to my success at social infiltration. But do not worry. That is just the official scheme of things. In reality I am a freedom fighter and I have come to save your country and, perhaps, the world."

He collected his rather meagre luggage, one suitcase, and headed for IMMIGRATION, the first really big test. The procedures around the world of this particular necessary-evil institution he always saw as a challenge. He had grown fond over the years of parrying looks, gestures, breathing patterns, arguments, documents, belief systems etc. with aggressive, power-crazy immigration officials, frequently entering into very abstruse explanations for his arrival in a country, as he found the simple answer was less likely to be accepted. Having learnt above all never to tell the truth, he had long ago realised that the more outlandish the story the better. Jean Blue was in front of him and he took his place behind her as she chatted happily to a bespectacled immigration official.

"I am so happy to be here to see your wonderful country. I have heard so much about its beauty! I can't wait to sunbathe on your golden beaches and sip your terrific rum punches," she said in what was quite obvious to Gerry the sweetest, falsest voice that she could manage.

"It is a privilege to have you here as a guest in my beautiful country, Miss Jones. If you have any problems *whatsoever* I can promise to help you sort them out. Here is my personal card with phone number. This special stamp means you can stay here for as long as you like," said the official, an extremely wide smile extending across his face.

Jean went on ahead, clutching her small handbag guardedly.

"Why de hell you decide to come here? Is there nowhere else you can go?," asked the official as he perused Gerry's gruff face and well-stamped passport with annoyance; "me can't read this".

"Well, it's because this is the only country in the world that I could think of where to come to work for a few years. You see I have a serious medical condition and Jaman has the only climate where my life expectancy can be extended," he answered with a formula answer which had none of the immediate problems of a simple, straight-forward interpretation such as almost any other answer would have involved.

"Work permit?"

"Here."

"Proof of authenticity?"

"Government stamp."

"Proof of authenticity of government stamp?"

"I don't need proof. I am a cousin of Senor Mauris."

"Ah. I see. Good. It OK then. Pass through, man. Enjoy the country and watch out for de snakes."

He gave the passport a hearty stamp.

With that Gerry made his way to the custom's area, hoping to catch up with Jean there. To his surprise he was approached by a smartly dressed person in an expensive suit, who announced himself as the representative of a Dutch Exportation Cartel and asked if he was Gerry McArthur. He was quite surprised to find himself speaking to such a person from behind the custom's area barrier. However, you learnt to always expect the unexpected in his profession.

Gerry had in fact been pointed out to this man by none other than the head of the CIA station in Kingstown, who was sitting up in the balcony bar sipping a rum and watching Gerry's every move.

The whole of the Kingstown Special Squad (Jaman National Security) had togged themselves out in waiters' gear and were themselves watching this head of station, serving him drinks, three or four cleaning his table at the same time and others sweeping the floor around his feet.

Meanwhile 'soldiers' of another well-known firm were disguised as returned Jamanese and American tourists (in boxer shorts, daringly rude T-shirts and dark sunglasses) and were observing the Kingstown Special Squad, who were their longstanding 'sworn enemy'.

This was quite a 'welcoming committee' for Gerry, he proudly told himself, and he also felt secretly warmed inside by the greeting from this mystery man, even if it was obvious that it might have shady/shoddy implications. Any recognition at all can be less lonely than no recognition, to those who have to work alone in dodgy situations.

Gerry felt humbled by this unexpected greeting and thought for a moment that perhaps he had a friend in high places who was out to make his path here a bit smoother.

"Yes, I am Gerry McArthur, but you must be looking for another Gerry McArthur. I am only an economics professor taking up an academic post here; surely it is some more important Gerry McArthur whom you wish to meet?"

The 'humility', the claim to an economic's professorship, were part of the game, a good ploy in the circumstances.

The Dutchman was a tall, blonde haired, ascetic-looking fellow and with very fine hands which looked as if they had been occupied with delicate, non earthy tasks all their life. His thin face looked down on Gerry from dark-blue eyes.

"I see that you are burdened with the belief of false humeelity. You are the very peerson I weesh to talk to. My employers have allowed me to geeve you an offer you just cannot reefuse. The top man weel not accept 'no' for an answer. You must tell me the truth." He gave a short guffaw, as if speaking like a criminal assassin was a big joke.

This guy gets straight to the point, thought Gerry, impressed.

"I have got a job here; I am not seeking another one. In that job which I am going to do, I feel that I will be actually helping mankind, not ripping them off. In any case, you do not know anything about me."

"I can tell you many theengs about yourself. The way for eenstance you came through customs without having to explain the gun you have een your pocket."

"Customs?"

"Exactly. Veery cleever. You walked past with me and everybody thought we were offeecials!"

Very cool, thought Gerry. He saw that they had walked straight through customs. This was, in fact, a welcome realisation for the gun might indeed have been a problem if they had searched him.

He now realised something else. Jean Blue had come through *without* her 'empty trunk', without any baggage at all.

Strange.

It was then that he also realised that Miss Blue was causing an unprecedented sort of emotional disturbance inside him.

This was not only strange. It was sinister, he thought.

"Eet is better I meet you first than some beeg crook. If you meet me at the Jamboree Hotel, the lounge bar, at six tomorrow you weel end up a wiseer man. Believe me, I know what ees best for you. Do not fail to be there. Meanwhile, may you be blessed een all that you do."

It was a strange way for anyone to talk, gentle and caring on the one hand, demanding on the other; yet even in that last sentence there was a note of threat. Gerry felt for the small pistol with silencer inside his jacket (in a secret compartment that would in fact have been very hard for customs to discover). This action made the head of station involuntarily move his hand in an impulsive feel for his own firearm. In turn, the Kingstown Special Squad became extremely edgy and they all went for their guns. Their waitering and cleaning tasks ceased momentarily as they stared at the said head of station. The 'soldiers of the firm', at the same time, also prepared themselves for action.

However, all normal tasks recommenced as soon as Gerry had removed his hand from his chest area. The serving and cleaning started up again.

"I'll turn up but there is some weird misunderstanding here," replied Gerry calmly, and the Dutchman walked away with a business-like stride.

He arrived in the terminal lounge and before he had even put his bag down he had ordered a whiskey. He saw that Jean had also taken a seat at the bar and was sipping a Martini or a type of cream sherry. Something in her manner made him decide not to speak to her; this was in fact the fear of a very public snub.

"Hello Gerry. Come and join me for a drink."

It was a voice that he recognised.

From far back.

But from where?

It sounded like the very same voice of a former colleague in the academic field, whom Gerry had intensely disliked for his ability, by means of a very suave approach to everything in life and a sophisticated personality, to make people revere him and to ensure that McArthur felt both professionally and personally unsatisfactory and inadequate in every way. He looked around expecting to see that old antagonist, Spud Murphy, sitting there. It seemed that his nightmares had even followed him to Jaman; and he was ready to pull out his gun and shoot Murphy dead on the spot if need be.

Then he realised that the voice was actually from further back. From Taran days.

"Jim McCall. I didn't realise that you were still around. I had heard that you had been dispatched to the next life in some experiment of the chief's."

Gerry felt a mixture of wonder and happy surprise. He and Jim had shared an affinity for whiskey long ago when they had worked together in the service. In fact Jim it was who had told him in Taran of the real, top secret nature of his (Gerry's) position as both a serving soldier and officer of an 'independent' service (that this duplicity was a capital offence, breaking the most important rule of the American Constitution, to salute the flag and respect each and every insignia on a soldier's uniform no matter what rank it was, was seen as a virtue by the anti-social lot who made up the brass in Military Intelligence). Gerry had replied that he had thought that all the privileges, the whiskey and marijuana they had been 'accessing' had been just another illegal black market operation, purely for the financial benefit of top people; he was then told that it was all a deliberate plan by intelligence to de-stabilise the defence establishment.

He had a sudden flashback to '65. It was as vivid as if it was only yesterday.

He had been ordered to take a bunch of 'boots' (new arrivals) to the hooches at the back of the base camp on the south slope of Monkey Mountain. As a newly promoted brown bar or lieutenant this was an extremely humiliating task usually left to some disgraced PFC to carry out, for all it involved was the men basically going to the toilet. Ever since the Can-Do claymore he had been something of a fugazi in the eyes of others; in his second, and last, patrol he had lost all of his men when they had taken a ferry across the river thinking it was a short-cut home only to discover, too late, that it was a Liberation Front vessel and it sank when half-way across with only himself making it safely to the shore, not being weighed down with heavy gear like the unfortunate, recently-arrived grunts. The incident had become a joke all over Taran and a propaganda victory for the enemy. To his immense relief Gerry found that he was not invited to lead a patrol again.

This particular assignment to the hooches was proving equally disastrous and insidious. No sooner had they reached their objective than a 6-By came past and at least twenty of the enemy inside started capping them, the dirt popping around and the new guys running this way and everyway. Simultaneously, some Big Boys opened up from somewhere; a real firefight began but with the difference that all the shooting was from one side only. Later, there was to be suggestions of diddy-bopping on the part of Gerry's men made by the S2 and other contankerables. He, again, had led his men into a Number Ten situation. By the time it was all over the guys were laid out where they had been taking refuge from the beginning of the 'battle', except that there was not much left of them, only mangled flesh and blood. Lieutenant McArthur, again, had had a miraculous escape. Hence the big breeze to make him feel guilty by those Security people (who, however, knew the real facts which Gerry didn't at the time). It was Jim McCall, whom he had met as he (McCall) sat on a stool in the sole remaining unscathed hooch sipping whiskey at the end of that same skirmish, who had a strange tale to tell him. At the time he didn't believe what he was told but later, of course, it all became completely clear.

"That was our own people shooting at us there," he said in his low drawl, a suspicion of satisfaction in his voice. One mystery, what Jim had been doing in all the shooting, was to remain forever unsolved.

"I suppose it might have had something to do with the 'toking up' incident," mumbled a somewhat disappointed Gerry.

There was another flashback-within-a-flashback and Gerry saw again the jeep full of pot freaks as clear as daylight and accepted the offer to 'climb on board and toke up'. He should have had his scruples aroused when he saw the battalion chaplain among the dope smokers. Gerry was carrying out a little intelligence work to discover the extent of dope taking in all the battalions in the Division; smarter brains were playing with the idea of placing a stronger chemical in the dope to ensure mind control. But when he made his report direct to the G3 all hell broke out between the S2's and the battalion commanders, the latter having been the main dealers unknown even to their own men. Ever since that time it had been policy never to give Gerry a straightforward assignment. He was simply too untrustworthy to be relied upon to notice the contradictions of life in a war or the clear hints of his superiors. He still seemed to think in terms of black and white, right and wrong.

Now it seemed the army was willing to do the job of finishing him off itself, even at the expense of innocent victims; what other explanation lay behind the shooting? It was very embarrassing for the authorities that the attempt had failed, especially after all that expenditure of bullets.

"Nah, it was just a training exercise, not a reprisal for your exposing the drug network," Jim had said in a matter-of-fact voice. "They thought you and a bunch of raw recruits would make for excellent target practice. You are paranoid, Gerry."

"I get the idea that you are kidding me, Lieutenant ...".

"McCall. Jim McCall. Call me Jim. Pleased to meet yuh."

"You're not making a joke, are you? There are a lot of bodies being transferred over there to the GR point. And I am getting the blame again."

"I know you feel guilty about splitting on the boys in the jeep. Everybody knows that you've had a spot of paranoia ever since. But you, and everyone else, know that it is customary to test the reflexes of our soldiers by unexpectedly firing at them occasionally (didn't you learn that in Training School?). Otherwise we will have a rusty lot when it comes to the real thing. Why, even top generals have been caught on-the-hop and ended up in the reefers after a simple exercise like this one. Forget about the dope and the dealers. War has always had those who will make a bit of money out of it. Nothing wrong with that. Look, why don't you settle things and just admit that it was you who supplied the padre and the others with the pot? Everyone would understand then. The heat would be off and then folk can return to their normal tasks. The top brass would be relieved; they might even reward you with permanent exclusion from combat duty."

He offered Gerry a sip from the (hard-to-get) Bushmills whiskey bottle on the ground in front of him. Gerry accepted it with a sort of desperate happiness.

This was the real beginning of his love affair with the bottle.

"Well, I guess I am starting to make sense of it all. Lots of strange things have been happening to me, especially since I became engaged."

"Oh yes. Congratulations. Col. Baxter's daughter, I believe?"

"That's it. The amazing thing is I have never met her."

"O.K. Well. The chief thing is, she's from a good family. She'll make you a good wife."

He gave a nod and a wink to Gerry at the same time.

McCall had not seemed surprised by Gerry's bizarre

revelation, one which McArthur would not normally have divulged to just anyone, at least not without a good shot of that old Bushmills inhibition-lowering factor.

"She's in college, back stateside. Her dad and my dad have been giving her 'action' shots of me out here in Taran. She wrote me a letter; it seems we once played together as children at a birthday party back in the fifties. She said that her dad had previously been putting pressure on her to marry the son of President Niceman and Niceman had even threatened to send her, and her dad, to a nuclear test site in the desert unless she tied up the knot with the budding junior politician. Then, apparently, my photograph appeared on the scene. She took to me like a drowning rat taking to a floating straw. Or so they tell me. Apparently she has this image of me as some kind of he-man or hero. I don't want to let her down."

"Classic," was McCall's comment.

"Colonel Baxter saw me here. He was in Taran on a morale-boosting visit to the intelligence boys in the hills, the ones who are all missing; you've heard about it; it seems they went AWOL. The official line is they are in the bamboo cages and Baxter's helicopter had a loudspeaker blaring out greetings and encouragement as he swooped over the jungle. He said to me that the only way I could ever get out of here was to marry his daughter. He then referred to what he called my 'suicidal and destructive tendency' that could be alleviated by a transference of emotions and fantasies to some external phenomenon; that in my case it should essentially be a woman. He could be a bit of a sage, when he wanted to be. The urgency of the matter made a quick marriage an imperative, he said. The sheer personality of the man and his psychological arguments impressed me at first, for it was so unexpected and out of character for a military type such as Baxter to speak, or even to think, like that."

"Well," was Jim's neutral comment.

McCall poured him another whiskey.

"After you get married let's go AWOL," had been McCall's sudden, surprising suggestion.

Later, he would look back on that as the one single suggestion which had led him into a new phase of his military career; that of conniving with the enemy.

Now here was the man again.

The last time he had seen McCall was in Washington in '75 when Jim had been suggesting that they blow up the White House and blame it on the WASP establishment. Then he heard that McCall had volunteered to be a guinea pig for a new 'Superman' drug and he had totally disappeared. Now, just when he thought life might be settling down and he could be on his last mission and would soon indeed be able to think of retirement and a cash gratuity here was the man again. McCall, the man of action as counterfoil to McArthur's anxiety-ridden character, had come into his life again at the most unexpected moment.

His worst fears were realised when McCall offered him a "quick jab of a new panacea I have discovered that will fix the brain in a millisecond; but you will have to get yourself ready for it first." □

chapter
five

Jim McCall was in fact the Head of Station in that backwood's island. That is what the 'rebel' had sunk to! This revelation came to Gerry in a flash as he sipped the second whiskey Jim had put before him. Jim had been the man in the balcony in the midst of all those waiters. However it seemed that he still liked to play the fool, especially before getting down to brass tacks. He said now that his ambition, as far as his real interest here was concerned, was in running a mission school in a remote corner of the island. That was vintage McCall. But Jim probably had a stake in every enterprise in the land, the hemisphere; maybe he even still had bizarre political ambitions.

"They tell me you are down here to spread the latest word from Harvard. What's it all about? I'm the last to know anything these days. Not that I really care. I've enough going for me at present to last me well beyond retirement; the less interference from the big boys the better! There is going to be a Golden Triangle of Progress extending from these islands to the mainland and I am going to be one of the hinges. This is where my charitable work comes in handy as a necessary front. I can always talk frankly to you, Gerry. I know that you will see to it that nothing happens that will interfere with my interests. We have always been pals; there are a lot of people here who would love to get their paws on you, especially to find out what's going on as regards CIA policy now, but I will look after you.

Somebody has been spreading rumours about you, about your ... disloyalty. Your private life has not been exempt."

"Look after me ... rumours about me ...? What have you put in this whiskey, Jim? Everything's all a-swim."

"Why are you here, Gerry? What's the real reason? You should be behind a desk in your own office with your own department by now. All this nonsense I've heard about ... coconuts and the economy..., they must think we have lost our marbles down here, due to the sun or something."

"I myself believe," said Gerry carefully, not failing to notice the aggressive, or was it defensive, tone in McCall's voice, "that I have been sent here to punish me for my past misdeeds and also in order to get me out of the way in the chaotic days during the installation of a new administration. I always get into their hair .... If it were not for Dick Warner ...."

"Look", said McCall angrily, "you are still producing the same old red herrings. You should be a millionaire by now. There are no excuses. I know we have been trained in the art of concealment and subterfuge and all that stuff is built into our very brain structure, but we should not let it rule our lives. I learnt to tell the truth a long time ago. There is nothing wrong with it; it's easy. Let me tell you the truth about yourself, Gerry. You are exploited. By just about everybody, including your wife. Let me ask you. Who spends most of your pay? No comment. You need a friend. You have been on your own for too long. Be open with yourself and the world and you will find that at least I will not let you down. If you require some midnight solace I have ...".

'Jim is trying the old pretend-to-be-honest routine with me and I must be careful for there is definitely a double-cross involved here,' though Gerry to himself;

'... or else he thinks I'm still a sucker.'

"OK. I'll be open with you, Jim. I am getting a bit fed up of the duplicity of the whole thing, of never being sure of people's words, of who is who, even of what to do. As soon as I arrived here I was approached by the first of the sharks. Even now I am not certain that he is remotely what he pretends to be, a businessman with an interest in employing my skills. I can see others around the place now, posing as waiters, cleaners and what not. Sure the whole business is so insidious that it wouldn't matter if I told you everything I know right now! I can always deny it all afterwards as you well know. You would never guess which is the truth!"

He continued in a slower, deep voice.

"Well, Jim, it is true that I have been sent here to overthrow the prevailing economic wisdom which states that urban and industrial is best, by the new Harvard theory that *rural and agricultural* is the way ahead. It is also true that we are going to concentrate on the coconut, a natural choice for these islands. Our bright boys have even come up with a scheme for introducing a new strain of coconut, though its development of course has been shrouded in secrecy and I haven't been able to find out much about it. I would always have a degree of reservation about anything these technical lads are involved in, but at the end of the day we have to live with invention. It is supposed to be the prelude of a major agricultural and technical revolution, a real economic transformation. There are some doubts about the viability of the present crop of coconuts, that is all I know about it. We just have to trust that these boys know what they are doing. Nothing could be worse than the present state of the Third World economies, in any case. All my lectures are going to revolve around the theme of rural development and its necessity here. You can be part of this new plan, Jim! We need all hands on board."

He paused, to let Jim take in the potential rewards that would follow from all this. There was no telling from his expression whether he was impressed or not, or whether he saw some cynicism in Gerry's offer.

Jean Blue had by now left the vicinity, Gerry noticed.

"Explain to me, Gerry, how the whole thing works."

"Well, we will work as usual on persuading the powers of persuasion first, and then the ordinary people afterwards. I will get the government to see that the common good comes before personal gain or ego-aggrandisement. As you know we can even work at getting our own preferred government ministers into power, using such old-fashioned methods as withdrawal of 'aid', character-assassination and so on. I will have to do some of the usual culture jumping, of course, Jim."

McArthur sounded like the tired old stager, a somewhat disillusioned professional who had done it all before and had become accustomed to the falsities and deceits of his profession. His words seemed even to have a symbolic, a mystical quality about them.

"You mean they are still into that discredited old rubbish about winning hearts and minds? Surely you don't believe in that crap? As for changing the government, meaning changing the names of the cousins who are permitted to use the fleets of Mercedes, well, nobody goes in for that now. You just go in and do your stuff and forget about the old bogey of political argument. It's the aim now of operatives in the field to keep the worst ones in office for as long as possible; that way there is real stability of government. Are you still espousing some ideology, Gerry?"

"We don't use that word anymore, Jim. Do you not get TIME MAGAZINE out here?"

He felt secretly sorry for Jim and other such-like permanent exiles, who always loved to pretend they had a luxurious way of life but who seemed unaware of the real changes taking place in the world as they continued in their obsessive efforts to make a little pile for their old age.

He continued to fight back against Jim's condescension.

"In the old days you were ahead of everybody, whether you were in a war zone or home in the United States. I know that you have never been the sort to do things the other fellow's way. Do you remember, Jim, how we got permission for that movie house in the Demilitarised Zone? You sure had the gift of the gab!"

Gerry was feeling a little contemptuous of McCall now. The man's grey hair was ruffled and untidy on his restless head; his eyes shot here and there, as if still looking for their first kill. Yet Gerry had always had an admiration for McCall's lack of what they called 'strack', adhering to the letter of military rules and regulations. It wasn't that he blatantly broke all the rules; indeed he always made a point of keeping them better than anyone else. It was that he simply had a way of rising above them. And here he was at the 'end' of his days and still 'striving' while the other members of his generation had either made it or given up entirely. Yet could such a self-serving man really be at the bottom of the heap, or was he into something big, really big?

"Movie House? Oh yea, I remember. It was the new Information Dissemination Centre, open to enemy and friend alike, on the pretext of seeing the latest from Hollywood. I had forgotten all about Taran. So much has happened since."

"What I mean is, do you remember how we got to build it?"

"How did we do that, Gerry?"

"It's like what you always said about not operating the other man's way. You said we should make friends with the enemy. Make a No-Man's Land, like on the Western Front at Christmas. Invite Guerrilla and American to laugh at the same jokes."

"And they believed me ...?"

There was surprise on McCall's face, even disbelief.

How the years change a person, thought Gerry.

"You must recap all that for me some time, Gerry."

Obviously a lot more water had passed under the bridge since those days.

It all went through Gerry's head like the rerun of some old movie, specifically, the Greengage Pop Concert at a decrepit theatre in the Taran bush, '69.

It was as if the sun had got stuck in the sky so slowly did time then seem to pass under the influence of an unknown, intoxicating fluid they had imbued, some said from the air itself. They were all waiting for the arrival of the Bug Eradication Section, Airborne Division, and the heat of the sun was like that of hell. The mosquitoes were large as helicopters, their wings and motors raising the dust so that the jungle glade became a veritable combat zone, the party of men ducking, weaving and firing off their M16s, M60s and M79s at the unseen enemy, at everything around them. Reports of a major battle got back to the Bin TOC. There were some airstrikes; then Spooky, alias Puff The Magic Dragon, appeared and the LZ (landing zone) became a No-Go area. This was the typical fugazi that accompanied every operation in Taran and was in fact a sublimatory reflex on the part of certain OPs officials who always liked to spoil things for everybody else. Then the smoke cleared and the pop group arrived and everybody made themselves as comfortable as possible, notwithstanding the mosquitoes. (The 'bug eradication pro-gram' had, once again, been delayed by 'others screwing up', and those keen, dedicated and idealistic folk in the chemicals division supped sorrow again that evening never once realising how they, and their vaunted chemicals, were being, and would continue to be, used throughout the war as simply a tool for the unspoken and extreme misconceptions of Harvard academics about Taranese ablutionary habits and their implementation, in practical ways, on the heart and mind of the enemy, and had nothing whatsoever to do with bugs).

Jim, along with Colonel Baxter's second-in-command, a weak man who was in McCall's pocket on all aspects of operations, had arranged, in secrecy and without the knowledge of the boss, for the Guerrilla General Van Cush to meet the Commander of the US Forces there, in non-uniform disguise and without the benefit of camera, media reporter or political person to mess things up. The concert was enjoyed by one and all, tensions were remarkably absent or at least greatly reduced and nobody even bothered about Gerry (he had lately been trying to get over his camera-phobia by practicing a lot with the same instrument) taking one of his famous, or infamous, photos of the two military commanders 'doing their own thing', sharing a beer and jokes over a table in a somewhat grotty scene. Jim McCall had manoeuvred himself into a position of some prominence in the background; his 'trademark' of Panama hat and slim cigar unforgettable even decades later, a smile, more a leer, deliberately exaggerated to suggest some connivance in a shady deal. It was the appearance of McCall's unwholesome visage that had especially unsettled the powers that be. It all seemed to suggest that the US Commander, the most respected man in America and the Western World, might have been involved in something that would not have been approved by Congress, president or even people; that there was something unsavoury about a selfless, risky and brave political act that would ensure victory in a grim war taken by a brave American soldier; indeed as time went on the revolutionary 'significance of the event' and the 'personalities of the occasion' were forgotten and McCall's 'rotten sneer', as it was later 'decoded' and officially designated by a secret committee at Langley, ruined everything and gave a completely different impression (in fact the opposite impression) than the one the authorities might had wanted to put over. Gone of course was the hope of impressing the Select Committee of the secret Bad Ideas Group which dominated all media input and thereby the highest level of decision-making. The culprit who had been responsible for the photo processing was an obscure lab technician in the Intelligence division (data processing section which always attracted the unreliable, sneaky types) who was later to rise to occupy the most powerful executive position in the outfit, that is, second-in-command, whom everybody knew as Dick Warner.

Instead of a much publicised Peace Conference highlighted by film showing grim stares across a large conference table, the world was inadvertently presented by the Secret Service with an unclassified photo of a folksy, nay 'hippie' scene involving the highest authorities in Taran and the US, including the major proponents of death and destruction in the land, who were now made to appear as amiable pals in a bar, dedicated to light-heartedness and idle chat. Inadvertently (in fact deliberately), McArthur's 'innocent' photo gave McCall the psychological edge over the military establishment and he was now able to persuade the Commander, General Rolling, of the benefits of going the whole way and making 'respectable' the presence of a social club in the DMZ by giving it the patronage of the US government, and even by having enshrined in its constitution the rules of the Pentagon Golf Club.

The power of the Secret Service was so secure now that they could go on to take even the craziest of chances. It was soon decided to take the side of the enemy and paradoxically use an escalation in the aerial bombing campaign as well as ground attacks to undermine the political and military establishment at home, by pounding the 'enemy' into the ground and thereby make everybody feel sorry for the underdog, so securing the 'enemy's' real moral or political victory that would then ensure the dismissal of certain hated, unpatriotic, inefficient obnoxious personnel in positions of authority. This would effect an overall improvement in the morale of the Armed Forces, the first step towards a real victory in the battle for the world. Such was the argument of the cynical McCall, who had, once, in a stupored state confided to McArthur that a beneficial side-effect of his plan would be the gaining of recognition for his private scheme to attract major entertainment events to venues at the remotest sites in civilisation; his dream at that time was to become a Pop promoter.

President Niceman was an immediate, enthusiastic convert to McCall's plan, although of course it was not presented to him in this form. He thought the idea of helping the enemy to win the war had the merit of being original as well as highly practical. It could only be done by destroying most of their unsatisfactory, poverty-stricken country in any case, a welcome scenario, and such a victory would not only bolster his re-election chances but would also help him with those difficult people over at Langley and the Pentagon. They were the ones who really got to him, but McCall seemed to be on his side. McCall had said so, according to General Baxter. The man seemed to be patriotic and loved American music. He had heard that the same officer had even been trying to encourage everyone in Taran, including the Taranese, to attend courses in American culture, golf, music and the like. He would excuse the controversial photograph by proclaiming its validity as a portrayal of democratic recreation, and as practical evidence of Free Enterprise in Taran, at future right-wing conventions. He would also point out that the practice of the art of photography had been brought to its cultural zenith by Americans. There was nothing disreputable about a good photograph. (Thus the ultimate patronage and seal of the presidency were given to Jim's social club, though a low media profile was ordered to be kept on its use by 'undesirable elements').

"You and your gift of the gab!," laughed Gerry, "I guess I sort of admired you in those days. You could persuade anybody, including me, of anything. I never realised that in what you said about photography, the playing of music and the drinking of whiskey and beer being instruments in the cause of peace, and indeed the salvation of the American way of life, you were just joking. I often wonder how it happened that you never got to the top. The trouble was, I took life seriously in those days. I was so keen on getting out of that place to somewhere I could live a sane, safer existence that I clear forgot how to operate as a proper intelligence officer. Unlike you. In fact I grew not to care even if I got killed, as long as I could get the hell out of there. Of course I worked out later that that was my value to the Generals."

Gerry sighed with what was a paradoxically fondness for those insecure times. Then, at least, nothing had been predictable.

"You know something, Gerry? They never meant you to come back. Baxter especially never really wanted you home to tie the knot, as it were, with Mary. He thought you were too well-read and a sissy into the bargain. He only approved the marriage arrangement because he wanted to annoy Niceman by marrying Mary off and he believed that you would never make it! He also wanted to appease your dad and get revenge for a snub by Niceman and his son, who jilted Mary when he heard that she had attended a June Boaz concert. Baxter told her some stories about you in Taran, none of which were true. They were supposed to prove how brave you were in action. That incident at the hooches was exaggerated and adorned with all kinds of embellishments. Mary fell for you on the rebound. That is the true story of the romance of your life, Gerry."

Gerry did not seem upset by these comments.

"Well I must admit that I did have romantic illusions about Mary in Taran. Especially when I was in dire straits or under fire. And it was one hell of a thing after we got married by proxy. Some questioned whether it was possible to have a legal marriage enacted that way, but Langley's legal department insisted it was. Her father started finding all sorts of jobs for me to do in Taran and he kept diverting Mary at home with visits to meet people at high society Washington parties. Mary had romantic illusions about me too, apparently, all of which stemmed from her childhood memories of parties as a child as well as the action stories from Taran; also the fact of course that she had never actually seen me in the adult flesh. This kept the marriage going, at least at a distance. The colonel eventually became resigned to it, but only after I confirmed to him there wouldn't be any children. I never figured out why he was so bothered about that . . . ."

"I could tell you part of the answer, if you like. That is, if you want me to."

"Oh? I reckoned it was just because he didn't like me. I didn't live up to the image of my own dad."

"That's nearly right. It was mainly because he believed that you had a transmittable mental disease which he didn't want to see passed on to his descendants."

"Is this true, Jim, or another one of your 'dummies'?"

"I kid you not. The whole establishment was paranoid about mental stability and 'split personalities' at the time. It seems they discovered a penetration by these split personalities into the third level of decision-making. It made everyone in every department a suspect and all their actions questionable. There was a right panic and childhood backgrounds became a focus for investigation. There was a story about a birthday party you once went to when you were about six . . . ."

"Where do you get all this stuff?," Gerry asked him.

"You were always an unknown quantity. When you let down your pants and watered the ground in front of the shocked guests they were not certain whether you had done it deliberately. It put a question mark over your whole reliability.

And I would remind you that, despite what you imply about my being the ringleader in Taran it was you who gave me a lot of the ideas that led intelligence into esoteric, daresay even macabre ventures, the credits for which were always laid at my door. It was you who first gave me the idea for 'Counter-

Retreat' and the application of liberal ideals in Washington under the guise of Conservatism. It was you who suggested that we get academics into Langley. What you did not realise is that your satirical, nightly inebriated ravings were treated as the outpourings of pure genius by more impressionable people. And all because it was said you had a degree in economics from Harvard University. It was a fine stroke by you that after you had sown the seeds you stood back and pretended that none of it was your doing. Even I learnt something from that master stroke! You left the practical implementation to others, placing all the responsibility for it on their shoulders. But there are still a few in intelligence who know your record, Gerry."

He spoke ruefully, but there was no bitterness in Jim's voice.

"I don't remember the mental illness craze, Jim. What do you think it was that brought such a panic on?"

"It can be traced to an incident which was a very bad social faux pas made by the Vice President at a function in the Swedish embassy. He started rambling on about uranium in Sweden and the latest thermonuclear gadgetry in the US arsenal in front of representatives of the Nobel Peace Prize committee. It lost Niceman the Peace Prize, something he had badly wanted before he had to escalate the war. So, they became a bit funny about advisors and speech writers after that and Dick Warner, what a bastard, started labelling people, officials, everybody as 'Schizo' and 'non-Schizo' to get rid of guys he didn't like and promote others. All this brought about the regrettable revolution when presidents and other top politicians began to read what their speeches said beforehand and even to make alterations. It led to that short, terrible phase in political life under Rodrigues when governments began to speak their minds and say what they meant . . . ."

"I'll keep you in touch with what I'm doing, Jim," Gerry said, "I'll make regular reports to your office and at the same time make sure I don't compromise your people if any foul-ups occur on my part. I have to get up to my lodgings before nightfall. And I believe I have to contact a professor of politics who is looking after my arrangements."

"That would be Professor Maria Gomez. She is very good on matters of political economy, actually, the international banking system and so forth, and public finance is her brief with the Jaman government. She has a big input into the various ministries here. Yet there is a great prejudice against her in the establishment, mainly because she is a woman who has a lot of brains. Unlike the men, it is very hard to get her to do what you want. She is very self-disciplined, though I bet she too will have a bottom line, like every other human being. But you will have to watch her. It is reckoned that she has the hand over the Jaman president, and the prime minister is jealous of her influence."

It was strange, thought Gerry, that there were all these different people hanging around in disguise watching him when his mission here was actually very low-priority; really just a stratagem of others to get him out of the way.

Or was there something else to it?

He considered the coconut project to be a bit of a red herring and he doubted the practicality of any such wondercrop, except in the minds of fanatical government scientists. Surely the multinationals would not be interested in seeing such a product come on the market which would make superfluous all their present profitable production lines? Usually he found that the free offer of some new American product concealed another, entirely different agenda. He thought it possible that his skills were being used in some other game, the possible outcome of which was unknown to him. The 'entertainment' in the coming weeks and months would be to try and guess the real purpose of his mission here.

"That's the top guy of the business fraternity," said Jim pointing at a half-drunken man in Bermuda shorts and sunglasses, a tubby, middle-aged fellow who was chortling over a Budweiser with other look-alikes who were clearly local well-to-do's. Rapt adherents, most likely, Gerry surmised, of the cause of Capitalism and the subjugation of subversion everywhere, would-be aristocrats who looked down on their own people and smoked only foreign cigars.

"His name is Raul Umberto and he is the general of the armed forces. Give him a wave. You may need his help."

Gerry waved at Raul who returned a smile that immediately became compounded to a worried frown, and then followed with a brief wave which caused the businessman/general to spill much of his drink.

"Who was that Dutchman who spoke to me?," asked Gerry in a curious tone; "he seemed terribly interested in my affairs. And he appeared worried about something."

"Ah, the Dutchman. He is the island's leading conman and that is saying something. He is always taking different poses. I would be very interested to hear what you find out about him. We have discovered one thing though, in a raid on his living quarters, that was unexpected. He is a sensitive poet, who is also writing a book about what happens to the average, ordinary human spirit in the poverty stricken, humid tropics. I have heard that he is into exploring the lowest levels of the psychological depths in their most pessimistic form. A bit strange for a reputed Mafia man. We do wonder about his mental stability too. Do you know, he has been trying to recruit *me* to his cause!"

"He didn't strike me as being anything like an unbalanced individual," said Gerry, nonplussed.

"Well, that just goes to show you his range of skills."

As it was customary for CIA people to steer clear of each other for a while on the commencement of a job, Gerry prepared to take his leave now.

"I expect I'll get the lowdown on everything in the Jaman educational system from Professor Gomez," he said, with little enthusiasm. He was already bored by the evidence of normal political chaos in Jaman, illustrated mainly by McCall's comments, by the haywire at customs, by the numbers of security people who had come to observe his arrival. Bribes to duck government taxes were probably the largest item in the national income here, he reckoned; hardware coming ashore at night on private yachts is likely to be the most lucrative foreign trade; but short-changing workers is probably a dying preoccupation as paid work itself is most likely non-existent. The idea of getting the nation enthusiastic about a new type of coconut monoculture seemed about as realistic as selling ice cream in the Arctic. He wondered whether it was time to retire, or else change his career for one of those illegal jobs ex-security people were so fond of. He did not really see politics or crime as a way forward though, he thought now, if for no better reason than his residual 'moral scruples' which those damn educators had instilled into him in his impressionable youth. Whilst Mary, and others in her circle, had been praying systematically over the years for his return to the practice of orthodox religion, Gerry apparently had been trying to put aside all that childhood indoctrination. Yet, he had once undergone what he thought of as a 'religious experience'. This was his survival of Col Baxter's subterfuges and Baxter's pre-deceasing him. To him this was the equivalent of the parting of the Red Sea. He felt that there must be some kind of God after all.

"Goodbye Jim, be seeing you."

Gerry lifted his luggage and turned away from McCall, staring hard to find the exit from the lounge. He felt muzzy from the whiskey. He now also felt very annoyed that he had missed the opportunity of talking with Jean Blue again and she had disappeared from sight. He still didn't know what it was in her that attracted him; it certainly could not be what most people would impugn; it caused a sort of uncontrolled, uncharacteristic light-heartedness making him wish for another long chat, a drink in pleasant surroundings, a little time spent with someone who was far removed from the intricacies of a complex life. Or perhaps he was just fooling himself and the attraction was indeed more basic.

He wondered about the value of his whole life. He had always been deeply involved in his work and career; he had lived, breathed and endured the practical details of his many roles, especially the teaching. The compilation of lecture plans and delivery of learned talks to critical, and frequently hostile audiences, sometimes gave him a buzz. But wasn't it, he now asked himself, the case that it was all part of a charade? Didn't his low boredom threshold explain his inability to settle for a stable career in a respectable office in HQ? Wasn't his liking for going his own way, sampling different varieties of national drinks around the world and seeing different sights from different bars and hotel balconies, more of an explanation for his life than any ideals or intellectual ambitions? Who knows, despite all the worldly wisdom he had acquired perhaps he was still just ... an overgrown schoolboy who delighted, as Mary had once claimed, in bad company?

Little did Gerry know what reaction his departure from the terminal building would have on all the people there. Jim McCall, the Dutchman, the Kingstown Special Squad, the Cartel Soldiers in their American tourist disguises, even the real barmen, all sighed in relief the moment Gerry had gone out the door, relaxed or even dropped their disguises, rubbed their brows and began to chatter noisily in relief as if some terrible disaster had only just been averted.

There was no obvious, or plausible explanation for this sense of relief, though anyone looking at their reactions would receive the impression that everyone there had known everything there was to know about Gerry already; also, that there was something of the jinx or 'spook' about him.

How is it possible to describe Jaman as it was at that particular moment, at that instant in eternity which never was before and never would be again, in its latent power, its pregnant breaths, its vistas of mountains and sea, the potential immortality of its beauty? He looked around him at the view as he left the building. It was a bustling, torrid scene quite unlike the mundane world beyond the island which he had just left; the hubbub of Washington DC and its functional, drab airport. It suddenly occurred to him, however, that despite all the national insignia that decorated this place; the multitude of uniformed officials, the fluttering national flags of green, yellow and black celebrating its richness of history, the colourful bunting arranged in orderly lines that somehow managed to look completely askew, to give a carnival feeling of spontaneous celebration, a sort of serious light-heartedness, exotic sounds of the strange local dialect in which plain English words were swallowed by humble minds and reproduced as eloquent, extraordinary poetry which was both musical and mysterious; all of this provided an insistent assurance that one was, indeed, in a place called Jaman. Yet it occurred to him that he was in fact in the same sort of place that one finds everywhere and anywhere, the place he had just left, the places he would go to next, that people around the world behave in just this way, show off in exactly the same manner, even in Washington DC.

Were not even the universe and the earth one? Hooligan had said so.

The whiskey was 'helping' his thoughts.

He stumbled a little. His thoughts came with the allure of insights to him. He wondered whether he was subconsciously already taking on reverberations of that version of Buddhism as practiced in some parts of Jaman; it wouldn't do to start becoming all mystical at the very start of a mission, or to set out on that path of cerebral altruism trod by the enlightened guru which would lead, as far as he could see, to an abandonment of all psychological self-protection. He determined to get some real whiskey or rum as soon as possible.

"Taxi, bossy?," shouted a man waving an arm out of the window of a battered old car (late 50's or early 60's) British-made Austin Cambridge, a machine, he had noticed, which was to be seen everywhere in these ex-colonial countries and he had often wondered about the magic of their popularity and resilience. He had even sent in a report for forwarding to GM in which he had enlisted the best technical advice from the NASA people, the Military and fields of industry, along with collaborating Japanese industrial spies, in order to give their opinion on a full break-down of this machine. Using computer printouts of the various technical strengths and unique engineering features, especially as noted by Gerry in both conversations with the drivers and as he himself travelled on journeys in the said vehicles, they had tried to crack its secrets. This was a project he had done in the days when he was trying to rehabilitate himself to some degree and re-establish his credibility after a series of very poor academic results amongst his students, and especially to get recalled from a humiliating exile among British ex-pat.s in a South Pacific colony. The mission there was to monitor conversations which might give a clue as regards future British intentions for the small coral island, as the US had designs on it as a nuclear test site. His penetration methods failed however, due more to the game of cricket than anything else for he was unable to understand any of their talk about the sport and was completely ostracised for his ignorance. Despite the failure of his top secret Austin Cambridge report to convince GM and others to start replicating the car's design (he was to learn later that there was an innate reluctance on the part of motor manufacturers to produce long-lived, efficient cars) he was recalled to Washington nevertheless on the strength of a number of suggestions he had made on Intermediate Technology which certain powerful people wanted to investigate further. They appeared to parallel some of their own latest patented or upcoming designs. It was interesting, Gerry thought to himself, that today, many years later, one can still see in the Pacific region, as indeed probably elsewhere, these same old cars plying the taxi routes, sometimes even on otherwise deserted, barren military testing grounds totally devoid now, almost, of a native human population.

Realising that the taxi man might be a 'set-up' Gerry nevertheless greeted him cordially and got into the Austin Cambridge with his luggage beside him. The middle-aged driver was smoking a large cigar and he pulled even more heavily on this as Gerry tried to make himself comfortable.

"That's a Jaman Royal you're smoking, isn't it?," asked Gerry in a friendly tone.

"Sure is, man, tho mos' foreigners can nuah tell de difference. Yo be'n here before?"

"I've been in many places in this world, but I've never been here, though it is quite likely that someone *like* me was here before. Everyone has a double, they say. It is amazing how many people swear that they saw you in some place that you never once set foot in."

"Man, dat's true."

"Now listen. I want you to pretend that you are heading in the direction of the town centre; then I want you to make a quick detour and come back this way to go on to a little bar on the east side. It's called 'The First Class'. My boss is still at the airport and I don't want him knowing all my business."

"Me understand. Yo know de Firs' Class?"

There was more surprise in his voice.

"It is recommended in a tourist brochure."

"Oh. Me surprised. Only very few tourists go there."

Unlike most eastern countries where locals employ a reverential diffidence when speaking to foreigners the Jamanese, due to the infiltration of western culture, had no such caution and people went out of their way sometimes to 'take over' a visitor and utilise the 'victim' completely for their own purposes. Gerry was aware of this and acted accordingly.

"I'll pay you ten Jaman dollars."

"Don't worry 'bout de money, man, we don't hask for money here. Jus' give me twenty five dollar American."

It was best to get this man on his side.

"Look, have one hundred US dollars. That means I now completely own you. Always remember that I can pay you more than anybody else. There are a few things you will have to do for me, no questions asked. You will be my regular driver, as long as you are honest with me. If anyone offers you money for information about me, tell me and I'll top it up with more. Do you understand?"

"Makes sense to me, man. Fine. Me used to Americans. Me tek himportant US government official round Kingstown once. Name Mr Warner. You know him?"

"No," said Gerry.

He started the engine and from the sound it was clear to Gerry that it needed some tuning, at the very least. They hurtled out of the airport area as Gerry reflected on his mission. He knew that he was here officially to carry out simple teaching duties; no more and no less than that. True, there was an attempt to spice up a humdrum task by referring to great, futuristic schemes of economic development that he would be involved in, mainly by explaining economic progress and inspiring the youth of the country to learn new ways of experiencing change, and so on and so forth. He would be expected to account for his success, or lack of it, in those repetitive end-of-term reports.

Nevertheless there was also something funny going on with regard to future American plans for the island, if not indeed the world. It would be just like his superiors to send him to the backwaters out of harm's way and yet, at the same time, give him an assignment which could prove quite momentously dangerous. He knew that the people at the airport had been there to see who he teamed up with, if anybody at all; that they were curious about his Harvard connections and they probably also were just curious to see what sort of a person he was (not to mention that they were also keeping an eye on each other). Everybody loathed and feared intellectuals, mainly for their unpredictability, their practical, every-day uselessness and their lack of influence on actual events. Yet they had an undeserved influence in other ways, the presidents always seemed to rate them highly, probably because they didn't look or sound like politicians and they could also be used to soften up public opinion by means of prestigious lectures and 'much talked about books'. It was going to be great fun to see how the business of the new coconut went down; how the multinational companies would respond to pre-empt competition in their own fields, how the MAFIA would try to get a share of the shady side to the business; how different groups would rush for shares in AMERFOODS INC., THE FARMERS' FRIEND. Their subsidiaries would soon be buying up all redundant estates in that crucial gap when nothing much seems to be happening and property drops steeply in value. Much of what would happen in the political and economic fields would be predictable, similar in fact to many previous 'subversive' economic schemes such as the introduction of Coca Cola to Russia and China, the manufacturing of Scud 'cars' in Germany and so forth. But there would also be the unpredictables, which is what the CIA would be mainly concerned with sorting out; and yet another unpredictable would be his own role. He sometimes went through great mental turmoil over his purpose in the CIA and in the world. Whether this was a spiritual or psychological problem, or else purely a matter of technicalities within the broad parameters of a profession and a professional job, was still uncertain. Was he really a 'spy on the spies' as had been mooted by more than one observer? Was he himself the victim of some plot, or was he the instigator of his own plot? Was he the supreme cynic, or else an idealist (is there much difference between the two?). Was he a loyal American or an untrustworthy, alienated anarchist? Were his suppose talents really only legend, a fable, based on no more than shadows of tales and myths inaccurately related? Had he behind him a life of achievement and feats or, alternatively, only a series of failures, lost in an alcoholic fog of lost causes? Was he really the brilliant economic theoretician, responsible for all US (or in reality CIA) policy since the 60's as believed for example by many of his students (he imagined) among others, or was he simply a FUNK?

No one knew; not even himself.

The Jaman licensed hire vehicle operator seemed impressed by Gerry's apparent street-wise knowledge.

"How you know about de Firs' Class?"

"I hear it is the place for an honest drink, no big knobs from upper Kingstown or supremacists from the local aristocracy hang out there. It's well away from where grumpy civil servants amuse themselves, and from the university campus and other dens of nosy parkers who bore and annoy you all night with stale observations on the world as they see it. If only they would leave their ivory towers and come out on the street and experience life as it is lived by the majority of mankind, people like yourself if I may say so, then they would know that it is absurd to impose their own fallacious logic on the keen, determined chaos and chance which is the natural world. Do you know what I mean?"

"Yeah, everyt'ing cool here ya ... Me tek life easy, man. Jus' let it happun, like you say."

"Yes, no point in taking life too seriously all the time," laughed Gerry out loud.

"Ho ho ho. Ha ha ha. Hee he eee! No man."

As he was 'humouring' the taximan Gerry was simultaneously thinking of various strategies and options to be followed in order to achieve successfully the objective of his mission, i.e. a hazard-free time and a safe return stateside eventually with perhaps a renewed appetite for life in the First World again. In the intervening period there would be the usual subversion by western teaching methods of established conventions and ideas in government, the university, the media and hopefully in the minds of ordinary people. But Gerry knew that common humanity did not control their thoughts in the same way as the educated elite; they did not measure or observe their thoughts. In fact they would be surprised by the revelation that every thought they had, every emotion, idea and mental image however poetically, roughly or stupidly expressed had a philosophical tag, a nomenclature in the files and grim registers of the world's universities if not also the records of government ministries and tax departments. Thus it would be necessary to translate everything he put over in his talks, lectures and seminars into the common parlance of the people of Jaman.

It had always been one of the challenges of his training, to explore these different lines of communication into people's psyches. Sometimes he thought that this was an inadvertent by-product of that intense indoctrination of the Propaganda Outreach Program in the sixties, when the aim had been to teach him a contempt for other people's beliefs, when in fact he learnt that it was impossible to convince a person of anything he or she didn't want to be convinced of, no matter what repetitive chant or torture was used. For instance he still listened to that undermining, politically unapproved, dissolute pop music. Brainwashing was a myth; people often just pretended that they 'believed' or 'agreed'. His other discovery, which he had always kept secret from Dick Warner, the CIA, the Harvard crowd and the government (probably to ensure that they maintained funding for his many research programmes, which allowed him and others to spend a lot of time in comfortable libraries) that *all people think exactly the same thoughts,* made his life much more simple. He even sometimes told himself, half in earnestness, that his inadvertent influence on events, if not also on the popular imagination, caused by the 'Taran incident', for instance, had been but the beginning of a long and brilliantly successful career in which he had entered into, and perhaps also affected, the global unconscious in ways unknown to those who had sent him out on his various missions. Gerry, as he grew older, was slowly beginning to suspect that his role in life was indeed a 'spiritual' one; on the one hand apparently following orders to impose US ideals on backward places and peoples, obeying the most facile and ludicrous pedagogic principles; on the other hand subtly letting his students see how absurd and ineffectual those ideas and theorems were. So that when he was, for instance, diagnosing their infrastructural and practical problems and propounding modern and socially acceptable solutions to their problems, they were sufficiently made aware, and confident enough, during the delivery of these lessons, by his irony and blatant sarcasm, not to mention his own deliberately instituted and obvious mistakes, to actually challenge immediately, not openly but in a subconscious way, all that he set before them. It was in fact the never-discussed sacred cows of conventional economic wisdom that Gerry really had in mind when everyone else, especially the 'curriculum' authorities, i.e. his bosses, thought it was some officially unapproved, condemned fallacy or heresy that he was removing from the consciousness of the young.

In the insecurity of his arrival in what was plainly a difficult country, as well as his own feelings of inadequacy, he reflected now on past glories as they drove along. The methods of Gerry's were seen to work, for instance, in the Tourism field, his ideas being taken on board at a significant weekend workshop on 'The Potential of Tourism as a Way to Civilise the World' held at the Pentagon. The great master plan was to persuade the chief citizens of the respectable countries in Europe to annually forsake their heartland for most of the summer months for faraway subtropical or tropical regions, allowing free access for American personnel to their own lands, homes and establishments, usually posing as tourists, sometimes as returned native cousins, and give them the opportunity to reconnoitre significant establishments and places. It was achieved essentially by the simple expedient of promoting the popular allure of photography and opportunistically released American films featuring so-called tourist meccas or sunspots, as well as various romantic locales. Anything could be used to attract people to where the Pentagon or Langley (not to mention Harvard which of course saw the anthropological potential of studying tourist movements) wanted them. The benefits of a suntan (again photography was the key, especially in tourist brochure advertising; significantly advertising was an international craze initiated from and controlled by the US), the promotion of a western cultural superiority to any found elsewhere in the world, by the provision of cheap American pop drinks and foods, especially in sunny coastal regions, etc., proved to be the key. So through a series of simple, apparently recreationally motivated proposals there was effected a major shift in world population and migratory balances suited to the free flow of American ideas, technology etc.

He congratulated himself on his own cunning, for with his double-crossing methodology he had been able to influence all the prevailing ideology in the way he wanted. For instance under the notion of Free Trade he secretly introduced the subliminal idea that *all* cultures, values and peoples were actually all of the same and equal value. The proof of this lay in the fact that although his own writings and the books of his department could only be read by about 10% of the world's population yet their ideas seemed to have passed miraculously into the common consciousness. It gave locals, and especially the people here in Jaman, as he had already begun to sense, the confidence to confront tourists in public and sell them their own 'spiel'. Gerry had turned what had been intended as a neo-imperialistic crusade into a triumph for the beach 'bum', the local craftsman, the frantic seller of native artifacts, the hard-pressed rickshaw puller, i.e. the little people of the Third World. Not that any of this would be welcomed or accepted back home. When he had pointed out the significance of these particular ideas to Dick he was 'rewarded' with frequent, demoralising postings to board meetings of The Reader's Digest magazine; and in fact his work was to become somewhat deflated by shortened versions of it unadvisedly appearing in that magazine, which probably had been the deliberate intention of Warner.

Now here he was in another place, another time and the job was still the same.

"The folk here have go bad since de Independence. It not the same since bwana left. We need education," said the taximan in a rather hamfisted attempt to ingratiate himself with, or to psychologically disarm, McArthur.

Gerry stared out the back window to see if anybody was tailing them, although much of the action was to the front of the vehicle where large, colourful country busses hurtled towards them at frantic speeds, forcing their own taxi into the side and managing each time to scrape or dent their unfortunate car (the driver laughed, saying that his taxi could 'tek anyt'ing'). It was worse than anywhere else he had been in the world, for here the manoeuvring was determined by the random positioning of potholes, leaving the final track a sequence of Russian roulette.

"Nobody behind us, relax man," said the driver happily; "tell me, why you here? By de way, my name Turbo."

"Pleased to meet yo, Turbo."

Gerry was already 'jumping' into a refrain of the local accent.

"I am Gerry. I think we can do business. I am here about the coconut, actually. What do you think of coconuts?"

Despite its apparently harmless quality this was a profound question with many resonances to it, and striking many chords in Turbo's subconsciousness.

"Gerry is good American name. Me love everything American. Now you ask me 'bout de coconut. Me never think about dem before, but now I think dey are GOOD to think about. They are nice. Coconut water nice nice and de tourists love it. Our Jaman coconut de bes' in the world. Only dey begin to get sick now."

"You know why they get sick, Turbo?"

"Some dey say it is de virus that come 'cross de water in de salt dat come from China."

"No, Turbo, it is not that. It is not some terrible disaster of nature. It is really something quite different. It is the last thing that you or any Jaman person would be expected to realise. It is the coconut's way of saying: 'we are tired with Jaman, with the way the people operate here. It is time there was a change in the living conditions of us plants and also of the people. It is time things were changed around here. Look at us, we are turning yellow and dying and bearing no more fruit. It is all extremely unhealthy and we cannot tolerate it anymore'!

"You mean, it is like a curse on us?"

Turbo sounded shocked.

"Sort of. I have come here to teach people to do better".

Thus, *'Better Mus' Come'* became the following year's election's Opposition slogan, inspired it is said by the original words of Gerry spoken in that taxi.

"I am what is called a US Government Development Expert. But everyone in fact knows that I am really an espionage officer controlling agents operating all over the world. I am the most public CIA official in the world and there have been to the best of my knowledge at least fifty assassination attempts on my life. Indeed some of my superiors have been trying to have me eliminated for twenty or more years."

"Why they not just fire you, man? Or shoot you? In Jaman that will be a quicker way. More merciful."

"It is a kind of game they play. Not for them the crude Chicago-style killing. That would be too easy. Nor would there be any logic in it for them. Everything in the CIA must have 'logic'. They prefer their ends to be achieved as the natural culmination of a long, preferably complicated process called a plan or a 'policy'. Everything can be justified if it falls into some sort of plan. But I have always been able to play them at that little game. For instance, it had once been intended for me to eat poisoned chocolate and fall over dead at an international symposium in Switzerland where I was stationed at the time. American chocolate wanted to take over the Swiss industry for strategic reasons, this was in Zurich in '80. But at the last minute, before the chocs were passed around, a bunch of anti-narcotic undercover police burst in (at my instigation) and busted the chocolates and suppliers. It was then that those present realised what was going on with the chocolates. They thought it was industrial sabotage. I knew it was a murder attempt on me. You see I am always one step ahead of HQ all the time; that is their problem with me. Your common Jaman criminal would have definitively made a better job of it than they have."

"Mac, I see it all. You is too smart for de boss. He no control you. You embarrass him all de time. You obey his orders but break his private rules. He confused. You too intelligent, not his sort. Yet he can nuah kill you too easy as maybe you have something over him, like maybe you marry de big boss's daughter . . . ."

Gerry's anticipation of a drink with Turbo at The First Class suddenly became a strong desire and he tried to relax as they negotiated some extremely large, rain-manufactured potholes; he also still occasionally glanced back at the road behind.

"Nobody follow us, Mac. Last three vehicles gone, run into potholes, break down, turn away and crash. Potholes very bad today." □

chapter
SIX

The road led happily, in the suddenly dimmed light, past the dusty, desolate cement factory to a siding of small shops and there, between a shabby grocery and hardware store, was The First Class. Gerry's eye was caught by the flashy sign on the roof, lit now in the dusk by red, white and green electric bulbs which emitted a weak glow and gave the establishment an air of exciting decadence. It might make it to a $5 A Night guide book, depending on certain facilities, he thought, contrasting reality with the glowing description that had been published about the place in a secret Harvard departmental handbook; it was said to be the place where you 'experienced all the delights of the Southern Seas in exotic tropical surroundings'. This information had been accompanied by a photo of an establishment which was certainly not the 'First Class'. A typical tourist brochure fib, or just a necessary deception? Of course Gerry already knew the answer to that, as he was the person who had been responsible for compiling the handbook in the first place. It was issued chiefly to roving academics who liked to combine long holidays overseas with work, usually relaxed spells in seemingly innocuous tourist resorts whilst doing intellectually challenging research or studying strategic and dangerous 'world security problems'. The truth was simply that it would have been in very bad taste to include facts which might have identified and prejudiced an innocent local premises; one never knew who might read these publications. As it was, The First Class was visited by the occasional foreigner who proved his/her worth in dollars and everything was kept low key.

He took his own luggage with him out of the taxi, realising that it would be daft to let Turbo even touch it (for it would have meant another large tip). At the same time he wanted to show the man that he liked him and wished to maintain their mutually relaxed relationship, which might be of benefit to them both. One learned to pick up as many friends as possible in his occupation. In a flurry of nervous activity he dropped his baggage on the road and picked up a scrap of a cigarette packet that was lying there, pretending to any observers that he was simply fiddling with his bag. He wrote down the address and telephone number of the place for a future rendezvous with Turbo, drawing the sign for $100's as well, and spelling out: 'ring me there tomorrow'. If Turbo couldn't read, somebody else would do it for him, he reasoned.

"Cha," said Turbo happily, putting the paper into his pocket; "but me stay a while yet to see you settle in."

Inside the bar there was a surprising scene. It was as if Gerry had been expected. His heart lifted, he *was* expected. A huge 'Welcome to New Boss' was over the bar and the juke box was playing 'Danny Boy' to a popular Jaman beat! Turbo too, it seemed, was very much at home here. The place was full of locals from nearby alleys, gullies and shanties. In a trice Gerry had taken in their respective status: gamblers, alcoholics, crooks, kindly but loose women, an embittered young idealistic 'student', beggars, idlers, ragamuffins, not to mention Mr Sher ('The Cap') and his wife Margarita who were in charge. The clientele's respective social standing, which in this context meant their relative ability to procure shots of free overproof rum at Festival Time, were in that same order, with the exception of course of Mr and Mrs Sher with whom it was always a case of 'the last shall be first'. They, in this unemployed, or unemployable neighbourhood depended on these 'engineers of ghetto society' for the maintenance of some 'stability' in local social life and the prospect of a little, however minute, custom. As with all struggling proprietors everywhere Mr Sher had a second string to his bow.

He was in charge of what was the HQ of the secret CIA, that CIA within the CIA in Jaman, all under the cover of what was termed a 'Tourist Agency', or glorified 'up-market' (for that neighbourhood) drinking hole. He was personally very proud of his secret post and he did not even discuss it much with Margarita, who was just as much proud of the fact that even she was not privy to information concerning her husband's Intelligence role as she was of the fact that he actually was an unofficial employee of the USA government, or of what was at least one of its (supposed) agencies. More often than not Mr Sher would put his wife through a whole series of non-OK dilemmas, brought on by his personal escapades such as disappearing with his cronies for weeks; or turning up at the bar in the early hours with a crew of drunken no-goods to threaten sleeping kith and kin; bouncing cheques put out by Mr Sher himself on his friends' shops and even on his own establishment; a complete inability to listen to reason, or to accept solid advice on matters appertaining to his good social standing with church and community; also a stock of very tall stories about his past that were quite believable if only for their stupidity which suited the man in a strange way. His wife accepted that he was like this simply for the good of the international community and, to put it bluntly, the freedom of all peace-loving people everywhere which, she had heard The Cap once say at a drinking session when he was wont to loosen his tongue and indulge in poetic license and expand on his many achievements, he strongly believed in. (He was named The Cap for the thin, blue peaked cap with the American Firestone

Company logo which he had worn on his head since 1952. He wore it even at night in bed, for he could never bear to be without it).

"Welcome, master. We have been expecting you," said Mr Sher somewhat proudly; "and how are things in Harvard?"

Gerry felt at home already. Needless to say Mr Sher's last five words were the secret code agreed for visiting officials. 'Harvard' had a defusing effect on overhearers' potentially hostile emotions as the resonance of the name equalled that of, say, the Vatican or of some sacred River of Pilgrimage in South Asia. Mr Sher had a strong belief that everyone connected with the legendary place of learning was unusually blessed, knew all that there was to know, and also brought in tow a special blessing. Gerry himself knew, intuitively, what was immediately required of him, before he had even bought that drink for everybody; a speech which spared no blushes and was not a 'wilting lily' in hyperbole or schmaltz.

"My friends, dare I call you 'colleagues', fellow travellers on the road to freedom and democracy and prosperity, I never cease to praise your courage. I admire your resolve in these dark and difficult times of unemployment. Even before the liberation of your land and its arrival in the galaxy of independent nations by many trials of constant struggle, enterprise, thrift and diligence in the face of adversity, I never failed to marvel at the bravery, resilience, competence, foresight, fortitude, prudence, patience displayed by each and every one of you over so many difficult, dark days and nights, indeed over the long, lonely years, as you dutifully, faithfully, carried out your intelligence duties here in the 'First Class'."

A sense of satisfaction, allied to bemusement, was felt by the bar's clientele, especially at the last statement as they reminded themselves of their real usefulness to the world, even though they just sat around most of the time, drinking cheap rum and discussing their own and their neighbours' lives. In particular much self-satisfaction was felt by Alfredo The Thug, chief character-assassination expert and Executioner-In-Waiting, who always claimed that he was destined to come out of hiding one day and implement his mission of liquidating various politicians and prominent members of society; he was only awaiting 'the word'. In the meantime he prepared himself for his lofty, future task by bullying his friends at dominos and roughing up customers whenever he took a dislike to them or was just feeling bad.

Another drinker, Idle Pete, was not feeling too bad now either. Pete was 'saving himself' for the big day when he would be called out from his enforced, long-term unemployment and take up his rightful duties at last as coordinator of all Gossip and Information supply in the bar, locally and in all Jaman. He had always reckoned privately that Mr Sher was an impostor and a usurper of his own rightful position as chief 'know-it-all'.

"If it were not for dat man ruling the roost, getting the contracts and acting the big goat we would all be better hoff and not be sidding around here without a job or the hope of one. Why should he be the one who gets to act big in front of the American visitor? Do you think me do all the work and let that fool get all the glory? No, not me ...", he muttered quietly to himself. He reflected now that the words of this man Gerry suggested that he might be someone who was liberal with the dollars.

Jos, the bar philosopher, also felt uplift and euphoria at the words of the eminent visitor. For most of his days, his whole life indeed, he had been struck by the futility of existence in general and his own existence in particular; life was 'a sham'; Big Eddie, the country's president, top personality and political leader for thirty years was 'a bum'; the normally accepted generalities of life were 'a plot' to be laid at the door of 'the Freemasons', whilst the bar was just a 'dive of wasters'. Nor was there life after death. He felt inspired now by the arrival and encouraging words of Gerry, for most likely there would be some dollars going around pretty soon. He had long ago reached the conclusion that money and material possessions were the only antidote to the miseries of life. His role in the Jaman 'Intelligence Network' was simply to undermine the confidence of anyone daring to speak up in favour of the government, the established political parties, all pillars of society or anyone with an optimistic view of things; with a bit of cash now he would in fact at last be able to face, and debate, these issues of life and politics in a little more comfort and style. The only problem would be how to get the available cash, or some of it, into his own pocket.

Barmaid Melanie, do-everything, see-no-evil and hear-only-what-is-meant-for-your-ears, everyman's mother, sister, daughter, girlfriend and provider to nearly just about everybody who was around, chief cook and bottle washer and healer of all wounds, now a not-so-young thirty years of age, was feeling ambivalent about Gerry's arrival. She knew that for a little while the men, or 'boys', would be going around with smart hats or shirts and their heads in the air, full of ideas and schemes on how best to serve Gerry and impress him with their own particular devotion; thereby fortuitously reducing the many immediate pressures and physical assaults on her, if only by default, her own presence being less important than Gerry's. At the same time it meant extra work, washing shirts that extra bit clean, begging an iron somewhere and then having to persuade The Cap to allow the use of his plug socket; even having to go and borrow some neat kerchiefs and bush jackets from the different church ministers passing the usual line about tragic funerals in distant regions. All this was to simply facilitate that great charade that men put up to show that they are masters of all around them. The politicians and government ministers set the worst example for these expensive fashions, thought Melanie; it was an on-going joke amongst the women of Jaman that the 'official island male attire' that was dictated by the minister of culture to be worn at all public engagements, who was considered to be the most ambitious and ruthless politician in the country, Magnus Rabid, i.e. so-called macho bush jackets, was only a reflection of what the men thought the women liked, and their style was all loudly approved of by the women simply because it made the male of the species look and behave in very pompous, but harmless ways.

However, Melanie thought that Gerry himself looked exceptionally sensible in his dark, heavy suit as it clearly made no allowance for modern male sartorial preconceptions and was designed for more utilitarian purposes than the Jaman style; its numerous, deep pockets for instance were very practical for carrying things, especially money, and its unsuitability to a tropical clime gave the serious-looking Gerry a studious, even self-abnegatory air; there was something about this man that was solemn and not susceptible to being played about with, she thought. She was even a little bit afraid of his somewhat mysterious behaviour here in the bar. She knew that all the others would look upon Gerry as 'the big boss' and as a 'sugar daddy'; hadn't the 'Travel Firm' been sending money sweeteners over the post for years? Yet she would treat him a little more warily, for she felt that there was something of the dark horse about him, a natural subterfuge that would put all the other men into the shade for sheer brazenness.

Just what was it, she asked herself now, that Gerry, and other passing-through Americans, found interesting, useful or exploitable in that locale, the bar, or the folk? It was all distinctly fishy to Melanie. It was not as if the locals were super-dooper criminals, subversives or *major* drug suppliers or anything obvious like that; and quite surely it was not those hilarious holiday guided tours The Cap put on occasionally for the odd tourist or two who happened to venture into the neighbourhood; forays into the 'bush' in search of the infamous wild pigs (yet to be actually spotted by anybody); or out on the sea for a tiring, dangerous fishing trip in shark-infested waters in a primitive native canoe?

Or was it really one of those cases of another affluent do-gooder coming to check on the outcome of donations made to another, patronised Third World development Project? They would have to pull up their socks now at the neighbourhood Community centre.

Whatever way you looked at it, there was no doubt that something queer was afoot in this part of Kingstown, she decided.

Then there was the idealistic, embittered young man, Paulo, from the rural hinterland.

"Here is the story of my life," he said, pushing a manuscript in front of Gerry whose head was by now swimming from the overproof rum which he was, as custom dictated, being forced to drink whilst making unconvincing grunts of pleasure.

Needless to say, this drink and all the other drinks the bar clientele were trying out, all the more expensive, rarely tasted treats, such as golden Appletons and Jaman Scotch, were 'on him'.

"*Chapter one* ... it's written in the form of a novel ... the police would be interested in it ... for the wrong reasons. Tell me what you think ... ."

Gerry was already back in the swing of things, it seemed, being asked to grade written work and give his opinion on a student's 'best effort'.

He did some speed reading, as he normally would, even if it was a Phd doctrinal thesis he might be assessing. He had once vetted such a thesis on 'The Rational Powers of Mankind as Evidenced by the Thoughts of the World's Decision Makers' by a young psychology student in record time, two minutes. It was later proudly published in an unexpected form, as a top-selling story of money, power and sex, but to his disappointment, under a different title.

As he started to read he began to feel a sinister, threatening atmosphere arise in the place, as if the whole population of the country was looking over his shoulder (his experience told him it was probably a sort of awe and envy emanating from those there, the majority, who probably could not read or write in even a rudimentary form).

He read:

"... *Paulo Costello, a penniless, temporary reporter on The Nation's Voice, the main newspaper in Jaman, or more precisely, government propaganda rag, sat on the bar stool, wondering about the possibility of revolution in the country, and at the same time contending with another revolution inside himself. The strong ferment of the country, the Red Label beer, the history of whose founding fathers read like the history of the country itself, the same Puerto Rico Family whose ancestral discovery of the liquid assets of the native aboriginals, combined with their own inbred 'business' qualities, had brought about a revitalisation of a moribund economy which had been depressed by the machinations of a dreadful, importuning metropolitan power, and whose many but close-knit descendants today constituted a network of families whose every sneeze caused major reverberations in the country's economic and political life, was causing a nauseous stirring in Paulo's stomach and a befuddled, if pleasant dizziness in his head.*

"This poison is what the country's wealth is built upon," he thought bitterly, wanting to spit.

The discontented rebel-in-waiting drank a long, deep draught speculating within himself that the people of the country were as much under the spell of this brew than of any other idol, ideology, religion or pleasurable attraction. Perhaps there was a link between the perpetually stupored state of three-quarters of the population of the country and the bad behaviour of citizens whose fights, arguments and foul language were evident at all times, with endless

94

quibbling and quarrelling over everything under the sun, the time of day, the clothes President Eddie wore on his Great Visit To The Countryside, the cost of a smoke, what day it is; only an hour ago he himself had been unwittingly involved in an argument with another customer over whose seat it was Paulo was sitting on, although everyone else knew that all the seats in the bar were the property of Mr—, the proprietor.

This little to-do had almost developed into a scrap and only for the intervention of the proprietor (much to Paulo's secret relief) there would have been another typical, disorderly Jamanese scene. He did not know what was bringing about this stagnation in politics, mores, manners, even in religion, where there was a proliferation of strange fundamentalist, inward-looking sects, led by the aggressive Church of Jah. There was a definite need for a revolution. He did not know how a revolution could be started or who could start it, but it was evidently something absolutely necessary.

Sitting glumly at the bar, his smart jacket too smart for that locale, making him look like an up-and-coming junior business executive or minor civil servant on a solitary bar-crawl uplifting the ambiance, his dark eyebrows and soupy eyes sunk in a dim conspiracy with the aromatic flavours of the beer, he bewailed the miseries of the country in a silent flow of thoughts. To start with there was the highbrow educational system. Its complex pedagogics and archaic classicism had succeeded in demoralising the people through subjecting them to the didactic ideas and alien values of a few, esoteric individuals, especially in examinations. The methods and gradings of these individuals were, he reflected, determined by their arrogantly low opinion of the ability of human nature as exampled especially in the average Jaman student. This might be expected from the blinkered and prejudiced ex-patriate teacher but was very hurtful coming from Jaman's own 'cream of the best', Kingstown's educated social elite. Such pedagogues, who had failed him and had him thrown out of the university, would surely be the first to go in the coming revolution.

He again drank deeply into his glass, enjoying the warmth and strength he obtained from its contents, and acquiring a stiffening resolve which helped to counteract the uncomfortable effects of having sat immobile and patiently there for the past three hours. These same people, he mused, were the selected representatives and spokesmen of a still smaller group of individuals, who had their own motives for keeping the people in ignorant and humble obsequiousness, and they in turn were just stand-ins for a yet smaller group, and they for a smaller group still. If you looked at it that way it all went back to one person. Who could it be, he asked himself, his lips moving noiselessly and subversively in the ill-lit bar; who could most profit personally by keeping the natural light of the citizenry dimmed, if not extinguished? The great mass of peasants (he was proud to consider himself as one of that mass) for instance, as they laboured away at the impoverished earth remained so uneducated that they were unable (he had found in his reporting from those destitute areas) to understand even simple things like the weather, complaining for instance about drought as if it was not a natural feature but some catastrophe planned by their enemies in Kingstown; or why, when it rained bringing havoc instead of bounty God was showing His vindictiveness towards them; why government promises never came true, or even why the country gave away bananas instead of eating them. In numerous, fact-seeking intellectual discussions with the sweating, toiling men and women of the land (some were his own, distracted relatives) he had found that they had no grasp of the fundamentals of life. They saw the earth as their foe, fate as certain death, and what should have been a boon to them such as a decent harvest was always seen as an unmitigated calamity as it usually portended a future bad harvest. One day on an enforced, unwished for holiday at his parents' humble cabin, brought about by a temporary suspension from duties at the behest of his employer at The Nation's Voice worried over his 'vehement truth-seeking', he had an involved debate with a peasant neighbour who was of the typical, pessimistic type.

"It's not this weather, by the heavens," he had said in his earthy, sweating voice, "that is our chief foe and cause of all our woe."

"And how is that?," the young reporter had asked, keeping his air of cynicism as low key as possible and looking at the brown, hardened face of the man with as much respect as their differences allowed for.

"The life-giving rain is often slowcoming," he had said in a resigned way, "like the gifts of promising politicians or the help of faraway relatives. It is also a mystery why, when the rain comes, it has at first an evil effect on everything, breaking up the soil and plants and drowning helpless people, removing the goodness from the land instead of refreshing it, running free but not partaking in the life of the parched earth. It is a hardship too that while this is a fertile tropical land the heat is too great, the winds too destructive and the air too parched with a great burning. It was never like that in my father's day. Then the government experts try to fool us with hours of 'farming improvement' courses, so that things worsen in our absence."

He stared, brow furrowed, out at the setting sun, licking his dry lips in a desperate pursuit of a little moisture. True enough, Paulo thought to himself: the poor man's harvest is often rendered null and void by the many enemies he has to deal with; and it isn't just hordes of minuscule ants invading from the east or pests such as the native fibre worms which bore away at everything before it has even been collected in, for sometimes a shining harvest, displayed openly by proud villagers in all its glory, is made useless by the incomprehensible word of some official who refuses its passage to market or else approves some dastardly price handed down by a similarly high-handed man of commerce, both acting with the sort of behaviour accredited by the superstitious to the petty, vindictive gods.

The peasant looked at him with sad eyes and spoke through still-unsalved lips:

"Oh, it's a whole collection of strange things that do cause what is happening in this world today. Did you know that the big American bomb that they let off not far from here is one of them

97

things that does make the bad weather, for I witnessed it myself make a smoky mushroom grow into the sky, and for many seasons we all collected the brown nuts that fell from the sky to plant them where they blossom in soil that would bear no other plant or crop. There are many other things that happen that bespeak a strange story of how the scientists and government do go about upsetting Mother Nature . . .".

As Paulo left him there, wondering about the Bomb but feeling a little tired at the simple man's primitive view of things, he went slowly back to his parents' cabin for an evening of talk and pretence about his successful goings-on in the big town."

(Here Gerry was impressed by the stark honesty and realism of the novelist).

"For a moment he had looked back to see the peasant, at the sound of distant temple bells marking the hour, sink slowly to his knees in prayer; Paulo shook his head in bafflement and pessimism.

Staring now at the hard, cynical faces of the other patrons of the 'El Conquistador' he thought it wasn't just the countryman who needed enlightenment either. Townspeople too were ill-informed about many things; such as where their food came from, what was the 'foreign' language they spoke and why they could not understand most of the rest of their fellow-countrymen; why they had to live in scrappy hovels with no breathing space between in a land of so much open space; and where there were none of the blessings of the countryside but all the disadvantages of extreme poverty. He would have to tell them right there and now of the dark cloud of hopelessness that lay over their homes and lives; of the tumultuous questioning and political restlessness that should have been affecting them promising great political change but which seemed never to have occurred to them; of their despicable acceptance of their lot, coming to the seedy 'El Conquistador' in order to escape any thought and effort when they could be outside enjoying life hopefully in the open air under a blue sky, leading active, fruitful, happy existences, earning by personal sacrifice and effort the right to live in fine houses, drive nice cars to work in government and banking offices downtown, being able to indulge in exploitation of, yet decry at the same time, all the no-goods and criminal elements hanging around street corners in the company of the only caste lower than they, the mad, in other words generally behaving just as their betters do now. He almost slid to the floor as he moved himself with great effort from the stool and tried to turn to the other customers; their faces he could not see. "Listen," he shouted in his country voice which had regained, temporarily from his recent home visit, its original resonance but which tended more to annoy than to impress his hearers;

"to one who can see it all coming. While you lot are sitting here the world is slipping away from under your feet; you'll all soon be out on your ears and the Puerto Ricos will be all the richer for the cents you have spent in here . . .".

He thought at this point that he could make out a moving mass, more a horde, of attackers coming his way and he never did find out what caused him to hit the floor with an almighty thud.

It was the herald of things to come . . .".

He had the mark of a novelist, thought Gerry, giving it a B, although he did not think that the irony which made the piece so attractive was altogether conscious. But this young man would be a useful accomplice in his plans, for he sounded like a raw, ambitious rebel. He wondered if the character in the novel was very much like the author; everything he had ever learned about such scribes told him that the identification would be more than 100%.

"What name do you write under?," asked Gerry, being especially careful here in order not to embarrass him with a patronising attitude, as aspiring writers are notorious for their sensitivity.

"Paulo Costello, my real name, and I can vouch for everything that is in the book. I saw it myself and heard the words of the characters with my own ears. The end is near."

"Have you finished the book, then?"

"No. It is half-way through. I mean I feel the end of the world is near. We are finished in this island unless we have a revolution soon and replace the status quo. I became a bit worried about that bomb after I thought about it for a while. What if it did really happen? The government has told nobody about any bomb, but many people in the country saw the explosion. However, if it does not happen in the city it does not happen at all, as far as Kingstown folk are concerned."

It was at this point that Gerry realised that Paulo was on the point of inadvertently blowing the whole master plan of Warner, a feat effected not by careful political thought or even counter-intelligence, but simply through a peasant's native superstition allied with the petty nationalism of a parochial reporter. But it was not yet the opportune moment to inform the population of the impending danger from Dick Warner, he had decided, for he was not yet sure in what form it would come. It would be a bit embarrassing for the powers-that-be (the people he was hoping to influence), and even for himself, if a young no-hope Jaman writer, one attempting to remedy his own poverty-stricken upbringing and low status by means of the only tool available to him, his partly educated, recently rejected, scholastic ability, should by means of what would be a scrap of local folk opera, probably finally converted into a piece of vulgar journalism or even into a popular hit song for the benefit of the masses, alarm the nation and cause mass panic. The real danger would then be missed in the confusion. Paulo would have to be silenced for a while. The methods to be used, Gerry's methods, would have to be more sophisticated.

He would immediately have to recruit Paulo, his student, as an accomplice and agent (even if it meant breaking that unwritten 'Hippocratic oath' of the teaching profession, never to manipulate or exploit an innocent pupil).

"Look, Paulo, I can help you achieve all your ambitions. I'll be working at the university (ok, the college as it's called) and I will have direct access to the very top levels of research and government departments. I can get you any number of scoops which might help you, amongst other things, get your job back at the newspaper. Perhaps I could even help you to get a proper job at the government information office. They often need qualified clerks like yourself. Also, you could use any inside information that you get in your book! You need a focus for your brain power, which you are wasting at the moment in wild goose chases around the country and hanging out here. There is nothing more heartbreaking for a teacher like me than to see wasted talent! Listen, I can even process some paper qualifications for you."

"Do you really think this book has some good ideas? It's only off the top of my head, really. I can do much better if I really think hard. I actually have some weird, deep thoughts which might surprise you, about the meaning of life and Armageddon and you westerners and such things. It all links up in one huge sort of explosive ending."

"Rule number one, Paulo, I give you advice as I consider you my pupil as well as a colleague, if you are ever to rise to a powerful position in this country, is never to come out openly with controversial information," said Gerry, looking furtively around him, "you never know who could be listening. You could easily be misinterpreted by some casual eavesdropper and land yourself in trouble with the authorities and your peers. Now concerning what you heard in the countryside, suffice to say that country people are more canny than city folk. Still, I would like to investigate everything that you saw there. In future tell me everything you learn about the places you visit. I may even be able at some point in the future to get you on a trip to Washington to make your reports and maybe even get to visit a publisher."

"I think that my life, which up till now has been something of a failure, is about to fulfil its real potential," said Paulo with enthusiasm, feeling that at long last he had come across a 'like mind', even a fellow-crusader. He looked up at Gerry, at his red hair, a sure sign of blessedness; at his wise, thought-lined face, which was also somehow marked with many sorrows, and was filled with admiration. This man had been to Harvard!

Gerry now made a request that he knew Paulo could not only not resist, but would be over the moon about.

"No doubt you will take me to see your folk and these country people whom you write about? I want to see the real Jaman and learn what is happening where it really matters, in the countryside."

"Oh boy. Si si si."

"Paulo. You will soon be hearing people saying this, so I don't want you to get a shock or surprise. It is no secret that I have been sent here officially by Uncle Sam as a spy and agent provocateur. Everyone here in the bar knows that, even if they don't actually say it out loud. It is one of those things you don't talk about too openly anyway. In fact there is nobody in Jaman who does not know why I am here. It is taken for granted by everybody that I am here to serve the interests of Uncle Sam, and indeed there would be great dismay if it was thought that I harboured any innate, deep sympathy for the Jamanese cause, especially by the Jamanese themselves! People have always found it comforting to know their enemies, which is why they more often kill their friends than their foes."

Paulo looked up at Gerry's face in confusion and it was clear that he had lost it as far as the present conversation was concerned. The beer had clouded his mind again, and he now simply pretended to agree with everything.

"There is this bunch of odd colleagues of mine, eccentric idealists, in Harvard who believe in helping the poor of the earth. They are seen by the powerful Econo-Military establishment as *the* great subversive threat to western civilisation. Such is the concern of the US government about them that I was appointed their 'mentor'. Instead, I have become their accomplice. My official duty is to advise the government in Jaman and the US on how to get rid of old peasant agricultural practices; along with these go ancient traditional beliefs and cultural practices as well; which are all seen as dangerously outdated, and bring in the new Supertechnology."

"Well," said a dazed Paulo.

"Do you know what it sounds to me like?," asked Gerry in a raised voice and adding to Paulo's perplexity:

"it sounds to me as if our fellows are already out there experimenting in the countryside. Agricultural innovations can be environmental disasters, you know. I'll bet there are young, idealistic experts around the place advising people on how and what to grow on this or that spot of ground in the new technological age. It wouldn't surprise me if this 'accident' you mention is really something to do with that. They are so enthused, talking about new hybrid wonder crops that will take over the world and solve all the problems of mankind! I happen to believe that misguided people in positions of influence have plans to hijack such new commodities and lace them with ingredients seen by the authorities as being *good for the people*. Believe me, I have observed similar collusion in other parts of southeast Asia, in Mexico, Africa, all under the aegis of the 'Green Revolution'. As mega-corporation plays off mega-corporation and governments are manipulated, a few rich farmers get richer and the only certainty is the continuing pain of hunger in the belly of the Third World peasant. My Harvard Special Study Group is trying to find out what is really going on. We have noted a link between the increased propaganda for vegetarian lifestyles and the promotion of these dubious hybrids. But I can't tell my bosses all this."

"What do you mean by *laced with ingredients seen as good for the people?*," asked Paulo with restored curiosity.

"Well," said Gerry, taking another sip of his rum and winding his face up with much repugnance, "these usually include special chemicals whose purpose is only to inflate prices and please the authorities who like to think that they are controlling people's lives and health. They will automatically, and immediately, want to curb any genuine life-giving vitalism and free availability of these plants, or whatever, by means of Civil Service checks, Health-Warnings and obscure, unfathomable printed messages on the packaging material. Haven't you seen it on the Puerto Rico products? There will also be attempts to allow only certain selected and approved farmers and established plantation owners grow it. As farming and social life is altered forever in Jaman and the world the commercial plant and all that goes with it will become not the property of the common man but of the rich, monopolistic owners."

"You know," said Paulo slowly, waking up a little, "I was thinking all that myself. It's like you have taken the words out of my very own mouth. You are helping me to think my own thoughts. If only I had a teacher like you before!"

"Paulo. Don't trust anyone who puts ideas into your head. Not even me."

"True, OK, Mr Gerry."

Gerry, well 'over-the-limit' now, turned to address everyone in the bar, all of whom were continuing to enjoy their free drinks, in a loud voice:

"You poor, exploited jackasses! Look at you all, sitting here with not the slightest bit of hope in the world. You look like dodos! Get up off yer backsides and go out and do something about your hopeless lot. Jobs won't come just by looking up to visiting, idle Americans, expecting them to give you handouts and solve all your problems! Is this how the other half lives? Full of self pity? Stand up for yourselves. You should be proud of your hardships, the mind-numbing boredom of life in a tin hut, the barren bush, the uninhabitable mountains and impenetrable valleys; be proud of your incomprehensible-to-the-foreigner dialect, your lack of supposed western good manners and any vain expectations of life! Be yourselves and demonstrate to the world that despite your poverty and misery you are free! Be proud of that which makes you most ashamed! That is the way forward."

There was a shocked silence. Gerry's eyes were now glazed over.

"I can even offer to train you all in military tactics. I see nothing wrong with that. A bit of discipline is useful even in civilian life; and the methods of guerrilla warfare are an essential skill in the Third World, if only for self-defence."

It was the offer of logistical help that probably saved Gerry's skin and made his audience forget their deep sense of personal and national insult and concentrate on what was positive in what the now-well-over-the-limit visitor had said.

"Can you get us any weapons, or bombs?", asked Alfredo The Thug with great gusto.

Idle Pete looked pleased too, but doubt and a certain shyness appeared on Jos's face. He started to stare glumly at the floor. Mr Sher, meanwhile, dreaming as usual, was imagining his bar becoming a great national monument of the future, with parties of schoolchildren coming to view the primary exhibits of the struggle for national revolution within its hallowed confines; a great car and coach park outside, a heliport, a library centre for students to pursue research into The Cap's (and maybe Jos's) philosophy.

"More drinks," shouted Gerry, waving his arm.

Another wave of self-confidence went through Alfredo, Pete (but not Jos) while even Mr Sher and Paulo felt inspiration at this basic, radical affirmation by Gerry of armed revolution and his promise of help with the necessary tools to bring it about. A cheer broke out in the room and more drinks were ordered at Gerry's expense. A dish of curry goat, rice and peas arrived at Gerry's table and he proceeded to eat it with some gusto.

Meanwhile the ensembled watchers agreed that Gerry was, despite his drunkenness, the best guy to come from the teacher recruitment agency for some time; ever since, in fact, the late, once admired and highly appreciated (for similar generosity and genial sociability) but now unlamented for the scandal of his professional failure, Mr Gusnud. He also had branched out as something of an educational expert but had unwisely embroiled himself in arguments with his pupils over controversial matters contained in the United Nations Declaration On Human Rights. One disreputable youth had tried to shoot Gusnud when the same irate pupil produced a hand gun in mid-lesson and was only prevented from succeeding in his task by the arrival of the headmaster in the classroom. The undiplomatic pedagogue had fled from the area in a state of nervous collapse, never to be seen again.

As he ate Gerry had a moment of deep introspection. He knew that achievements of a cerebral nature were seldom self-evident to the public and it was the more mundane sort of accomplishment that had any appeal for ordinary people. He would have to be very down-to-earth with the people here. It was the likes of these people in the bar who might be the sort to help him out in this assignment. But Gerry knew what they were *really thinking*. His totally relaxed, uninhibited behaviour here, his drinking, his formal attire (though he had now loosened his tie), his determined intelligence, would be a wonder to them. To look at him now, dining and taking refreshments in a local Jaman bar with such a motley crew they would certainly think perhaps that here was an unusual person, a foreign chap with surplus cash enjoying a drinking spree, perhaps to relieve the heavy professional load that was obviously on his mind. But he would appear also to be an educated man. Certainly one not unwilling to share time with those less fortunate that himself, to show that he did not go along with that old, traditional custom of keeping aloof from the native.

They appreciate that.

That is what they are thinking.

Gerry by now was quite high and somewhat careless in his next choice of words, even though he meant it all as a joke:

"I will have to leave this downtrodden slum now and go and find the place of my residence, which I hope has running water, a proper toilet and all the essential mod cons like toilet paper, on the college campus. Don't be surprised if you see me on tv soon, arguing politics with the prime minister. You can then say, 'we know him, he drinks here! He is our friend. He is no friend of the top knobs. He is secretly working for us!'"

He paused to catch his breath and examine closely his glass.

"Well, this rum seems to be counteracting the effects of that dubious whiskey I had at the airport."

"Yes boss," said Mr Sher, coming over to his table; "we hear everything you say. We know you have come here to save our nation from the depredations of the hyenas and the vultures. The dollars and newsletters that your people have sent over the years for the pioneering Educational, Health and Social Welfare activities of The First Class Institution and Community Centre have sustained us around here in our times of desperation. The whole community, which has immensely benefited, is grateful. And we know that there are some who are envious of our friendship with you and many who will try to kill you. But you will be protected by the ordinary Jamanese people! We will protect you! You are safe in The First Class!"

Gerry was not sure at all if this should make him feel better or not.

So, *that* was the secret of the secret CIA-within-the-CIA, Gerry imagined McCall and Dick Warner speculating to their agents who might right now be observing Gerry in the bar, to 'buy up' or control odd bars or small peasant holdings here and there and perhaps the occasional fishing boat, a co-operative even, all around the Third World so as to be able to observe and manipulate politics at grass roots' level.

Already, Gerry had Jaman almost sown up.

He felt proud now.

To ingratiate himself with the doubters, especially with the hard cases among them, he now stated proudly:

"I served in Taran, you know. I have battle scars."

His speech was followed by a stumble. A hefty arm (Mr Sher's) steadied him.

The others looked at him. Mr Gusnud and all that was in the past. This man Gerry looked far more amenable and foolish and they would be able to pin him by the tail quite easily. They now all began to fidget as it was not clear what might be expected of them next, as a constantly positive attitude was not usually possible with these shanty people; and they had been positive all evening.

"Time to go, Mr Gerry, they getting restless ...", said Mr Sher with some concern. He knew that even a brief moment of silence, inactivity or indecision could lead to immediate trouble with this lot; a fight between two rivals to impress Gerry, a subversive outcry from an untrusting street urchin against Gerry, even a fulsome riot over an imaginary issue of honour. It was time to get things on the move again.

And the mention of the Taran war had not helped.

As if by a secret sign Turbo appeared from somewhere and through his body language (a firm, friendly grip on Gerry and a guiding of him to the door) McArthur was made to realise that it was exactly the right moment to go. Melanie took his empty dish away and whispered:

"You is good American. You eat up de dish clean."

Gerry congratulated himself. He knew that by a hearty appetite he had not only made a friend, he had insinuated himself at a stroke right into the heart of the local culture. The juke box was now playing some very popular tune, judging by the swaying body movements of the clientele and sung, he was informed, by the top island pop star. As the bar joined in the singing he was told it was number one on the hit parade. Gerry asked the name of the song as well as that of the singer (all this would be useful information):

"Slangman Stardust, and he sing 'Cane Juice Sugar Bitter'," said Paulo enthusiastically.

'Cane Juice Sugar Bitter', thought Gerry. An idea came to him. He would pen a song for this man and put in it sublimatory, subversive messages he wanted to promulgate here. He tried to recall old memories and data on the music business he had picked up with Jim McCall as he watched the inebriated 'dancing', reflecting on the marvel of this popular idiom . . . .

He now proceeded to give Mr Sher some last minute hints should any suspicious-looking Americans turn up, but The Cap was convinced that Gerry was raving somewhat; he was certainly not making sense. He seemed to imply he was being followed and spied upon. At the same time Gerry whispered a question:

"When will you get me the plant specimens I mentioned before to you? I need them for my agricultural research."

The Cap replied reassuringly.

"Soon as Little Man get back from bush. No worry, Mr Gerry, it come like sun in morning, moon in evening . . . ."

Then he was back in the taxi, with no recollection of any farewells to the bar crowd, and forgetting his baggage at Mr Sher's, settling into the passenger seat as the rum began to take full effect.

"That rendezvous spot you tell me. You really mean you wan' go that place?," asked Turbo in an agitated voice;

109

"that is where them crazy holy Jahmonks lives."

Religion in Jaman was an anarchic affair with multitudes of wayward sects vying with each other on the streets and rooftops. These represented the unspoken yearnings of ordinary, normal people who are always obsessed with anything weird or bloodthirsty in life and even philosophy; and each found in his or her particular choice that their sect generally gave them a sound sense of participation in, and oneness with, the great 'Out There'. Above these, or beyond them, were the Jahmonks, the Established Religion of Jaman, whose main role was to denounce the sects and indeed Jaman society itself. The Jahmonks had little to do with the mainstream of affairs in any case and mainly tended to look after their cathedrals and take part in obscure rituals revolving around the person of their Lord Jah whom they actually placed as living on earth, though it was not clear where he was. The other thing about the Jahmonks was that their's was considered a very 'earthy' religion (akin in some ways to the version of Buddhism found in some districts) and they had a most elaborate dietary system. In particular, they were said to hate foreigners.

Why had Gerry chosen the Jahmonks' monastery as a secret meeting spot with Turbo the taximan?

Another puzzle.

Gerry's boss in Kingstown, the person whose role it was to oversee his term here, had called him in.

"Mr McArthur, where the hell have you been? We have been looking all over for you! You arrived at the airport and failed to follow the normal procedures. Customs have made a complaint. Fortunately I know the Chief Customs Officer. Look at the state of you. Drunk as a coot and you barely one day on the island. You upset some important people at the airport, before you had even officially entered Jaman. You must realise that this is a very small place. Everything is spotted. It was even noticed that you had your eye on a young lady there! Woman chasing is a problem at some of our institutions. I hope you are not going to be another Don Juan. You are supposed to be setting an example. And then you vanish from sight. To some seedy bar, no doubt?"

It was the US ambassador, Mr Delroy, speaking.

Gerry's lately sleek suit was now crumpled, his tie was gone and his top shirt buttons were open. He was perspiring heavily and there was a flush on his face.

"Screw it all, Mr Delroy sir, I just went to see the sights and have a sip of the local brew. There is nothing wrong with getting to know the 'ground'. We were always taught that in training college."

"Look, Gerry, everyone knows your problem. Your predilection for booze, your terrible marital problems, your inability to hold down the same job for any length of time, your fantasies about helping the poor of the world, due no doubt to some strange guilt complex, and which involves you in hare-brained schemes which have put lives at risk in the past. How did you ever get into this job ...?"

Not realising that this was a rhetorical question Gerry answered:

"I volunteered for it. Originally, as a way out of going to Taran."

Mr Delroy was clearly impatient with Gerry's hang-ups, his imaginary grievances.

"Taran! That old excuse for everything! Actually, I may as well tell you one thing. There have been rumours going around for a long time. I have been told that you have been suffering from emotional problems. We like to take an interest in the personal problems of our staff. I have heard that your poor wife, completely against her will, is having to consider a divorce. It appears that her Church is insisting on it. Nevertheless, I think that they have recommended you to work here because they seem to hope you might benefit from a change of surroundings for a while; or maybe they just want you out of the way. But we don't want you stirring them up with any ideas of Social Justice, do you hear? Because if you do I'll have to have you put in a dry house for a year. And you wouldn't like that."

Gerry was impressed by Delroy's forthrightness. He could do business with this man. Perhaps he was indeed on the level; US ambassadors were usually innocents put in their posts purely as puppets by the powers back home.

"Ha," laughed Gerry, "they always say things like that. That old mental jibe has been going the rounds for a long time. They are simply afraid that their own agents can't be trusted. It all goes back to the time of the Triple Agents, remember? When even the Vice-President of the USA was suspected, with good reason, of working for the wrong side? It was I who sussed him out, but they didn't believe me. They can't face reality, can they? It's an old story. It's what Freud said about suppression. Freud is a much maligned man .…"

Mr Delroy was perplexed by Gerry's talk (being an innocent also in the world of espionage).

"You're very drunk, McArthur, You don't know what you are saying."

"I'm dead sober when I'm drunk, Del. Dead sober."

Mr Delroy now incomprehensibly and suddenly changed his tack and his voice became very soft.

"Actually, Gerry, I could do with your help and support here. I know you are a man of the world. I have run into a spot of trouble with some of the hard cards about the place. Mr McCall, the director of USAID, the man who calls the shots, who is the paymaster and chief advisor of the government here and whose word is the bible as far as everyone is concerned, and especially the educational establishment which is mainly funded by him, is laughing behind my back. Because of his seniority he seems to think that he can treat me just like a …

simpleton schoolteacher. He is trying to further his department's influence both at my expense and that of the US government."

"Don't worry about McCall. I worked with him long ago and I know his Achilles Heel. Number one for McCall is Jim McCall, just remember that. By the way, I believe that he also controls much of the import and export trade here?"

"There are many stories concerning him and his activities. I would be grateful for any information about him; anything that you get for me will be appreciated. I know that you two were buddies once. I could recommend you as a head of department somewhere, some place you really like."

"They say that he is patriotic," said Gerry quietly.

"Well. That may be so. Anyway, how is your room at the college; I trust all is in order, or haven't you even gone there yet?"

"I came straight here from a bar. Must have been up all night. Where is my luggage? I never notice the most obvious things around me, like I've left my suitcase somewhere."

"Maybe you are a deep thinker, like they say you are," said the ambassador with some beginning of respect, for Gerry was not like other US officials, who always held an unspoken threat over him, based on superior talent, experience in the field or higher academic qualifications, feeding on his inferiority complex. Gerry seemed harmless.

"Actually I have decided to sleep in different, unforeseeable places as much as possible while I'm here, just in case of any security problems. I'll probably have to take to sleeping in cupboards or under the bed. You know the sort of thing. Better to be sure than sorry."

"I always feel a respect for you ex-military guys. You never lose your old habits."

This bizarre attitude in Gerry served to increase in Mr Delroy a suspicion of unusual wisdom or esoteric knowledge in the man. Eccentricity in an official could be a very useful ingredient in his business. It can be blamed for everything.

"They are expecting you at the Ministry of Information and Education at 12 pm. It's officially at 8.30 am but I've learnt to always add three and a half hours to appointment times here to allow for the 'soon come' syndrome."

"Three and three quarter hours, actually," said Gerry.

"Fine. In the meantime you had better call into McCall's office. It's not likely he'll be in, but you can always say you called if he asks."

"What's McCall's status as Head of Station?," Gerry asked, taking a risk, knowing that Delroy could easily snub him and ignore this 'impudent' question. It was like asking the Pope who he went to for advice.

The question seemed to make something in Mr Delroy snap.

"No such thing as 'status' here. He's beyond the Pale. He controls nearly everything. Except the Jahmonks, of course. Even I'm completely under his thumb. I happen to know he's a little worried by your arrival though. He can't get to the bottom of it. He wonders if you have been sent over to make an independent report on him, i.e. one that nobody is sure who gets to read it."

"I'm only here to teach them about the coconut," said Gerry quietly, as if there was no way that he'd get involved in any underhand or political doings.

"Where can I get breakfast?," he asked.

"Try the Pegasus Hotel. They like Americans there. By the way, how is the photography?"

Mr Delroy proceeded to laugh in a very silly manner.

"I suppose you were told to ask me that?," replied an unimpressed Gerry.

"Have I insulted you or something? They said that it was just a big joke that everybody was in on. I hope I haven't offended you . . . ."

"There's been innuendo for years over a reputedly, supposedly disgraceful photo of me. But the truth is, there is no incriminating photograph. I happened to once take a picture of a very high US official having a social discussion in relaxed circumstances about the American Way of Life with a Communist leader. That is all!"

"Gosh," said Mr Delroy, stuck for words. □

chapter
seven

As he sat in a chair in his room, lackadaisically contemplating a lesson plan for that first important impression-giving lecture in what was sure to be a crowded, even excited classroom, Gerry started to doze.

It was not long before his nightmare returned.

The Coconut Experimental Laboratory at Langley was in the highest Security Category possible, ZZ. The Director was not only not allowed in, he was not even allowed to know of its existence. When he would walk past he either ignored the place or reflected (once he even commented) on the nice house plants that decorated the sills, giving him a warm feeling that his authority and management were rewarded in a happy staff. Dick came in to have a look. He always tried to be on first name terms with everyone, though he usually got it wrong.

"Hi, Adolf," he said to Gustave, "and how is the new enzyme? Very sticky by the looks of it."

Dick knew nothing about science. He believed that hard mental labour, such as that associated with serious research, was for the fairies. He liked snap decisions in everything. He was a person who kept his fingers crossed that luck and bluff would see him through. Gustave had his fist deep in some dark, treacily fluid which was gyrating in an aluminium tub, much as brown sugar is extracted from molasses in a cane mill. But the point of this stuff gyrating was not apparent at all; it was a puzzle as no change was appearing in its essence. It rather reminded Dick of one of the 'nutty professor's' fantastic experiments.

"Well, yes, Mr Warner, by courtesy of the world's best known soft drink we have here the secret elements for growing the Supercoconut. We have at last cracked the hi-tech problem faced by all hybrids, the need for expensive inputs of high grade fuel and fertilizer. This gunge does the trick. You would never guess what that noxious company uses in its drink. Pure tar essence. That's what! Here, I'm just getting the feel. It's good, try it."

"It looks very impressive to me," lied Dick, who was aware of the billions of taxpayers' dollars that had been spent on the project;

"and the concept of using the choicest, most useless of capitalist products as a catalyst for fuelling the mass production of what will become the most essential element in the future diet of mankind will very much appeal to our new Capitalist-Communist class. Now how are the new red cells getting along?"

Gustave went over to a VDU.

Dick followed him, his chest puffed out with an expansive, childish enthusiasm, as if he was going to view the treasures of some Aladdin's Cave. The scientist called up on the screen the blueprint of the great coconut improvement; the new red cell had pride of place; this had the 'hostile gene' whose strenuous boosting of the plant and its fruit ensured no limit to their 'biozone', i.e. their aerial or horizontal extent. One forecast had put the size of just a single nut at 12,700 cubic metres. But there was no way of knowing anything for sure about the potential capacity of the plant; this was what made the whole enterprise exciting.

Dick now indulged one of his most annoying personal habits, rubbing his hands exuberantly and humming joyfully with some great, emotional release, like a child ecstatic over a new toy:

"President Hooligan is delighted with that new slogan we have coined for the benefit of the media, to fit in with his Practical Politics policy: *'Money Is Democracy, Democracy Is Money, You Know It Makes Sense'* (some interfering do-gooders find it morally objectionable, why I don't know, who has ever found anything wrong with money, a bit of cash, especially in the hand?). I have now worked out how to take Hooligan's policies on board and make them fit into the scheme of things. We must henceforth establish that Money be seen as the Golden Grail of all our endeavours rather than outmoded 'politics'; it is absolutely crucial to persuade both Houses to accept my own, novel idea of establishing politicians as a hereditary, monied caste, as well as privatising the international waters (we already own the moon and most of outer space anyway) to the highest bidders, as ways of getting revenue as well as outsmarting the United Nations and all those insolvent new nations with their tedious, nationalistic 'territorial waters' claims. Everything in the cosmos must be in the hands of private enterprise, which means us. The influence of the people on the Spiritualist wing of his party is waning, but Hooligan now needs a foreign policy Knockout. As soon as the first coconut pod is in the ground down there I will invite myself over to the White House and 'spill the beans' as it were; i.e. that he himself will henceforth be responsible for the welfare of the whole world; that we will shortly control the world food supply. He could not have imagined in his wildest dreams a more perfect fulfilment of his own political philosophy. There will be no waste anywhere, anymore! You, Adolf, will then have what you asked for, your own laboratory in Harvard University."

"That would be so good. I have so many better ideas for the future. This ... is only a sideline."

"Your services are respected and valued here, Adolf. I will continue to mention your name in high places. I hope your future plans come to fruition; though remember I would always like to be informed of them first. Now listen here a minute. Is it true that these new plants have a military and strategic value as well? I have heard it mentioned that they might have some lethal consequences, or something to that effect?"

"Yes, it is quite possible. Maybe we can always kill the two birds with a one stone. Ha?"

"Very good, Adolf. It's people who are the problem in this world. Our new ecological awareness makes us determined to defend nature, the plants, some useful animals that are being exterminated by primitive people all over the earth. Plants need to breathe and grow at the expense of man. The problem is that there are too many people, the population explosion. We may have found the remedy, Adolf. If these new hybrids can squeeze out human populations in their respective zones we will be on our way. If they can, as I have heard rumoured, starve the areas of oxygen during the hours of night then that will be all the better. The process will be quicker. When our agents in the pilot project areas have ensured that the governments adopt the new plants as part of an Anti-Poverty Drive (everybody loves that phrase!) there will only be hours for the few in the know to get out of the place. The ambassador will forewarn all US citizens and aircraft carriers will be employed in the usual 'hostage-scares'. But we have a man there named McArthur who is acting as a dummy for us. You met him once at a cross-curricular departmental meeting. He will be left behind, supposedly to explain the after-effects of government policy but in reality to expire through lack of oxygen, hopefully. We always eliminate some agents in successful operations, Adolf. Nobody ever even notices. This McArthur has always been an extremely untrustworthy character, pretending that he is simply only a good-intentioned college teacher and criticising me behind my back all the time. We have been trying to get rid of him for years. But he has this personality problem, which means he is very unreliable, an unpredictable sort. He never turns up on time for my staff meetings, will go to the wrong appointment or rendezvous, doesn't finish a job, doesn't even turn up at all sometimes. He has defied many of our better-laid plots to get him, mainly because he is so extremely hard to nail down.

Now listen Adolf. I realise you have been living under certain harsh restrictions here, not being allowed to communicate with other people and so on. There are good reasons for this, as you know, for there are many who would like to get their hands on you, and your special skills. I am very sorry that you took our threats of torture, surpassing in brilliance even that of the Gestapo at their very best, so seriously. It was all meant as a joke, you know. But that gene is money, and money attracts the hordes, just as democracy does, and if anybody manages to get their hands on the hostile gene before it is properly tested by us who knows what might happen? It could destroy us all. As soon as the danger is past we will release you from all the restrictions and I *promise* you a professorship as well as a laboratory at Harvard. In any case I want somebody there on our side to fix that Professor of Economics who is of the discredited, old-fashioned school, holding that Political Economy is *not* an exact science. Such a view runs exactly counter to President Hooligan's stated beliefs, I am told on the best advice."

Dick was talking to Snakey and Spooks (now promoted to global overseer) a little later in his private office.

"We have lately discovered that there is one of our renegade people in the Jaman area named Jim McCall, who is the richest man in the world. He is the rogue who was permanently sent abroad after a Superman drug experiment went wrong. The full story is classified. He has been establishing himself in the archipelago and region over the last few years covering all the comings and goings in that strategic focus of shipping and air lanes. He could upset things for us if he wanted to. However, I have now put in place Project K which, with the indispensable help of your two departments, will see him eliminated in the very near future."

Gerry woke up in a sweat, just in time for his next class.

"I must warn Jim McCall," he said worriedly to himself, as he hurriedly put his shoes on, with no time to tie the laces, trying to remember what it was he was going to teach.

He entered the classroom in his usual manner, slowly, head and back slightly bent downwards as if all the knowledge and problems of the world were ensconced right there in his brain, of which soon he would 'deliver of'. In his hand was no precisely thought-out lesson plan but an old book, one he had found in the stockroom cupboard. It was dated, in fact, 1948. Quietly, having forgotten to greet or give any recognition to his pupils, he wrote in chalk on the blackboard the title of the first chapter in the book:

'The Coconut in Jaman, its physiology, climate and economy'.

The telephone rang in the ambassador's office. A Jaman government agent, the cleaning lady, answered it.

"Hello. My name is Mrs McArthur. I believe you've got a Gerald McArthur working for you there. Can I speak to him?"

"Ah, Mr McArthur. He just leave, miss. I give him a message . . . ?"

"I am his long-suffering wife. I can never seem to get him on the phone."

There was a sniffle, whether in sorrow, anger or frustration it was impossible to say.

"Are you are an office lady?"

"Yes, ma'am."

"Can you help me? He is on the run from home. His pay cheque hasn't come through this month either. The children are starving. Is he still drinking heavily? Or gambling away the housekeeping money? We are trying to send our very bright son to college. One of our daughters has a very bad illness. The medical fees are astronomical."

"Yuh poor woman!"

"The scoundrel has been trying to persuade the church for years to annul our marriage by concocting such tall stories! There is no bottom to which he will not sink. Do you think you could keep an eye on him for me? You tell me anything you can about his activities there and I will reward you ..."

"He in Jaman only de few days. Me suppose he is only ordinary CIA man. As far as me see he is drinking the rum all de while an' going to de clubs at de late hours. But he at de work job now ... ."

"I'll tell you, here is the deal. If you keep tabs on him for me and ring my number regular with all the info, I promise, not only to send you some dollars, but to see about arranging for you to have a 'holiday' in this country. In the good old USA. How about that?"

"OK. But I have serious responsibility here. I de Jaman government agent in de American embassy. Me very important to de chief. I mus' be careful. Me doan wan' lose me job."

"I am used to dealing with these situations. I will give you your code name. I will call you Gloria. Gloria, here is a bit of information that your prime minister will be pleased with. Tell him that your boss, Colonel Urquhart of the Jaman Defence Force's intelligence section, is working for the Opposition there, the Jaman Labour Party. You will get a pay rise for that information! Send me reports on Mr McArthur and there will be more of that to come. How about it?"

"How you know all dis, ma'am?"

"I keep my ears open here in Washington. I go to all the parties."

"It ok ... It a deal to me, ma'am. Sounds like a very good idea to me. Send de dollars in international money order. What your number? I can always ring free from here ya."

Gerry was dozing again. His lecture had tired him out. The blood runs thin in the tropics, or thickens, which was it? Before long, he was having another colourful, interesting and yet unnerving dream. He dreamt that he had a wife back in America and that she loved him so much she was moving earth and high heaven to win back his devotion. Then his dreams took on a more morose flavour, with gunbattles, explosions and shady characters in black coats and hats hiding around corners. Afterwards he tried to figure out in which order these dreams came, for each had a special meaning.

Jim McCall and the Dutchman were relaxing in the best-known beach house in Jaman, drinking the purest rum of the country, hobnobbing with the flashy, newly-rich business whizzes of the capital and the odd drug dealer and both of them were reading books: 'Building Up Your Self-Confidence' was McCall's and 'Teach Yourself Philosophy' was the tome in the hands of the Dutchman. They had not bought these books but had obtained them free-of-charge from the CIA library where they were used as examples of what the enemy liked to read. It was always considered form to be able to 'get inside' the opposition. One curious feature was that McCall and the Dutchman were really 'into' the books; they seemed to be enjoying them for their own sake.

"Hey, listen to this," shouted the Dutchman to McCall; "this is amazing. I theenk it is maybe one reason why McArthur deed not turn up last night at the Jamboree Hotel. It says: 'It is left to man to exercise his dreadful freedom and construct hees own order; then he alone ees responsible for what follows, thees is 'Existentialism.' I theenk McArthur made the Existentialist decision *not* to turn up at the hotel for our appointment because he ees used to thinking in an Existentialist way; fundamentally his philosophy ees Existentialist. I think he was afraid of making . . . a real decision. Yes?"

"Look, er . . . Hans, that is not how Americans think. He did not turn up most likely because he was drunk and was incapable of making any decision. Also probably because he thought you were a messer. Look. If we are to work together and get our hands on the import patent for the new crop technology that Gerry has so kindly revealed to me, you had better leave that old schoolbook alone. Read something like this one I've got. It would help you with all those scruples of conscience that you complain get in the way when you have to conduct business. It says that when you have to tell the biggest lie and con someone (actually it never puts it like that, with its fine words about 'powers of persuasion', 'bolstering the ego of the other person', 'feeling good' and 'pretending that all is positive when disaster looms') then you should look 'em in the face and just spit in their eye."

McCall spoke with what could best be described as a raw, adolescent cockiness. His coarseness would make any psychologist wonder where the 'mature man' was, or if there had ever been one. A life of continuous action and material achievement always has this effect on human nature. Something like this thought might have been expressed interiorly by Hans if he had let a certain judgmental awareness inside him grow to full fruition right then, but he always tried to suppress this critical aspect of his character. Instead he just said:

"You Americans always theenk big, yeh? But we Dutch are more clever with our schemings. The coconut idea sounds a bit like a . . . dangerous venture . . . as you say . . . to me. And still you do not yet know how or when the big coconut is coming to the island? It must be the most carefully kept secret in heestory; most times a few hundred people always know a secret."

"We must ensure that we are right there at the point of entry. Then, effect a takeover in the name of law and order and present what we will assert is the only import license valid at that moment in time; which will be a document you, in your capacity as the

Dutch Expo's rep., will get forged at the Ministry of Industrial and Trade Matters (go to the political families section). Now when you think on it, where do ya think they will bring it in?"

"The airport?"

"Hell no. Not this one. It will be somewhere private, a spot nobody will notice, where no one gives a damn what goes in or out. A run-down port out in the country, in other words. And there's no better place than Mobby Bay, you know, where we send out the drugs? Where the government built that Space Launching pad? So much contraband stuff moves through there that nobody will pay much attention to the arrival of a crate of coconuts (they just might think it a bit strange). And the area around Mobby Bay is good plantation land, ideal for the new crop."

"Pleese do not mention thee drugs. It makes me feel like a crook. You know I only agree to thees business because eet makes less drugs for the youth of Jaman to be addicted on."

"Oh, you and your conscience! Of course you, we, are only doing it for the right motives, Hans. Just make sure you get the correct piece of paper"

"Now that we are working together, Jeem, we should share all our secrets. There should be no secrets held between soul brothers. Tell me, what do you inteend to do weeth all your money when you die? Are you leaving eet to charity?"

"That is a secret that will die with me," replied Jim, smiling; "of course if you tell me where the prime minister keeps his overseas bank account, something I've been trying hard to find out for years, I'll let you into the details."

"What makes you theenk I know about the prime minister's money?"

"Hans, your people have contacts all over the world. You know where everybody keeps their money."

"It's a deal. I need to know more about your last will and testament and you need to keep an eye on Prime Minister Stanley. It ees where nobody in the whole wide world would suspect. It is no wonder it is a great secret. It ees in the Great People's Socialist Bank, Addis Ababa, where eet is put in trust for the Great International Repatriation Fund."

"Sounds like a great idea to me."

"It ees."

"Ok, Hans. I know I will have to give up all my cash one day. It is not an easy thing to do, I must say. All my life has been spent working for a nice nest egg. Yet I know that I have to face death, as you have so kindly pointed out to me. I have been a very important man in my time, you know."

"I know, Jeem. That is what makes eet all the harder."

"They are all in my pay, actually; the Director of the CIA, the President of the USA, the Secretary General of the United Nations, even the Queen of England. Did you know that? Sure I run the whole world."

McCall's face was suddenly very strained.

"Oh, I theenk you must be exaggerating a little. You are making me a joke!."

"No, it is the case. I have private hotel suites in every major capital in the world. The KGB rank me as their best man abroad; in fact I am a Colonel in the KGB. I own Aeroflot, Air Transamazonia and American Airlines, under a false name I should add. I have been given thirty million dollars as an advance on my forthcoming memoirs, and the Nobel Prize people have told me that if I write a novel, or any kind of written work at all, I am guaranteed the Nobel Prize for Literature, for three years in a row! Among the talents and skills I have picked up in a busy and eventful life, a life indeed fraught with many life-threatening events, are those of the surgeon (from having to deal with the injuries of my own loyal, elite band of soldiers sustained on secret inland missions, including amputations); I can fly a Jumbo as well as the rather tricky U2 and the Stealth Bomber; there is not one world leader who does not come to me for advice, even the Pope . . . ."

Jim was clearly entering into the throes of some critical psychological crisis.

"Ha ha, cut it out Jeem, I have not time for joking. Do you theenk we have time to fool around?"

"It is very important to have a reputation. But you would not understand. Well, you've told me your secret and I'll tell you mine. Sometimes I wonder which has been more important in my life, the making of money or my artistic achievements. I ask myself, would I give up all my wealth for the sake of, say, having produced the biggest musical hit of the 60's?"

"What was that, Jeem?"

"Well, it was me that brought Motown to Taran, the biggest concert of all, for its political content. Not to mention the military strategy. But the Woodstock thing was me, too, you know. That was my doing. The CIA had a field day. Anyway, that is all in the past. I am leaving all my money, which is held in a bank account in Grand Cayman, to the poor of Jaman. That way I can help redress the balance in what is obviously an unfair world."

There was frustration in Jim's eyes, even the glint of a tear. He was suddenly all tensed up. He looked like a man still chasing a dream, even though he already possessed most things the world can offer.

"That is a greet thing for you to do. Eet weel make you feel a lot better. You were een Woodstock? That is great, Jeem. Everybody knows the Woodstock."

Hans was trying to cheer Jim up, as the man was obviously feeling a bit down.

"Hell, I could have sung there."

"Why did you not, Jeem?"

"I was in hiding at the time, couldn't, daren't show my mug on a million television screens. I had a class act. But I had to stay backstage. That was my ... tragedy ... ."

He stopped speaking; he did not look like his old self at all now; he was having some kind of flashback. His face was very strained.

"But, about another matter. The CIA would not trust Gerry with a really important assignment here in any case; unless there is something *else* going on. I do not like being outsmarted. There is something really *funny* here . . . ."

"Don't worry Jeem, you will outsmart them all, going by what you say you have achieved in successes. So, you theenk Gerry ees not . . . kosher?"

"Screw Gerry. Why are you so interested in him anyway? I'm telling ya, I wrote Woodstock."

He went quiet for a moment, trying to recollect himself and his emotions. He continued in a low voice.

"In some ways I envy Gerry McArthur his failures. He has done something I never could have: he has avoided the ultimate emptiness of all this . . . power. He has that great empty space inside him where no assignment has ever been successfully completed; no fame, esteem from peers, approval from head office or even any comfort in knowing that he has done something with his life. Instead there's just a great impotence, a great failure with no sense of satisfaction. And yet, he has something I have not, the potential and promise of actually doing something positive in the future that he has never done before, some success, of whatever sort, or however small. Me? I have already done everything. Oh, what I would give for . . the futility of McArthur's life . . . ."

"Jeem. This McArthur is a fall guy. You cannot envy heem. You told me, he betrayed his country in the Taran War. He is a brainwashed ex-Catholic, married badly to the daughter of one of the baddest Americans who ever lived who ran the American Forces for his own private benefit and glory. He ees a jinx. He causes embarrassment to his employers and colleagues, and that ees why they are always sending heem away."

"Well I don't accept completely your analysis of McArthur's role but there is an element of truth in it. He is a jinx. He always seems to get out of the most terrible fixes quite easily.

The real trouble is that no one can figure out how, or what he actually *thinks*. In the old days he was a great man for the talk, about progress and ideals and all the things we went in for in those days. But when you thought you had pinned him down to some clear belief or statement he would introduce various red herrings to put you off the trail. Nobody knew him better in the field than ol' Jim McCall here, but even I never got to know what he really thinks. However, I am wise to his ruses."

"What about hees wife, Jeem? Has she not had a good influence over heem?" I heer that she is a good Christian woman. Does he still ... what is the word ... love her still?"

"Mary Baxter? The marriage has always been the talk of the CIA, ever since their engagement was first announced. She works for the Agency as one of its chief internal operatives. She keeps a sharp eye on all the important political wives and the domestic doings around Washington and Virginia. For years they have tried, with her help, to get an insight into Gerry. To no avail. It is generally and firmly believed, from all-night surveillance spread over a period of many years, that they have never shared the same bed. Even the presidents became concerned, starting with Janson, and extending through Niceman and Rodrigues; I expect Hooligan is making his own inquiries these days. The love-life of the McArthurs' is a matter of National Security. And why? For what? Oh, they say it has always been on top of the file in the Director's desk. I bet it goes back to the time of Baxter himself. The McArthurs are nobodies compared to me! Look at all that I have done and achieved in my life, yet I bet that Hooligan has never even heard of me! Niceman I know for certain was browbeaten by Warner with the threat of my power around Washington, but never to the best of my knowledge did that president ever make even one personal inquiry about me or my private life. What is the purpose of my breaking my back in the public service if that is the recognition I get?"

Jim McCall was clearly upset. He covered his face in his hands and this time emitted a croaking sob.

"Why does thees McArthur trouble you and your people so much? He seems like a ... dreamer ees the word ... yes, a drunkard and dreamer to me. That ees all. I will soon have heem in my hands."

"I believe it was Gerry who destroyed Baxter's confidence in the end. We all know he ended up a disillusioned old man who had to be put out to grass as Attorney General of the United States. It was something to do with the psychological profile the military had done of his son-in-law. It obsessed Baxter a lot. And Gerry, deviously, used to play up to that old profile of his quite a bit, deliberately I think. I really would like to find out, even at this late stage, what makes him tick ... or see that profile."

"As you well know, Jeem, it is the policy of my cartel to capture the minds and hearts of every American official and of every person of high position in these lands. We often approach our more difficult subjects with offers they find hard to refuse, such as Eternal Happiness, or Death and Damnation. I intend to catch up with thees Mr McArthur; he must have hees weak spot. It is not always wise to have such people, such outcasts or indeed lonely people, operating independently under the pretext of 'acting morally' or 'following their consciences'."

"I agree with you entirely. It would upset the balance of nature and the world itself would be a worse place if people were allowed to control their own destinies. There is nothing worse than moral anarchy. I know I have stretched the moral rules during my own life but, should there be life after death, I will answer any charges of unscrupulosity with the assertion that the world would have been even worse without me to preserve a tight control over the underworld. Can you imagine what would happen if we did not control the arms trade, the drugs trade, those hick politicians? In less responsible hands it would be certain that the world would either fall apart or blow itself up. So much for good intentions! They have only ever led to trouble and strife. Look at religion! Look at well-meaning politicians! Thank heavens the world is in the hands of crooks like us!"

"Some of our associates are only een it for the money, Jeem, and to hell with everything else. But you are more principled than that. I see that you are still maybee affected by the things they taught you in Sunday School! Ha ha. You are now beginning to wonder about a good world and salvation, even after your own very worldly, dangerous life in which you probably keeled many people. Well, life is strange indeed," said Hans seriously, adding, as if as an afterthought:

"but I would not be so quick to blame religion for the world's troubles. It has its uses also."

"True enough. But I would hate to see the day vice falls into the control of unscrupulous hands. The time has not yet come when we can entrust the making of money and the pursuit of power to the Pure of Heart."

"True!"

McCall seemed puzzled by something.

"But surely McArthur cannot be of much use to you, Hans? He is yesterday's man."

"As I have already tried to say, my bosses are a beet funny about Americans, who are their biggest financial contributors; and they are especially interested in, and worried by, people who refuse to involve themselves een crime. It may be to do weeth the fact that they love the sinners, as they have greet influence over them; but the eennocent are not so easily cajoled, or put on the right track. They see non-criminals as a dangerous species. I tell them, when they want to persecute innocent schoolteachers, social workers, priests, ladies who help out weeth the blind or people who show peasants how to make useful theengs instead of putting up with the old hardships and penances, hey, leave theem alone, they are not about to undermine your Edifices of Faith and Morals; but thees straight talk only makes the bosses madder and then some of them want to send them to Anathema. I think it ees best for me to get this McArthur on our side. Then there weel be peace and I can go back to my old office!"

"What is your 'old office', Hans?"

"Saying my prayers!"

"Ha ha."

"Ha ha ha."

Jim McCall tried to think deeply for a moment. With his sort deep thought cannot last longer than six seconds; after this time it becomes simply a total withdrawal from reality.

It was possible to tell he was conducting a serious inner consultation by the glassy look in his eyes and the flicking of his cigar ash into his full glass of American rye.

"Man, you're a genius! You've just given me a great idea! An idea which has appeared in its due time! Well, well, why haven't I thought of it before? You said about getting McArthur on your side. That is exactly what you should do! Boy, you are a genius!"

"I do not understand."

"Of course you don't. You probably didn't even realise you were jogging my old skills at plots and behind-the-lines action, just like in the old days. Let your lot take McArthur! Kidnap him! Pretend to hold him to ransom, or do with him whatever it is you want to do with him. You need have no fear of retribution, as I will cover you from this end, and the US government will only feel 'outrage'. Or will they?; I reckon, in fact I know for sure, that most of the top establishment will be greatly delighted and may even want to give the kidnappers a reward for lifting him! There will be many 'deadlines' passed with 'no word from the kidnappers', the usual bull. Everybody will be happy, except McArthur, at first. Until he sees it is for his own 'good'."

"So, the plan is, from your angle, to play your game with Uncle Sam and to get McArthur out of your hair. Me myself will have heem at my mercy and be able to have a long, persuasive chat with heem. For that is all I want; in order to get heem to work for us. But what else do you want, Jeem?"

"Well! Boy, this is just like the old days. I'm sure even Gerry would enjoy the intrigue. I will arrange a little rescue plan, or maybe an escape plan after he has had enough of your good self. He will then owe his life to me; he will be at my mercy. In fact I may even organise a little of the old action stuff from the Taran days just to impress him. Or, of course, I could simply leave him with your boys to dispose of him as they wish. Hey, this sounds like a bit of fun!"

Jim's depression had lifted, probably at the thought of this new cloak and dagger stuff.

"I have a nice den of thieves up een the hills right now who sometimes come to work on our farm and meanwhile grow de precious poppies, who weel love to kidnap him to kill the long time between planting and reaping. They geet so bored up there that they often practice shooting at each other to pass de time. Russian roulette is an old habit with them which we have failed to cure. They hate boredom. They also hate Americans."

"Wow. Meet me later this week and we will work it out in detail. I'll find the right go-between for the operation ..."

"Nobody must get hurt too much."

"I promise, Hans."

The Dutchman gave McCall a worried look; he was hoping that things didn't get too much out of hand .... .

"Is that your girlfriend sitting over there by the dieffenbachia, Hans? The blonde woman who looks like a movie star?"

"No. She ees my sister."

Hans took his leave of Jim. He was touched, not to say a little amused, to see how excited Jim had become at the mere thought of some subversive action. How an old dog finds it hard to change its spots!

After a breakfast of saltfish, ackee and weak, tasteless Mountain Coffee (the best island coffee was exported by the cartel to Japan) Gerry made his way to the Ministry of Economics and Information, still without his tie and breaking the dress code of the employment authorities. He walked slowly up the boulevard past milling citizens and visitors from the country-side and from abroad. The slow walk was in aid of his objective of arriving for the 8 am. appointment at 11.45 am precisely.

Gerry normally did not bother much about correct timing, but he always made sure that he was in time for an appointment that he wished to keep. Even then he was usually behind schedule; probably having a drink or simply lazing around his pad, deep in interesting contemplations of life, considering unusual questions such as *why* do cockroaches, rather than skulk behind greasy pots, not use their obvious intelligence and clever tactics to extend their territory, or at least take up a more civilised way of life; or *why* do John Crow vultures wait so patiently for their prey to die, instead of indulging themselves immediately on fresh, living flesh? He was still suffering somewhat from the fatigue of adjusting to the tropics, but he knew he mustn't miss this important appointment. First impressions are what count in these situations; first impressions, he had found, become the eternal folklore no matter what else happens thereafter. If he should happen to slip on a banana skin or inadvertently wet his trousers on his way up here, this would be celebrated in prose and song long after he was gone, even if in the meantime he had saved the country from war, famine, built two new cities and founded a major university in the island he would forever be known as 'wetpants' or 'he who walks straight onto banana skins'. He was determined now to give a good impression (strange how strong this desire appears when one's career or status is beginning to slip a bit), as it would also be his great opportunity. A good show in the next two hours would save him a great expenditure of effort later on. He would be able to relax and do what he liked for the rest of his stay, enjoy himself, watching the results of his secret work, and not worry about anything, just let events take their natural course, which they always did in any case, anyway. Another thing, it had to be remembered that the natives of a country did not like their guests to be seen to be sweating by the brow or worrying too much, as if they did not depend on the locals for everything; they were, after all, guests of the country and it was important to always behave as such. The first rule of success was to keep a low profile; not make too much a nuisance of oneself. He certainly intended to stick to this rule!

What impression exactly he should try to portray was another matter. He would play it, as usual, by ear and suss out the terrain as he went along. He would have to figure out what these people considered as virtues and vices; this varied greatly from country to country and his experience told him that Jaman, also, was a place likely to have its own eccentric ways and habits. For instance, in that first lecture he had given, the initial apathy and languor that he had found, rather than the expected keen interest, had given way to what appeared to be a mini-riot when he had mentioned, innocently, and not realising its potential effect, that farming as they knew it was going to disappear forever and that a future on the land was going to be something of the past. He had asserted that the masses of the country need never fear having to slave and sweat in the cane fields again but would have rosy futures hanging around in the shanty towns, or, if they were very lucky, get a low paid job cleaning the toilets in some nice tourist hotel; or migrate from the country where they weren't wanted to another country where they were even less welcome. The shouts of disapproval and anger that greeted this revelation had raised the roof.

(Soon there were exaggerated rumours about this lesson and an inquiry by the relevant authorities into what had 'gone wrong' in the class, an investigation which eventually reached the Board of Management, with repercussions).

It was also possible, he now ruminated, that here in the Ministry a certain degree of intoxication and madness at top decision-making level was something to be admired, whilst a dour face and laborious expression in people was disapproved of as they only portended bad news and disaster. The way to tell what-was-what was to study the attitudes of everyone as you came into their presence *for the first time.* Who was smiling, sitting back relaxed, who was bolt upright with a strained look and who was studiously ignoring you as you came in through the door? He could read each one's past, present and future in their expressions, the way they initially spoke and sat. It all told a tale, the body-and-face language of people.

At one point he stopped to watch a disturbance outside a store in a small shopping parade; he had time to spare and he wanted to see how these people behaved in such situations; were the police capable of dealing with the trouble for instance, or did they only succeed in making things far worse than they were at the beginning?

The owner of the foodstore, a Mr Joong, was holding a mob at bay by means of a machete in one hand and a gun in the other while his two assistants were aiming spearguns of the type used in the local Marlin fishing competitions. Here was body language spoken 'in extremis'. A number of people were writhing in pain on the ground and the crowd were 'baying for blood'.

"Doan ya 'ave enuff," screamed Mr Joong, his face streaming sweat and his eyes wild with anger and anxiety;

"come awn if yo waan more!"

Gerry calmly observed the faces of the crowd which had surrounded this grocery store entrepreneur and was a motley collection of men, women and children. The most obvious emotion was one of excitement, excitement at having caught their prey, even at the expense of a number of their fellow-rioters lying dead or injured on the ground, excitement in the anticipation of the coming kill. He had seen that look before, on a pack of stray dogs that had cornered an injured cat in Boston; at a siege by the Taranese Liberation Army outside Da-Lay-Bac City; on the faces of a group of literary critics and authors at a Book Competition Awards' ceremony in Washington. There was, he knew, only one way to quell the commotion and prevent further unspeakable horror, personal intervention by a sane, responsible individual such as himself.

However, Gerry had a secret weakness, one which he had always been careful to keep hidden in the past, by the use of a method well-known to gamblers, bluff.

For, despite his inebriated fantasies about guns and revolution, he had a loathing and fear of physical violence.

This was a handicap that had plagued him all his life; it indeed explained many of his more 'unworthy' escapades, actions and omissions. Yet, strangely, for much of his life a macho front had been all-important in confronting his many adversaries and enemies, both open and covert. It was as if he always had a need to walk this tightrope over danger and death.

He had always considered this apprehension to be a vice, especially in the days whilst serving in the armed forces when it was a matter of personal shame and guilt. It implied a serious moral flaw, a deficiency of character making him suspect in his deeds and even in his opinions. There was still well-remembered, for instance, his unheroic, clever ways of deserting duty when there were upcoming battles, delegated walks through minefields or along dangerous, booby-trapped village tracks.

Then there was his ever-present fear, one which continued to give him many nightmares, of ending up a prisoner of the enemy, captured, held as a helpless hostage in some grim room somewhere.

He had always assumed that he would confess under torture and give away any information that was required, and more besides. He had never disposed of the official issue of two cyanide capsules from the underground days and while doubting his willingness to ever take them, he generally anticipated that he would swallow them if he ever faced a certain, slow death.

He was perpetually thinking of ways out of such desperate situations. He practiced at imagining 'no-way-out' impasses, and then would relieve the ensuing stress by imagining different, possible solutions. His schemes of self-protection, of evasion, had reached a fine art; with strategies of great subtlety and novelty stored in memory. He it was who devised the art of 'going over to the enemy' as perfected later by better known figures. He was especially adept at infiltrating the camp of the enemy. In these predicaments he always, immediately, put all his cards on the table. He would often go further, not deny who he was and offer 'the world and her brother' to the opposition. It was one way of staying alive. It always worked. He gained the respect of both sides and no one dared to eliminate him in case he was of value to their side. Everybody believed he was working for them. It was more than just 'sitting on the fence' or 'rowing in both directions'. He was in fact working sincerely for all the parties concerned, discerning in every situation what was best for all. He sometimes thought that this duplicity was no vice at all, certainly not something to be deeply ashamed of. It was even perhaps a sort of virtue. Yet there was that ennui in his life that bothered him, gave him no rest and made him feel that he was not as other men when it came to the things of this world. He sensed that all 'achievement' was so ... meaningless. He was never interested in 'self-assertion', or ambition. During recreation periods in

Taran it was hours spent, albeit fruitlessly, trying to comprehend Kierkegaard, Plato and Nietzshe (in parts) that engrossed him rather than football or drinking the gross beer; (however, he also remembered spending many long hours enjoying McCall's whiskey and a cigarette, reflecting happily on nothing at all behind a shed or, following Jim's example, in the Corps privy). Or he would lie 'sick' in bed, perhaps taking a rest from the tedium of his own internal conflicts, instead of behaving like more normal colleagues with their oppressive chatter and childish games as they enthusiastically flocked off to baseball or informal, off-the-cuff meetings on more ways to infiltrate enemy lines or how to doctor high explosive bombs to blow up in the face of some no-longer-required allied colleague. No, it was better not to be brave about life, especially in a war zone. After all, the greatest strides in human progress were often made whilst retreating from the affairs of war and carnage; the ages of progress in great civilisations were times of peace, weren't they? And fear was often a greater innovator than bravery.

Even his flight from Mary's discipline and her fierce strictures was a positive thing, for how else was he to gain the freedom to achieve his hope of bringing about a radical change in the world?

Oh, he suddenly realised, here he was 'thinking' again; instead of considering what was at hand, in this case a dangerous riot. He had been day-dreaming again!

"Yu r-o-b-b-e-r! Rob de poor an' tek bread from we children mouth! One dollar a pound fe chicken . . .!"

Considering the exchange rate and local wage levels this was an extremely high price for chicken, he thought, a staple food in the diet of these and all Third World people; it represented in fact 50% again on the price level of chicken in the USA at that moment (CIA people always had current international statistics running through their heads, from The World Book Of Facts

19–, published by the Central Intelligence Agency in conjunction with the IMF). This man was certainly asking for trouble and no doubt he had done a deal with the other supermarket entrepreneurs and chicken producers islandwide. It was always the way that these guys were in the habit of pushing it to the last cent and that they intermarried. He remembered Paulo's novel at that moment and the 'families'. Families have a lot to answer for, he thought, including his own! They were the cause of all the world's divisions, and yet they seemed to be necessary for the natural upbringing of the human species. Blame God again, he supposed. At least it was possible, sometimes, to escape from them!

Well, it was decision time. Mr Joong had retreated with his back now up against a wall. He felt sorry for the man, a father probably of a large and demanding family, who certainly worked from early morning till midnight all year round, who realised how easy it is to lose everything on a bad day or in one bad deal, who did not cheat out of pure greed or maliciousness but of desperation over the uncertainty of ever being fully financially secure; in some ways a man just like himself as regards self-doubt and apprehension. The sound of a police car siren came to their ears and Gerry did what he had to do; all his training had prepared him for such an action and it was one that he had found, despite his aversion to physical force, increasingly easy to carry out the more he *had* to do it. He took out his handgun and shot Mr Joong dead there in the street.

He turned around and the crowd was gone, as if they had melted en masse into the surrounding walls and buildings; there was not a soul to be seen and even the bodies had disappeared from sight.

At that moment the police appeared, guns at the ready. By this time Gerry was also making himself scarce with the thought:

'Better that one man should die than all the people'.

He still got to the meeting 'on time'. It was with some disappointment that he saw that they were expecting him, for the doorman greeted him in a familiar, friendly way as he entered. He would have felt a good deal better if there had been no acknowledgment or any sign of pre-knowledge of him on his arrival, only bafflement or even hostility; as would have been the case in most normal assignments. If now, at best, there was a degree of awareness of him there could only be, also, expectations. He would certainly have to quickly find out what these were.

He had entered a Developing Country government building which had the typical cost-cutting furniture and paraphernalia noted of such establishments: especially coarse but large notices saying DO NOT ENTER, KEEP OUT and NOT OPEN TO MEMBERS OF THE PUBLIC; wall posters from the well-besmirched ancient printing press of the capital's official newspaper (owned by the Puerto Ricos, naturally, being run by Carmen Puerto Rico who had been so glad to sack Costello as she could not stand a peasant around her office), depicting scenes of crude death and despair with the literal warnings DRIVING WITHOUT LICENSE CAUSE DESTRUCTION, or EDUCATE, COMMENSURATE, HESITATE referring probably to those who came to complain to government departments, and one that gave him cause to ponder: THE COUNTRY NEEDS YOU. YES, YOU.

His first urge whenever entering these establishments was always to speak loudly and rudely to the person, whoever or whatever rank he or she was, or wherever he or she happened to be, who was the least busy, most idle person in the place. To find this person was a harder task than one might suppose. One had to know the signs of pure idleness. It wasn't just a matter of someone sitting in a comfortable chair and chatting endlessly to a friend or relative; or else lolling about quite drunk and

141

abusing everyone. It was more a matter of defiance, a defiant look in the eye, a defiant lounge in an armchair probably behind some mammoth collection of paper but not necessarily; the biggest knobs liked to have nothing on, in or behind their desks; a defiant silence when asked anything and, eventually, a refractory tone in a single syllable 'answer' to whatever was asked. When this person is singled out it is an absolute certainty that you are looking at the boss, or at least one of the bosses.

"Where is *your* boss, the top boss?," shouted Gerry at the uniformed official who sat in her chair looking quite blase, as though she were doing the seat itself a great honour.

"Ha," was her reply as she extended her arm out slowly to a telephone at the side of the desk, surprising Gerry by the speed of her response (his question of course had been deliberately expressed to be as provocative as possible, as nothing else would have elicited any useful reaction), but it was then that he knew immediately that she had been forewarned of his imminent arrival; normally the reaching for the telephone takes twenty US minutes.

"Him 'ere."

There was a group of three important-looking executives standing more or less together in what appeared to be a self-conscious attempt to put on a united front, in the executive suite to which a porter with a most miserable countenance (caused by his low pay, actually, which did not cover his bus fares to work for the week) had taken him and to whom Gerry, knowing that it would annoy all on-lookers and might disarmingly appraise them of his 'innocence', gave a 50 CENTS TIP. To the three Gerry immediately gave the code names Mr 1, 2 and 3. This later became Magnus Rabid, Minister of Culture, Education and Chancellor of the Exchequer, Erico Mauris, Information Minister and Mr Stanley, Prime Minister.

Stanley was a typical Third World leader. A Puerto Rico on his mother's side, he was paternalistic, well-read in some of the more atrocious verse of Blake, Kipling as well as possessing some apt Shakespearean cliches, a sampling of Irish Literary Romance and a distant admiration of 'The Romans' with a neurotically-engineered exhortation of their 'discipline'. He approached every person and object with a grave, unnervingly long laugh that had the effect of investing both himself and said objects with a strange solemnity and awe. He thought that Americans were the next-best-thing to the Romans and he always had the belief (and secret wish) that one day they would have to come, with their helicopters and aircraft carriers, and save him (and his island) from the anarchy and self-righteousness of the smart asses and irresponsible upstarts who abounded in the place. Mr Stanley, fortunately or unfortunately as the case may be, for much depends on a realistic appraisal of the value of such leaders for making inspired decisions in a cruelly logical universe, was a dreamer.

Erico Mauris, the Minister of Information, was actually too small in build and casual in expression for such an important position in life; but he was an irredeemable gossip and had got the cushiest job in the cabinet by pleading desperately one night over drinks with prime minister Stanley, claiming that he knew all the sneaks and liars in the land and that he had the low-down on the main island homosexual circle. This latter information clinched the deal for him with Stanley, who had a particular aversion to the strange stories he had heard related about such people and wanted to keep an eye on them.

Magnus Rabid was the most effective and powerful of the three politicians. He was a thin man of medium height and Caucasian appearance and looked surprisingly like a hippie from 60's America, with long hair and a taste for fancy rings and body ornaments. But he was a native Jamanese of mixed race. He was an aggressive sort; it was he who ordered, for whatever ulterior motive, that every male public servant in the country wear the bush jacket (a light, though formal looking tropical jacket manufactured by Magnus's own textile firm) in all government offices and all public places; he was the first one now to speak to Gerry, in an effusive manner that embarrassed one by its false obsequiousness:

"Greetings, Professor Gerald McArthur, Phd, Honorary member of the Society of Washington Intellectuals, Dip. Sociology."

Gerry was horrified. How ever did he find out about that Dip. Sociology?

"As one economist to another, as one doctor of learning to another, although I myself cannot claim *many* links with your illustrious Harvard, I welcome you. We already have many brilliant graduates working here, such as my junior colleague who gives me much advice on the economy, Professor Maria Gomez, who, believe it or not, is a woman and yet has graduated from the famous London University with top honours in the Dismal Science! So we are not unaccustomed to intellectual discussions here!"

Why is he being so ... effusive? Probably it is either pure bafflement, or curiosity to do with my Harvard connection," thought Gerry to himself.

"Professor Maria Gomez. I am told that she has the most brilliant mind in the country. I have been looking forward to working with her," he said now in an earnest voice.

He looked for any effect this laudation might have on the staring, wondering men in front of him. He had always found from experience that to praise a professional woman in front of her male colleagues often had the effect of bringing about a reaction, not the least one being to believe that the person speaking was a bit of a dolt, someone it was safe to assume knew next to nothing about matters of real importance. In this

144

way Gerry hoped to ensure that they actually began to think now that he was, after all, no cleverer than they and not much of a threat.

"Oh yes, she has performed some useful work producing economic plans for the country but of course it is myself who does the real work. And only I make the important decisions," said Magnus, annoyed.

"Of course," said Gerry.

"I believe you have many good ideas on the theory of economics," said Magnus, now looking more critical and becoming somewhat inquisitorial:

"I, and the rest of the government here, will only be too glad to hear what they are. Your first lecture went down with a bit of a bang, apparently."

His voice had a slight note of reproach in it.

"Who told you that?," asked Gerry, hoping to cause a diversion. He did not want to be questioned about the 'Dip. Sociology'.

So what, they would try to get him crucified on the altar of the most detested academic subject in the world? His economics portfolio had always been a cover-up in any case for his real qualification in sociology, a qualification which he had kept secret throughout his long career. He had always managed to pass himself off as an economist at these job interviews, such as he was attending now. He had picked up enough about the subject along the way, and especially about the methodology of economists, who were the biggest bull-artists in the world, to be completely well-read and conversant in the so-called 'dismal science' in all its aspects, even in the most academic of circles. He had never doubted his ability to pass himself off as an economist of the top school in any gathering. Nobody at Harvard had ever even suspected that they had a rogue sociologist in their midst, and even his colleagues at the Pentagon had long since forgotten his real field of theoretical knowledge (after espionage, that is). This of course was the most frowned-upon subject in the world. He had long ago realised that sociology was the subversive subject of the Humanities. It looked objectively at human behaviour and included many different schools of thought, giving its doyens a rare skill, the opportunity to think and write about society in a cold, dispassionate way . . .

At the back of his mind all the time was an unspoken, near-superstitious belief that somehow or other the matter of his academic credentials would lead to his downfall one day. He had been in so many tight situations with them, frequently just getting away by the skin of his teeth.

Here they were, already perhaps doubting his qualifications and testing his mettle. If he was not careful he could find himself removed from his post. It was all to do with that problem of being over-qualified, he consoled himself.

"I have heard some very important people say good things and bad things about you," said Erico solemnly; "it seems that you have had an interesting career."

"I have come here to help your country," said Gerry genially.

"Yes," said the prime minister, "we are more worried about the bad things. We know your record. We read that you have academic achievements in many fields, but also that you are headstrong and undependable. Your last employer, in his reference which I have here, does not pull his punches."

"Mr Warner is a fair man."

"It's a very thorough document," he continued, pointing to the piece of paper on the desk, a facile grin on his face. He was obviously just repeating the information from the said reference, it being the only source of information he'd got. The reference itself was probably a diplomatic memo, photocopy-third-level secret document.

"Ha ha," guffawed Gerry to himself, but the croaking laugh slipped out and was immediately interpreted as a sign of embarrassment by the others rather than disdain and irony; an incident of cultural misunderstanding which had a fortunately non-damaging result.

But Gerry was being careless.

"OK, gentlemen. Let's get down to business," he said now with enforced bravado, deciding it was time to draw the conversation away from the matter of his credentials and show that the real discussion was now to begin, one between practical men, between equals. He still liked to play the down-to-earth, go-ahead American at times.

"Let's face the facts, your country needs people like me; I have some ideas about improving things here."

"Those simple, innocent days of the expert from overseas coming here and changing everything are gone, Mr McArthur," said Magnus, "we all live in a different age now, a changed world that our forefathers would not recognise. The old sayings are useless. Our enemies are our friends and our friends are our enemies. We need you because all our best brains have gone abroad."

"Hounded out by your threat to make every college graduate spend a year working in one of your factories to learn how to work with their hands," said Mr Stanley, looking sourly at his precocious minister.

"No. By your lack of solid leadership! But I don't think Mr McArthur," said Magnus, "let me call him Gerry, has come here to listen to us agonize over our national problems, most of which were created by your attempts to copy everything American. Such as when you broke the country's finances ordering the building of a space-rocket launching station in the rural backwoods simply to save TEN votes! An expensive White Elephant where I believe the goats graze now but for which you still insist on holding out, at local election rallies, the prospect of an eventual launching, or hear us wash all our other dirty linen in public . . . ."

Splits and tensions between the members of government were showing themselves; the previous display of unity was already breaking down, to Gerry's satisfaction ...

"Or ... ," put in Erico Mauris, "the catastrophe that hit the university and the Ministry of Economic Affairs recently ... ."

"What was that ... ?," asked Magnus turning suddenly to face Erico and speaking in a sarcastic, but hurt voice.

"Do I have to spell it out in front of our foreign guest?"

Erico was clearly having a bit of fun too.

"I don't care what you do."

"I'm sure Professor McArthur would like to know all about the Foreign Hippie Cult, in the form of the post-Independence foreigners who took over all the lectureships and professorships at our university and thus infiltrated the 'Thinking and Policy' department of the Economics Ministry with their weird philosophy and teachings. These we all swallowed as words of wisdom that we were fortunate to receive from such wise gurus. Of course nobody realised at first what was really going on, putting down the absence of note-taking and the general boycotting of exams to free thinking and student revolution and identification with the oppressed. All this eventually culminated in the conventional wisdom of 'Money Is Bad For You' which proceeded to take over our entire culture; the 'beads instead of money' philosophy I call it; and, now that today nobody has any money, the truth is beginning to dawn at last. For today, if any money appears anywhere it immediately disappears again! If an ordinary citizen happens to get his hands on it at any time he immediately gives it all straight back to some shopkeeper or somebody else who 'asks' for it, more often than not with the proviso that he will also promise many further, larger sums (in a scam these hippie professors glorified as 'Social Credit'), all in exchange for something the shopkeeper, or other person, is only too keen to get rid of and doesn't want himself anyway, a dollop of margarine, a pint of adulterated cooking oil or an hour of labour at some task the seller could not be bothered to carry out himself or herself.

Then there is the All-Powerful National Money Rejecter, which sends away any-and-all foreign exchange cash as soon as it has been earned to unknown foreign parts, never to be seen, or heard of, again, by every known and unknown route out of this forsaken island. This is applauded by the experts and financiers as being 'good for the economy' and the more efficiently the money disappears, the more the feat is celebrated. Under other appearances, some of such said money is then lent back to the country in rather smaller amounts at supersonic rates of interest to finance hopeless projects (indeed if any proposed projects do show any promise of real success they are always rejected as 'socialist'). That is how we got landed here with those development follies your own ministry is responsible for, such as the President Niceman-Eddie Hydro Electric Dam, which successfully blocks up the only worthwhile river in the country, ensuring that no water ever reaches the parched peasant lands (that in itself is seen as good for 'Enterprise' as it presents our farmers with a Great Challenge to work harder ...)".

Magnus then had it rubbed into him by Stanley that it had been his responsibility as Economics minister to solve all these problems. And he had failed!

"We economists have a lot to answer for," said Gerry attempting to neutralise this situation of obvious animosity between the cabinet ministers, "but I think I can help you here, Mr Rabid. You will find that most top economists are foreign to the English-speaking culture and all their development theories come out of textbooks written by people who have never been to Jaman or the Third World, but spend their days in libraries and ivory towers playing games with statistics. My own knowledge is based on the real experience of world problems picked up from having, perforce, to live in many countries and I am here, as a non-politician, to offer unprejudiced expertise.

That, actually, is why most right-wing and indeed left-wing academics hate my book, 'Aid to Economic Theory', and ban it in many colleges. My theories make no sense to them."

There certainly was such a textbook, and others, written by a 'Gerry McArthur', but it was to come to the notice of some people-in-the-know later that there was another Gerry McArthur, professor of business studies at an Australian university, who claimed to be the author. Not even the librarian in the CIA data section had spotted this one.

"Aaaah, a cynic," said prime minister Stanley, showing an unexpected sense of humour, "a very old tradition from the days of the Ancient Greeks. They have a lot to teach us. I remember when I was a young man. I was an ordinary classroom teacher, the most noble profession in the world, much sunk to the depths these days and no wonder, just look at the practitioners, no offence to you, Mr McArthur. When I was indeed very young and raw and green ... ."

"Stop blathering and give the man his instructions. We can't be standing around here all day, Mr Stanley; some of us have jobs to do," said Magnus in a haughty tone.

Gerry could not see anybody speaking to an American president in this manner. Then he remembered. They were all 'family' here.

"OK.," said Stanley, using the vernacular, perhaps hoping to ingratiate himself with the American by showing that he, too, was a man of the world; "here we go. Your mission is to talk economic sense to the populace. I am tired, and the president, leaders of commerce and finance, advisors, newspaper editors, are all tired of having to make excuses at election time for our supposed economic failures. We inevitably lose elections to the opposition, and this is inconvenient even if we do share power on a rotating basis ... ."

"Hurry up, prime minister," said Magnus, moody now for he had been smoking cannabis that morning, "or I will miss my meeting with the delegation from Fine Tobacco Inc. on ways to beat the US embargo on our herbal exports. Tell him the facts about this new policy which we must adopt now in our country."

Well at least, thought Gerry with some relief, they have dropped, or forgotten, the question of my qualifications.

"Listen, Mr McArthur. I want you to teach, to persuade, to exhort the populace in the Way of economic truth. Brainwash them, cajole them, trick them, whichever way you can get them to listen to reason. Tell them to stop asking for more. It's More, More, More all the time! Neverendingly *more*. Show them that it's economic sense for a few to have the whole wealth of the country and for everyone else to have nothing. Say that this is the Supreme Economic Certitude. They will believe anything you say, for you are an academic and you have written books on economics. Economics is a sacred god to the masses. Persuade the country that poverty and unemployment are the way forward. It should be a simple task. It is the easiest thing in the world to get people to understand that they are the victims of Grim Impersonal Forces. Tell them to work without pay. Tell them that our value-less government paper money is the greatest patriotic treasure on earth. Tell them that their economic reward is to be able to feed the more worthy, powerful nations with sugar, coffee, tea, tobacco, the fruit of the trees and to forego their own selfish needs, for this is Pure Capitalism, the only economic system never yet tried out on earth. Show them how postponement of one's present needs for 'future' fulfillment has been the darling of all true economic theories. We will give you full access to all our media pundits to give them what we will call The Big Message. That they are a wonderful, unconquerable, brave people who must realise that *scarcity* is the true economic condition and that any idea of economic progress is pure bullshite, if I may borrow an American word."

Gerry was nodding his head as if he already had grasped the idea; as if he had known what it would be long before he had even entered the room. He spoke, trying to show the maximum of respect for the trio and their policies:

"Gentlemen, these are times for recognising reality, as the new US president would put it, and what America does today everybody does tomorrow. Yet I often ask myself the question why it is that leaders in faraway, small struggling countries, like yourselves, usually show far more intuition when it comes to the harsh realities of life? You are to be credited with a discovery that they are still only coming to terms with in Harvard; that the masses can be bombarded with sufficient economic data to be able to accept the most atrocious conditions if it is done with the aid of an irreproachable textbook; be it Marx's theory, Keynes's jottings or my own 'Aid to Economic Theory'. Equally useful, however, are the media, especially pop music, the opium of the people, a basic cultural form here in Jaman with, for example, the likes of Slangman Stardust and his well-sung 'Cane Juice Bitter' and its references to the alienation brought on by working conditions in the sugar industry. A friend of mine, Jim, he's called, is very good on pop music. I could myself, or get him, to write a song encouraging the growing of the coconut tree once more. For the coconut, believe me, is the food of tomorrow. It will feature in all my lessons"

They were impressed by the evidence of methodological flexibility in McArthur's approach and his apparently novel techniques. But the reference to sugar industry working conditions caused an angry expression to appear on Magnus's face. Before he could point out the subversive element in all this 'new spirit of learning stuff' the prime minister interrupted.

"Aah, mass communications are a great miracle," said Stanley in the deep voice he put on for solemn statements; "the Ancient Romans were wonders at it. They used to crucify criminals by the hundreds of thousands . . . ."

"I don't think that is what is meant by mass communications," said Erico sarcastically; "although they did use Latin all over the empire and later on they were into art and homosexuality and all that."

"I think we should stick to the issue here. We would ask Dr McArthur to present his message in as many big words as possible, to stick to abstractedness and technical terminology and to make sure he uses his broadest American accent at all times. In that way he will succeed in persuading the masses that our new policies are a good thing," said Magnus Rabid.

The termination of the interview had a slightly unsettling effect on Gerry.

"By the way, Dr McArthur," Stanley suddenly asked, looking at Gerry oddly, "are you bringing your wife to Jaman? The nights are long in the tropics, what with the heat and the bugs. It wouldn't do for you to start going unbalanced, as too many do who come over here."

"I always work alone. It is the best way."

"It is not natural for a man to live alone, as was once wisely said somewhere. I view with suspicion anyone who lives without a woman. I would strongly advise you to get a woman for yourself. There are plenty of them around the island."

"OK. I'll see what I can do about that."

"I hope, also, that you are not going to continue to hang around certain bars in bad company?," said Erico Mauris, catching Gerry somewhat by surprise.

"Also," said Magnus is a low, admonishing voice, "from what I hear you should see what you can do about discipline in your classes. Unruly classes never learn anything." □

chapter
eight

Gerry felt shaken after the interview. He had, for the first time in his life, experienced a slip in his self-confidence. Fate seemed to be threatening to close in on him for he could not, he now realised, continue to carry on these supremely self-confident 'acts' for ever. The years were slipping by; he was losing the virtuosity of his youth. He was starting to feel a bit old. They all seemed to be watching his every move now, scrutinising his personal life, whether it was by means of The Firm's agents or through Erico's Ministry of Information, poring over every petty, mundane detail of everything that he did. He felt a bit desperate, as if all avenues of escape were fast running out. There were only so many countries that he could go to, or which would even accept the benefits of his expertise. Would he end up in a comfortable, dead-end office job in administration back home, or laboriously de-briefing immeasurably more successful agents in some suburban 'safe house', the dream of self-respect, of liberty, gone forever ... ?

The reality was even worse. Already he could feel the suffocating tentacles of that bourgeoisie, ancient world closing in again, the nightmare that he had long been trying to escape. Everything was coming back now, as he walked out of the building. He remembered the reason he had turned to economics (for was it not that powerful ingredient which promised solutions to the problems of a desperate world); away from all dogma (the cause of all hatreds); the detestation of all social convention (which stultified the human spirit). It was the war in Taran that had been the catalyst of his guilt. He had lived since that time a life that was at odds, indeed at war, with 'the world'. And now he could feel in his innermost being that the old world was coming back like a black cloud, to cover him over this last, and for all, time.

Mrs McArthur had put down the phone to her old friend and adviser, Father McCarthy, who had called to inquire 'how was the lad?', when it rang immediately with her friend and confidant Peggy Dunne asking 'what's the news?'

"I told Fr McCarthy that Gerry was away on another assignment 'helping the less fortunate' again, this time in Jaman. He said that he still held the hope that Gerry would do great things for the church one day. He said that our marriage stood out like a beacon to all upright Christians; that if we went for an annulment there was the possibility of a medal from Rome. He already knew the details of Gerry's posting and that the Cardinal said that they were keeping an eye on him over there . . . ."

"Gerry would return to the Fold, according to Fr McCarthy," went on Mary, "when he is spiritually ready, and in the process bring many others with him into the Church. Well, I have my doubts about that but you know how it is with these unworldly priests. One doesn't want to give scandal to them so when he said that maybe one day the Pope himself will be able to present Gerry with a Papal medal or even a Counthood I said nothing. Sometimes I wonder whether the clergy are miles behind us in the affairs of this world, why they even bother to try to convert the likes of Gerry. Or else they are eons ahead of us in the next! It seems I am the only person in the world who knows the real Gerry. I understand why he doesn't face up to life. It never ceases to amaze me the extent, and distance, to which he will go just to enjoy a boozing spree with any disreputable friend he can find."

"But ... I have always believed he was sent to places where his skills and knowledge were indispensable and he had important jobs to do for Uncle Sam? That is what you always said, anyway. Doesn't he work for the US defences, or something. Isn't he supposed to be one of the hardest necks in the espionage business?", asked Peggy Dunne, incredulity beginning to sound in her voice. She had always imagined Gerry as a cloak-and-dagger character; it was even possible that she carried for him a 'small flame'.

"He is a lot of things, my dear, but Mr Indispensable he is not! I have had to cover up for him many times in the past. I painted a more glorious picture than the reality. I'm afraid I am getting a bit tired of it all. I am more resigned to the full truth now. He is just another, no-good drinking husband."

"Oh, really," said Peggy, sympathising with Mary's sadness, "I am sure he does wonderful things for his country when he is in those places. Don't you dare take the shine off his image. You can be proud of him, despite everything. And ... I'm sure only a very few people still remember the way he was sent home from the army in disgrace. Is it your place tomorrow night?"

"Yes, seven o'clock. Danielle Warner is coming. She's Gerry's boss's latest wife. She runs that man like an Armalite automatic. Funny how all his other wives came to a sad end though. It makes you wonder how some of these men can be left to make important decisions. Ho ho, she's good for a laugh anyway. You should hear her on Hooligan's penchant for certain strange yoga positions."

"Ha ha ha."

Mary put the phone down and proceeded to internally process all the recent phone conversations. She had been speaking again to Gloria who had informed her that Gerry was meeting important government officials that day and that, to all appearances, he was now sober. Mary had then, as a reward for this information, informed the lady that she would find Gerry's secret 'black book,' his diary with all his spying reports on Jaman's politics and strategic installations detailed there, in a secret pocket inside his trousers and that the only way to get a glimpse would be to catch him asleep; something even she herself had never yet succeeded in doing.

"Whaa? Yo never catch 'im asleep?," Gloria had laughed down the line.

"You don't know my husband. He is thinking hard when others are fast asleep and he is asleep when you think he is working. He is the hardest person in the world to get to, when he has a mind to it. I'll leave it to you to see if you can sneak a look at that diary. I, too, would love to know what is in there. By the way, your dollars will be in Jaman by the next post. And I will soon send you an airline ticket for New York Kennedy."

Fr McCarthy was 'an old family friend', a term which always has sinister connotations, especially when it comes to members of the clergy or political parties.

He had once been dragooned in to help try to persuade Gerry to fulfill his marital obligations; or at least to take them more seriously. It appeared that the said 'family man' Gerry had taken up a dilettante attitude to his marriage, a devil-may-care disposition concerning the important, essential function normally associated with this irreplaceable social contract, this holy bonding of matrimony. How word of his 'sin of omission' got out was never clarified. Whether its disclosure by Mary occurred in the confessional, or whether somebody leaked Gerry's files from the Pentagon record office, remained a matter of conjecture.

Gerry seemed to believe that bringing home the pay cheque was enough. Then one weekend he had come home to find Fr McCarthy sitting in the kitchen having a cup of tea ..

"Is it yerself young man that's in it?", the priest had asked jollily, and as there could be no doubt that it was Gerry standing there, annoyed, presumably the Fr had thought that a traditional Irish greeting would relax things.

"And how are you and Mary getting along?," he asked later over the Irish whiskey, referred 'jokingly' to by the clergy all over the world as VAT 69.

"A marriage made in Heaven, as you might say," replied Gerry unhappily.

"Let's discuss it, just between you and me. No further than these four walls. Mary is a wee bit upset. Sure why wouldn't any natural woman not want to have children? More guests at Our Lord's table. More priests and nuns for Mother Church?"

"Is there a problem, then, Father?"

"You tell me, Gerry."

"We can't have babies, Father."

"And why not, young man?"

"Some of the vital works were irreparably damaged at Can-Do, that Taranese village years ago in a bit of an explosion. Her dad knows. It seems it was the traumatic shock. Also, some of the water works are not quite operative."

"Excuses. Good Lord, man, what sort of an explanation is that? You are still obliged, by law, to go for fatherhood. Any old excuse seems to be good enough these days. Be your own man. Stand on your own two feet and do what is expected of every Irish American. The next thing we'll be hearing is that it is unwise for women to have children as it hurts too much when they come out. What is the world coming to? This feminism business has a lot to answer for, if you ask me. Sure how can you call it a marriage if you don't ... ? Let me tell you, Gerry McArthur, your good Mary has grounds, you know. Grounds for an Annulment."

"She can have one any day," said Gerry sourly and this was the end of the discussion for the time being.

"That is just Father McCarthy's round-about way of telling you to pay more attention to me. It's his way of saying 'try to show some affection'. You can't expect them to come straight out with it. They are rather shy. He does not approve of your career path either; he thinks it verges too near Liberalism," was Mary's comment later to a somewhat perplexed Gerry.

Mary now poured herself a whiskey-on-the-rocks and sat down at the kitchen table (a very expensive oak table, at which to sit with her friends, was one of her self-indulged compensations for her trials, but Gerry had put many scorch marks on it with his cigarettes), to plan her next move. There was no doubt that her long-term master plan was in real jeopardy.

She thought back. Things had been slowly improving after Taran and then Gerry and his colleagues had that row at Langley (it was over a silly thing really, the issue of whether the window should be left open or closed in the middle of an October afternoon) and things had then begun to go from bad to worse both at home and in his career. It seemed he had undergone some kind of breakdown and had more or less engineered that 'argument'. He had been in a huff over their rejection of his thesis 'The Illogicalities Of Human Thinking And Consequent Policy Making' which destroyed many years of research, tediously pursued by him with a view to the proud publication of his work as a handbook for civil servants. He had, thereafter, refused to conform to any aspect of departmental policy and had made himself a pain in the neck to management, debarring himself from any promotion. He had taken up the unsatisfactory career path of field officer, knowing that, when he would be sent abroad to deal with a problem that needed sorting out, there would be sighs of relief all round.

So much for Mary's plan to have him promoted to a good Washington job and cure him at long last of his obsessive drive to 'make the world a better place'. He was still trapped in a dreadful youthful idealism, while the natural cynicism of increasing age served only to fuel his drinking and even deeper 'thinking'. If only she could have kept him near at hand she could, she firmly believed, have reassured him that the world had no need of his help, that God was in His Heaven and 'worrying' and 'influencing policy' served no useful purpose. She was particularly convinced that if he would indeed return to the consolations of religion (which he had consciously rejected apparently when, as a student, he had discovered that God was apolitical) they could start a normal family life and Gerry's quest could finally end. Of this at least she had been convinced by Fr McCarthy.

She took a short, sharp sip from the glass. She only ever drank whiskey in private. In public it was Cinzano Biancos or light Champagne. Her private moods were subdued, serious; her public image was outgoing, daring, even jocose. She thought now that her relations with Gerry had always been conducted in an unusual coded form; generally the opposite was meant when something was communicated. This she must have learnt early on in the marriage. She put it down to his training in *the importance of what was not*, the symbolism of an arcane code. He had become an expert both in the practice and theory of grandiose delusions, the implementation of paranoid plans, and the execution of bizarre ideas, all in the pursuit of an unstated, secret Higher Cause. He had once explained it all to her one evening, when he had been in an expansive mood and he was feeling comfortable as they sat together in one of their rare fire-side drinking sessions when, as Gerry talked and reminisced in his long, lonely, rambling way, she acknowledged in a somewhat begrudging though resigned manner that at moments like those he treated her just like 'one of the lads'. He was a lonely man at heart, she had always known that. Most other women would have left him by now. But she was made of sterner stuff; she would stick by him through thick and thin and would make a settled man of him, yet. Indeed her chief ambition had always been to make him in some way 'house-proud'. Hence her efforts to decorate the home at some expense. His indifference to the tasteful furniture, the posh artifacts, the beautiful curtains incorporating exotic artwork, the woollen carpets, the magnificent kitchen, the lush bedroom, was accompanied only by his ability to mark or damage the furniture. He simply seemed to be always at odds with her.

Yet she comforted herself that just as it is possible for those who are furthest apart to have deep, intimate understandings so, for those who are closest, it is equally possible for there to be between them light years of misunderstanding.

The phone rang again and it was the 'Director' of the CIA. At least here was a hope of some moments of temporary relief, as he was another of her acquaintances who liked to cry on her shoulder. For it was in the sharing of the troubles of others that she could escape her own woes.

"Hullo Mary."

"Hullo Tom. You got my message then? It's about the new gossip that's going the rounds. Well, you won't believe it. I was at Cheryl's bridge party the other evening in the National Security Council room and I heard that there is, apparently, a big experiment going on in the CIA at the moment. All hush-hush. They are saying that Dick Warner has a mad plan that involves taking over the world in the name of the CIA. This is not by the old established means of military power, multi-national corporations, the media, the latest fashions and so on. He apparently has arranged for spare radioactive materials from our's and the Russian nuclear arsenal to be issued to Third World farmers in the name of agricultural progress. There is also a new bioengineered product, a secret weapon, in the pipeline whose effects are amazing and the inclusion of which in the world food chain is expected to change the planet's population/environment balance. So I heard anyway."

"I never knew all that. It's the first time I've heard it. I don't know why they get up to all these things without telling me. But it would not surprise me at all, not one little bit.

But what I'd like to know, Mary, is: who is responsible for placing all those strange plants and flowers around the place? It's either that there seem to be different ones every day, or they keep changing their appearances. One day a plant has blue flowers, the next day it's the same plant but with red flowers, then what were green leaves change to yellow overnight! I can't figure it out. If, as I thought at first, it was only a case of civic pride in my members of staff I wouldn't mind; but is there, as I am now beginning to suspect, another reason for all this display of horticultural curios?"

"You are really bothered by them, aren't you?"

"Well, I must say I am, now. I feel very uneasy these days walking around the corridors. The place is too quiet, and apart from those weird house plants, it is all too clean and well-ordered. I think somebody is covering up something. I know I shouldn't be saying this about my own staff, but I don't completely trust them now."

"Well, let me put your mind at rest. The plants are only old Gustave. He is a bit of an eccentric, and he is Central European."

"Sometimes I wish my information sources were as good as your's, Mary."

"There are a lot of con artists in your outfit, Tom. My Gerald is undoubtedly the biggest one of them. If it had been me in charge I would have done something about them a long time ago. Gerald himself would have been far less trouble if he had held a good job in some White House department, or a secure lecturing post at a decent university, away from all that agency stuff. You know he needs to feel he is changing the world."

Mary now spoke bluntly, for she had grown tired of Tom's diffidence over the years; one never seemed to get anywhere with him.

"It is always said that they have something over you. Is that true, Tom? Why didn't you arrange to have them all kicked upstairs years ago? I happen to reckon that some personal problem is causing you great embarrassment. Tell me what it is, and I bet I can help you find a way through it."

"Well, I am in control all the time. Really, Mary. It only looks as if I am not. I like to let them carry on as if I am not there. I get satisfaction out of watching them and all their funny ways. But now that you mention it, I do have a personal problem. Between you and me, I keep getting this feeling that I am ... inadequate. I find it hard to look people in the face. I look at strong, really successful people and I feel so envious. I find it hard to ... mix with people ... ."

"Oh, shut up Tom. You are making a fool of yourself. If they heard you talking like this you would be locked up, and pronto. Get a grip on yourself. The next thing we know is you will be blubbering down the phone."

And this, sure enough, is what happened next.

Tom was crying gustily. Exasperation filled her.

"Look, Tom. If you do one little thing for me, I promise I will see to it that those jumped-up clerks at Langley sit up and take notice of you. If you can set in motion, through Warner, the procedures to get Gerry promoted to, say, Secretary of State, where he can still feel he is important (Lord mark the spot!). I can guarantee that they will really respect you from now on. All I have to do is have a word with their wives. I know them all. I can easily pass on, for example, a few hints that you keep a secret correspondence detailing your friendship with J. Edgar Hoover and Senator McCarthy. Something like that. That should do the trick."

"What's so special about a friendship with those two?," asked Tom.

"Oh, Tom! Don't you know anything?"

"Well, Secretary of State! That might be a little hard to arrange. Would something equally important, but less high profile sort of, do? The last time I set him up for you he wouldn't play ball. Remember?"

163

"Sure. Although the idea of collecting the garbage around rural Virginia didn't appeal much to him, even if you did think it was the best job for him at the time. But he is older now. See what you can do. It must be something that really attracts him this time."

"But I can't seem to do anything right! I only fill a plum political post," said Tom unhappily; "in fact my lack of ability to prevent all those disastrous policies has been the chief underlying reason for my unwillingness to blame, punish or chastise anybody. Not even in the CIA. I just keep out of the way. Oh, but I do know what they get up to."

"Your poor record in office is nothing unusual. Somebody has to carry the can. That is your unavoidable destiny, I'm afraid. You are the one they will all blame in the books and tv memoirs. Your colleagues' feats of supreme neglect of duty, domestic as well as professional, abandonment of all moral positions, support for the undesirable and alien and uptake of all that is un-American, will be seen as just brave, individual actions or at worst, unfortunate but innocent mistakes. Yet, I think that is why I ... tolerate you; for we are told to love that which is unlovely and accept human failing. Needless to say, there are times too when I even play tricks on Gerry, such as putting on a big show of indifference when he leaves for foreign parts. Indeed I always ensure that there is a good, flaming row. It is good for a marriage. You have got to learn how to deal with people, Tom. Don't despair, there is hope for you yet. All you have to use is your head."

"Thanks, Mary. I know you have the wherewithal to put things right. Put in a good word for me."

"And you put in a word all round for Gerald."

"Will do."

There was one other call that day. It was to the Cardinal in Boston. Another old friend, at least of Mary's dad. The prelate owed a lot to that family; contact with the Military Industrial

Complex at the very least, plus very valuable information on the moral lives of people in secular and religious circles worldwide. To learn via Mary from Gerry and other operatives of, for instance, the religious and heretical obsessions of prominent or potentially powerful people around the world, the gleanings of long-night chats over whiskey and card games and from off-the-cuff, revealing remarks, was extremely useful. Plenty of impressive guff for whenever he met with the Pope. The new man in Rome was a great gossip and consummate politician who could give and take it with the best and worst of them. Why the Church was such a powerful and respected institution today could partly be answered for by the contributions of the likes of millions of such informants all over the world, by the inadvertent or deliberate revelations of even irredentist atheists and compassionate humanists to the clergy in their oft-denied, yet paradoxically loyal service to an institution that they believed they abhorred.

But then, all real whiskey drinkers are complex.

"How good of you, dear Mary, to call me. Has that bad lad of your's been up to his old tricks again? Has he mentioned, or been talking about, another nest of activity working against Mother Church? Ha ha."

"Your Eminence. From your own sources you will soon get to hear of moves to appoint Gerald to a very high post in government. Add your own weight to the process, for I will ensure that he will continue to be useful to the Vatican in whatever new position he occupies. They tell me he is now monitoring a very unorthodox religious sect in Jaman. As soon as I find out anything I will let you know."

"Ah, Mary, leave Gerry where he is. He is more useful to us doing what he is doing than in filling some useless high position here. Sure how else will we learn about what is really going on in the world? And also, we can't have him home here all the time making our juridical and moral theological systems

165

malfunction with that personal problem of his. In some ways I feel, Mary, that his return to the Fold would be a problematical thing; I have tried to convince the Jesuits of that, but they never give up."

"The Jesuits have gone to the dogs. Look, Cardinal Rice, it is payback time. I am tired of all these promises I keep getting from you lot that it's all for the best and so on. I am calling in my dues. At the risk of being rude, I have made a decision. It is time that Gerald came home for good. I have made that decision, not anyone else. I expect that you will unhesitatingly support any application that is made on his behalf, with the understanding that should you fail to do so, I will reveal to President Hooligan and the press all the ways you have exploited and abused Gerald's failings over the years."

"Of course, Mary. How silly of me to argue with you. I will certainly use all my influence to push Gerry's promotion. President Hooligan is a fanatical golfer and I can always threaten him with being blackballed from the cardinals' golf gala in Philadelphia next season. But the old question remains. Will Gerry co-operate?"

"I believe he will run out of steam one day. See to it any way you can, your Eminence."

When Mary had put the phone down she drank another sip of whiskey. There was only one weak link in the chain of command. Gerald himself. For one thing he would see any offer of promotion as a scheme by his enemies to get him finally under their control. Then there was also the formidable obstacle of that phobia of his, his 'path of inner integrity', developed in the early days in Taran, or even before, of avoiding anything that called for real responsibility or significant decision-making.

Sher's bar was now the scene of an intellectual argument. Gerry was sitting in the back room, keeping away from the other

166

drinkers and meditating in peace, writing up a lecture plan entitled 'The Future of Jaman', relieving the strain now and then by imagining what it would have been like to have been really married, or at least have had a normal job. This lecture, he believed, was going to be the most important discourse of his life. At least he hoped it would keep the lid on the explosive emotions of his hearers, for he was obviously facing here a very volatile youthful generation. He heard the commotion of the beginning of the argument; but it was best for outsiders to beware of such 'discussions'. What started as an outbreak of bad humour at a winning 4 key in dominoes soon extended to bad-tempered comments on Gerry's recent speeches and, thus, the clienteles' own understanding of their inherent importance and place in the world came into question.

The bar was in a rollicking, saturday night mood, the locals congregating outside as they did not have the hard cash to enter but instead subsisting on narcotic weeds of types unknown as yet to scientific or legal authorities. The blare of the sound system shot out the 'island rhythm' in a thunderous 'dum dum' that reverberated to and from points unknown; the inhabitants rollicked to and fro with this music and their repeated chants of 'revolution', 'de solution', 'for de nation' had a certain hypnotic quality with the rhythmic motion of the dancers suggesting a subversive connivance with the music bespeaking a secret desire, a promise for the future. Ragamuffins of every age between 1 and 14 tore around under the feet of their elders. Sellers of peanuts, cooked fish and ice drinks (cool pops) sang their wares as the mad dogs of the neighbourhood, of which there were a great number, were going berserk, barking uncontrollably and chasing each other in wild flourishes that inevitably proved mutually cowardly when it came to the showdown. Up above on the electric wires the rats of the vicinity observed the proceedings; with no flies on their tails they knew exactly what, where and when to do their own thing.

The moon herself was like a drunken spectator at this saturday night hooly, bobbing around with a witless, sick look on its face.

Alfredo the Thug had lost the game and was screaming his head off at Jos the Philosopher and Paulo the Intellectual.

"Cho, dat no way to play! Dat way out of order!"

He slashed down on the table with his machete and just failed to sever the arm of Jos. Jos sat back and smiled calmly while Paulo had taken up his drink and flung it across Alfredo's face.

"Baabwe!," screamed Alfredo and he upturned the table as he continued with his diatribe against the playing tactics of the others.

"It no way to treat a friend. A friend ah tell yo! You mek me an enemy! Give hup de game; hadmit yo lose it!"

"No, no, no, Alfredo. Yo lose hit fairly and squarely. On me grandma's life."

"We a grow hup together, we heat, drink, cry together and still yo play de game like dat. Yo should play de 4 hearly in de game!"

"Dat is not cheating," shouted Jos as he swept his arms across the neighbouring table and knocked bottles of beer and rum glasses to the floor. The occupiers of that table sat back happily in eager anticipation of the rest of the discussion.

"You will soon mek me lose me temper! Soon yo mek me a raging bull. Shut up de mouth. Yo as big mouth as dis Gerry man fool from hAmerica. An' he a clot naw wid heven de power or de respect. He a fool fool CIA man. Fool like yo. An' he mislead dis Pedro here who writes de books. He lead the youth astray!"

Alfredo put his arm around Jos and proceeded to emit loud sobs. Paulo could not hold back his own tears. He was bewailing the death of the detached observer in himself. There was disappointment elsewhere in The First Class that the argument had ended thus between the contenders. For a short space of time there was unanimity in silence. Until The Cap spoke.

168

"Who insult this here man Gerry? Who 'ave de nerve to upslight my friend? Speak hup!"

Alfredo, awed by nobody and welcoming the opportunity to raise the heat again, did not baulk from Mr Sher's challenge.

"Me did. He a big charade, like yo."

"Ha ha, Alfredo, it's jus' like you to have de big doubt 'bout Mr Gerry. Cool it, brother. Dis Gerry is a good man an' a good teacher. He will have works for hus all! Every day he is wid de government, speaking hup for hus."

Paulo was thinking, meditating and gestating his latest chapter at that precise minute. He had learned from the tuition of Gerry, who had showed him how to express himself in an unselfconscious way. In an incongruous coming together in his head of reality and fiction, day time dreams and bone-headed games of dominos, imagined vistas of incredible drama and silly, nay stupid, quarrels over nothing, revolving around dead-end illogicalities in the minds of unschooled folk who preferred the excitement of high noon confrontation to the cool evening of calm meditation, he experienced that marvellous flight of words which he commenced to put to paper in his head right now.

'Paulo was upset and confused. He tried to remember back to a time before the unpleasant present, the unpleasant past; back to a time as far back as his birth, or even before. Then, the spheres remained on their unchanging course, the great and hoary legends of former times were unaltered; the vivid, stark landscape unblurred; and the harsh shock of life was unchecked as Paulo Costello was born in the early sunny afternoon. He made his personal appearance in this world in the little homestead of the poverty-stricken peasant family in the foothills of the province of San Michel. It was mid-day in June with the rash heat of the high tropical summer absorbing the energies and aspirations of the people and all of nature swelling and shining and preening itself for further bounteous events.

His mother remembered the birth for its smoothness, its ease of transport, compared to her seven others, as well as for pleasure at *seeing the handsome, rounded features of her third surviving child. His father could only remember, right then, wondering if his new son would be more like himself in temperament than Juan.*

For Juan, at twelve years of age, had proved himself something of a disappointment. He had expected that his wife would 'produce' a robust, energetic offspring to follow in his own footsteps. But nature presented one of her periodic surprises in the form of a boy who was indented in shape, thin, delicate, timid and now apparently totally unadventurous in outlook; just everything it seemed that he could not admire, or even like.

But ... little Paulo gave all the appearance of being different. With his shining brown skin and dark hair and light-giving eyes with a faint tinge of good fortune blue in them, he promised well. Perhaps, his father had thought, the genes had got mixed up along the way and nature had made a mistake (country people have seen these in strange aberrations in the fruits of common plants, cuckoos of the harvest), and the one that should have been born last had been first and Paulo was the son he really deserved.

Submissive, unspeaking mama, accepting the failures and losses of her children was now unusually hopeful for Paulo; she foresaw a sunny future for him. Perhaps it was indeed his 'blue' eyes. He could not fail to be successful in life with such a good 'colour'! In that religious, less developed society there was a contradiction in that worldly success was not frowned upon, but admired. It was not simply a matter of the material trappings, a clean shirt, a suit of clothes, a pair of shiny shoes, a healthy complexion, the prospect of some hidden wealth, but also the incompressible reality of community respect, a ray of hope in the family, something that people could look at and admire, touch even and feel, or come to know for its healing power.

That was what they had in mind for Paulo.

There would be more than just the prospect of a life of grim hardship on the rugged land for Paulo. In a mysterious way he was to carry the hopes and aspirations of all who knew him, the conscious and unconscious desires of a weak, humble society.

They both reflected over that birth now, hunched over the kitchen table, she crying soft tears into her best white handkerchief, her husband (Roberto) grimly holding the edge of the table and his perspiring, pallid face filled with perplexity and panic.

It seemed now that his birth had been the highlight of Paulo's life; his childhood a glorious age, the rest barely remembered shadows that had no bearing on his destiny. It was not possible to understand what had brought Paulo to his present plight, word of which had come to them from the capital; or what unnoticed calamity during his birth had been responsible for such a thing.

What had been the sign which neither of them had noticed at that joyous time? What was the mark or blemish? What accident?

They might even have themselves to blame. But ... but ... . Juan, standing nearby, his tall, loping body slightly adrift but nevertheless more powerful for that ungainly strength which comes with maturity, felt a deep concern for his distraught, now-seemingly aged parents. As he tried to comfort them he found the same old reluctance on at least his father's part to accept any offering of sympathy or friendship. It struck Juan that not only had they both aged overnight but they seemed to have been drained of all life's goodness, their faces shorn of hope. Juan, in order that they might openly vent their anger and sorrow over Paulo's disgrace, imprisonment and imminent death by firing squad suggested that it all had something to do with Paulo's grief over Maria, their dead sister.

Their minds went back again. At five Maria was delighted at the arrival of her new brother, Juan being far too old and grumpy to play with. She took charge of baby Paulo and it was to Maria rather than his mother that Paulo turned to in any danger, in a crisis; Maria growing to womanhood as perhaps his only friend, in their smallholding in a remote location where the region's stagnant politics and movement outwards of population also added to their isolation. Not even the bold spirit of boyhood weakened Paulo's rapport with Maria; there developed for a period a slight doubt in

171

Roberto concerning his son's masculine spirit and determination. Paulo was happily content to let Maria share his life; their mother, her health always it seemed declining as the years passed, was only too glad for the help of Maria. 'Maria is the best one for keeping secrets,' Paulo had said to Juan and Juan had shook his head, never having understood Paulo or fathomed his younger brother's nature.

When Maria left home to work in the family mansion of Senora Fitzrobbino, one of the Puerto Rico clan members albeit a less important one, far away in the capital city, Paulo had at last begun to develop independence of character, while at the same time a spirited belligerence began to appear in his attitude. At the age of twelve he had the reputation of a bright, lazy, friendly but stubborn child. A year later, in stages, the news came: Maria was ill, Maria was in hospital, Maria was not in hospital, Maria had died, Maria had not died, Maria had died slowly, Maria had died suddenly, Maria had been hurt by someone, Maria had been killed in the commission of a crime, Maria had committed suicide, Maria had somehow brought about her own death, Maria had been injured in a fight with her employer's husband, Maria had tried to kill her employer's husband, Maria had inadvertently been killed as she tried to kill her male attacker in a case of self defence, Maria had deliberately been killed as she tried to defend herself against her male attacker.

To her parents it only mattered that she was dead. To Juan and Paulo it mattered not only that she had been killed but that they could not avenge her death. Paulo became morose, withdrew into a world of his own. For Juan this was not evidently a sudden or complete alteration in his brother, with whom he had always been on cordial if mutually critical terms. A pre-existing thing had come to the surface while deep down in Paulo some other dark secret continued eating away, awaiting its full-fledged appearance.

Then the day came that Paulo himself had left home for the bright lights of the city.

"Ooh," cried Roberto, "they killed him too. He turned into a wild one. Those desperadoes! Those banditos! Those murderers!"

He cried, failing to understand that which he could never understand. His tears were faults to him; he was surprised, shocked at being so weak; he decried the validity of sorrow to his family . . . .

Meanwhile Paulo sat in his cell, intense, thirsty, his body bruised and beaten . . . .'

Mr Gerry would be very pleased.

"De Americans keep promise hus everything," Alfredo was still arguing, "an' dey no deliver. Naw deliver! Dey tell us we are de pride and joy of hall de professors hin hAmerica an' dat we is de prototype model for de Third World community. Dey conduct all de experiments on hus for hall dese years and send de students and big names hout to see how we hare doing. Dey mek us answer strange questions such has: How we wash de teeth in de morning; how we able live from de hand to mouth; what we think of de prime minister or de pope or de God; what we think of de American way of life; what we think of Jaman way of life; what we do if hAmerica drop big bomb nearby. Dey give hus little monies to do crazy things like build big-big shed of which we have too much already and call it 'Community Hall', or buy funny American cowbull that kill hoff hall hour cows, or build dat place down dere wid hall de books dat noone can read. Now dey have hair-brained scheme for big Tourism for dis rundown, God-forsaken district dat nobody wan' live in. Me tired o' being American experiment . . . ."

"It still a good idea; it bring in de dollar; you can't blame de Americans for everyt'ing," said Jos the Philosopher.

"You a philosopher?," shouted Paulo, suddenly unexplainably angry with some inexplicable grievance inside; "if you are a philosopher then I am a rich and powerful politician. Shame on you for saying the dollar is more important than our national culture. Next thing is, you say any old job is worth more than the truth!"

"You shut up boy. We honly tolerate you smart alec in here. Yo t'ink yo is better than hus. You say yo know more than hus.

Do you know how we city folk live wid no food in dese here back streets? How we fight hoff de criminals when dey show dey hand here? All yo know his donkey an' bush! Show me yore *scars*," shouted Alfredo the Thug.

"I remember," said Paulo in his most sarcastic tone, "the last time you had a fight; when those bully boys from the government party came out here with guns and demanded we close up and go down vote for Premier Stanley. You and Jos were nowhere to be seen then. It was me who stood up to them, in the regrettable absence of Mr Sher, and saved the situation. Me ensured that we could all remain drinking peacefully here all day by telling them that Stanley had our loyal support and that we had voted for him already. Brain power is better than muscle power any day. Especially run-away muscle power."

"Cho man, I'd 'ave sent dem tails flying if ah had been 'ere," said Alfredo somewhat subduedly.

The Cap came in and intervened.

"Hail. Stop arguing brothers. Remember. Always remember. We are the Prototype Model Community of the Third World. We are PROUD. Hall de professors in America talk about hUS. If dey knew yo be fighting an' cussin' like dis dey be disgraced!"

"What you mean, Prototype Model Community of de Third World?," Alfredo demanded to know.

"Dem pick hus many years ago, in de 60's, to be de typical folk an' spot o' de Third World for dem to carry hout hexperiments hon. Dey come 'ere an' try heducation, radihation, television, remember dat in de bar here, then hit vanish one day. Den dey give hup an' concentrate on hus alone because we more hinteresting than their hexperiments. Dey say, leave h'em has dey hare for dey hESSENCE o' de whole Developing World! Is true! We famous! Now dey have new plan to mek us part of BIG NEW COCONUT SCHEME to change the country. Soon, hall de beer will be FREE!"

"Ha ha, we hear same story from yo each time," said Alfredo angrily; "jus' de same. The president pay you."

"Not true," said The Cap, "not true."

"Me know if Mr Gerry lying," thought Paulo to himself, "if dat big job promise don't happen."

Gerry had missed his lecture appointment and, drinking rather a lot in the privacy of his apartment, was feeling somewhat alone in the world. His room was sparsely furnished, except for a bed, chair and writing desk. It reminded him of a monk's cell that he had once stayed in during an investigation into the life of the dissident Trappist, Thomas Merton.

What the heck was life all about anyway?

Did existence continue after death? He opened a bottle of the local rum, 'Cane Juice Rumbo'. He drank with a sigh of relief.

In fact, how did life ever come to be on earth in the first place? It had all the appearance of a plot of some kind. And was human nature a part of the natural world, as scientists had always assured us, or part of the supernatural? It was quite tedious to contemplate humanity as both natural and super-natural. Man was certainly a strange concoction, even more strange than the rest of the whole world of nature put together. The natural world ... was at least understandable for its ... banality. But humans ... there was always something suspect about them ....

He drank another sip and felt marginally more optimistic. Perhaps it did all have a meaning hidden away somewhere this Cane Juice Rumbo certainly tasted different a new liquor always had the effect of making him look afresh at life yes there were many meanings to life mainly when one looked at it from certain different angles there was one angle for instance now what was that he had difficulty remembering it he did remember one drunken old man sketching for the benefit of a bar audience the outline of a continuous self creating circular universe long before the logic of such an idea had become scientifically respectable String Theory the same sage had also conceptualised before it had ever even been heard of when the fellow had announced in a slurred yet convinced voice that *reality is strung together in some weird way* but he was losing touch with the main argument ... this was ... angle numero uno ... this juice sure was terrific he would definitely stockpile some the number one angle was to see in the asking of the question the answer so suppose he was suddenly subjected to an in-depth hostile interrogation right now where would that leave him logically probably spilling out all the information freely and willingly but that was simply how he felt dedication was just not worth the effort his old friend his best friend Jim McCall how much he admired that man how he wished that he had the talents the achievements the cynicism the hard neck of that man Jim was his hero getting depressed just like on the flight down here where was that lady now what was her name.

Thinking was a strange business. It did not strike him as realistic to deduce that consciousness was simply an accumulation of physical or material sensii that impinged on some invisible mirror in an overhyped manner. But that at least was the opinion of some more qualified minds. Freud, Marx for instance, two favourite hate names of Mary's father, Col Baxter, who had been a sort of embryonic intellectual. If the universe was a momentous, technical miracle then Jaman, too, was a wondrous creation. Now there was a serious, useful thought! He was not losing his touch after all. Each and every human being in Jaman, from the most talented (Paulo?) to the stupidest, basest criminal type, harmonised within his or herself all the great secrets of existence that ever were. Now this was a fact that could be logically deduced and was not to be contradicted in any way by scientists who loved to contradict everything around them. Here was a mystery beyond normal comprehension; that even the contemptible Stanley, Mauris and

Rabid contained within themselves the whole mystery of the universe!

At the very least, he would face all these people with a different, more respectful attitude tomorrow.

He had better stop thinking for a while. He was supposed to be meeting someone that evening. He had better get himself ready. It would not do to miss any more appointments. That lecture he was supposed to have delivered had been a crucial part of his master plan.

Prime Minister Stanley was on his way to see President Eddie. A meeting had been called, ostensibly to deal with a complaint about the new man from the embassy, Mr McArthur, but ongoing internecine politics would undoubtedly intrude into the proceedings. President Eddie wielded the 'people power' while Stanley controlled the political machine. Fifty years previously as a young Trade Union leader Eddie had gained for the workers a 5% increase in pay, something that had never been matched since. It assured him immortality and total political power (as long as he stayed away from the day-to-day political mix), but all Eddie ever wanted after that early coup was popularity, the greatest elixir of all, and the position of Head of State, with a veto over the appointment of prime ministers, leaving all the opprobrium to fall on Stanley's, or Stanley's predecessors', shoulders. The only fly in the ointment of this happy arrangement was that Stanley, too, ached to be president.

"If only I could be president. I would be on equal terms with President Hooligan, kings, queens etc. I would be ... immortal. My name would survive in Jaman history. I will use the Americans to get rid of Eddie. They know about his socialist record in any case. Perhaps Mr McArthur can help me. Oh why," he moaned silently to himself, thinking of the great palace coups of those times, "couldn't I have been born in the great Roman era of natural justice?"

These were his thoughts as he was driven along Kingstown's Avenue Eddie to Jaman House, the residence of Eddie. Oh, those Presidential Flags! Those streamers! How he ached! The Presidential Guard blocked the gate as usual.

"Identification and Password please," said one of the officious young guards, a typical secretarial type, obviously trying to impress.

"Do you know who I am, young man?," demanded Stanley out the window, shocked to find that he hadn't simply been waved or saluted past.

"Identification and Password please," asked the young guard again.

"Put me on the phone to the president, "demanded the prime minister angrily.

"Yo speak to the prime minister, man," said the driver impatiently to the guard; "this is one of dose times yo skip de rules."

"Me nuah skip de rules," replied the guard haughtily, dropping his Standard English;

"we need de discipline in dis society. Yo could be de enemy in disguise."

"Discipline? Yo call dis discipline?, "shouted Stanley; "what do yo know 'bout DISCIPLINE? I will tell you about discipline . . . ."

He became speechless for a moment.

"The president is on the line, sir," said the driver.

"Good day, Your Excellency, this is Prime Minister Stanley. Your guard at the gate is being very difficult. We have an appointment at 4."

"Ah, Prime Minister. How nice of you to come. Your name is Stanley, you say, not the previous Prime Minister Huang Sang? I am glad it is you, and not him. Huang Sang too damn difficult. Can you give the guard your I.D. and Password and please come in?"

"Oh, here is my official seal of office. The password is 'The UPPLA LIVES'. Let us in."

The gates were opened and the guard gave a weak salute. There was a smile on his face.

"Get that man's name, rank and number. I will pass it on to general staff and see that he is never promoted, not even to corporal. He will live to regret this day." Stanley's face was flush with anger.

UPPLA; United People's Party for Progress, Labour and Anti-Colonialism. The founding party of the country and now completely removed from its roots as a broad-based mass movement with popular appeal. Hence the 'lives' addendum. With the only other party, the Jaman Labour Party, it shared a secret agreement that there would be no third parties tolerated in the island. This was why inconsequential foreigners, such as Americans like McArthur and other outsiders, aroused much suspicion and usually had to take the rap for anything that went wrong. It was pointless blaming anybody else.

Stanley was led by a butler into the presence of the president in the august (this was how Stanley described it to himself) meeting hall. President Eddie was his old, hobbling usual self.

"Ah Prime Minister De Souza. How nice of you to come. Reminds me, what happened to that man, eh . . . Stanley. A bad sort too. Would never give his name, rank and number. Should have been in the army, like I was, the real army, the British Army. I have many fond memories of my days with His Majesty's forces. I saw action in the trenches too, old history now. What can I do for you?"

"Your Excellency. The Americans want us to export coconuts again all over the world. They want us to concentrate completely on this crop to the exclusion of everything else. Forget sugar. Forget bananas. It's to be the new coconut from now on. It will look after itself and labour will be no longer needed on the land. American advisers are already here preparing the people for a major turnabout. All our economic indicators are to be regulated from a computer on Wall Street. They just need your benediction for the project. Mr McArthur, that new CIA man I have been telling you about, has been disturbing the people with madcap ideas he has been propounding in his classroom. He is threatening to upset future plans. He has been raising expectations beyond what might realistically be expected in our poor society. There have been ructions on the campus. This man Gerry's teaching about progress is already spreading like wildfire around the island. Just one lecture and already people are becoming disturbed and threatening to oppose agricultural innovation as everyone knows it. It bodes ill for our political peace. Our towns are under threat. It will set back the coconut for decades."

Premier Stanley was passing the buck. Eddie would now have to take the responsibility, whichever way it went.

"Ah, progress is great. That is what the party has always been after. I remember the old days when you could measure progress by a few pence on a man's wages. NOW IT IS COMPUTERS IN WALL STREET! My! We have come a long way. But I want to see the American first."

"Which American, Your Excellency?"

"The teacher, of course."

"His name is Mr Gerry McArthur. We knew from his references that he was an expert on economics, but also that he had his own, particular personal flaws. But then you know how hard it is to get qualified people to come to work here in our comparably less well-endowed educational establishments."

"Well then, send this Gerry to me at once. What is keeping you man? And while we're at it, what's this I hear about the prime minister's office overseeing the Annual Military Parade? I am in charge of all things military, not you. Any more of this and you will be removed from office, Stanley. I hope you are hearing me?"

Eddie was still a tall man, despite his great age. Some referred to him as the Jaman 'De Gaulle'. His thin face, white hair and beard and narrow, intellectual eyes behind expensive spectacles, concealing great benightedness, told of a once-prominent figure now reduced by handicaps of memory, sight and hearing to a shadow of his old self. The problem was that his moments of unique, great lucidity (probably that biblical wisdom associated with the old) was accentuated by a vehemence that was also new to him, that had all the marks of insanity.

The insanity of the wise, or perhaps the wisdom of insanity.

The meeting now became one of those 'family' occasions marked by an intimate, incomprehensible bantering.

"I will send Mr McArthur up immediately. As for the Grand Annual Military Parade, I was only saving my beloved Great Grandfather the tedious business of the nitty gritty involved in organising things. I am conscious of your great age and mounting infirmities, evident to one and all. I wish for you to take it easy in the interests of your longevity and for the sake of your beloved family. Think of the COUNTRY! You should consider what is in the best interests of all."

"Thank you sir. I am actually considering taking up a more active interest in the affairs of the country. I am going to have your office moved up here. I don't see the need for a prime minister, in fact. I can do all that. The parliament is a bit of a waste of time, don't you agree? Always arguing and making a public nuisance of themselves. I am going to have a chat with General Umberto about locking up the troublemakers. Would you like a job, prime minister? I can always find something for you."

"Like what?," asked a shocked Stanley, stuck for a moment for words.

"The prison service?"

"Thank you, Your Excellency. Then I will have to get the army to lock you up as you are displaying the paranoia of a totally insane person and you are a danger to yourself and the country," laughed Stanley, his moustache wriggling with forced mirth as he put on the face of a court jester.

Loud laughter greeted this 'riposte' on the part of Stanley amongst the various individuals standing around there.

Eddie looked stern at first; then he put on a scowl that temporarily halted the laughter; then he clearly made an objective decision to take the matter lightly and he gave a soft chuckle. This chuckle was followed by a rise in the volume of the surrounding chuckles; then Eddie gave a loud guffaw and slapped his knee with surprising agility for an nonagenarian; this was greeted with peals of the loudest laughter imaginable from the others.

Stanley was both relieved and hyper-anxious. He knew enough not to be taken in by any of these shenanigans.

"Let me see President Hooligan's envoy at once," demanded Eddie as soon as Stanley and his party had walked out the door.

"You mean the ambassador, Your Excellency?," asked his secretary who, himself, was now busily trying to decide who was to be the likely winner in the coming power struggle and was already formulating a plan to bug General Umberto's place for his own advantage and not anyone else's. That was the trouble with these people put in charge of things; they were never satisfied with the bit of power they had. Everybody wanting to be King or Queen, instead of being content to be just sit on the 'Board of Management'.

"Not the ambassador, idiot. This man Gerry. He obviously the CIA man here. He under secret presidential orders. This how they operate. Me no fool. They here to find out if me or Stanley win."

Stanley and his car were ignored by the guards this time as they drove out through the gates. □

chapter
nine

Gerry took out a tourist brochure for Jaman that had the travel agency 'First Class Hols' publishing imprint. This, of course, was a CIA cover; but in the context of a shortage of educational materials he would have to use this booklet to decipher Phase 2 of his mission, (Phase1 had been simply to arrive and deliver his first lectures, a task that had still to be completed).

"Let's see what these jokers in Langley want next," he muttered to himself, drinking a hot cup of coffee and beginning to recover from his brief bout of depression. What did the past matter? Here he had a new opportunity; and he liked the country; they all seemed a rather sophisticated lot in their way.

He opened the brochure at page 3, the denoted key code number for all the missions he had ever been on. The idea was to take the first letter after every punctuation and from it assemble the instruction, a simple code that fooled the best counter-intelligence. He read:

'Hold a party in Jaman, and you will never forget it. Very many already have; each one wishes to return. You will love it, or simply ecstasise over it! Under the coconut tree, round by the bar, sitting on the beach, eating coconut pie, lolling scenic views, foraging in the souvenir shops, kidding with your friends, it is all wonderful! Don't delay, name the day. And have the time of your life. Promises, prayers all lead the way to beautiful Jaman today. Eat

your fill of bananas and rare exotic fruit, drown yourself in coconut water!'

This now gave him: *Have yourself kidnapped.*

It made sense. A typical Byzantine CIA scenario. It should be easy to arrange with the lads. Even Jim McCall, in his prime, would have been proud of such a plan! Perhaps it would prefigure a marine invasion; or some swift local coup. Whatever, it would definitely throw all those schemers who were out to undermine him; place everybody in a compromised position and allow him to set his own terms; he would not have to worry any more about 'spreading the message' as the publicity would do it for him. It would also be an exercise devoid, hopefully, of any physical danger. Well, he would certainly arrange for his own escape too. There was just no way Dick Warner was going to give the eulogy at his funeral! He had often pictured the scene, the bunch of flowers in place of the missing body (too gruesome to return to relatives); Warner hyping it up in front of the dignitaries; Mary thinking 'I told you so', the Cardinal full of platitudes about Western democracy, the primacy of conscience, the threat of despotism, the Glory of God, everything in fact Gerry's life hadn't been about.

No, he would come out of this alive, whatever else.

As he went up to the hotel, past the gullies and the backstreets for the meeting with the Dutch businessman, he noticed that the children of the neighbourhood had their own nicknames for him, shouting out various, incomprehensible appellations such as 'Popeye' and 'DaDa', and different names again in the next street or alley. His fame was clearly spreading! He had sent on a message apologising for missing the first appointment and assuring the gentleman that he would be on time for this one. This sort of guy was going to be either extra-serious, or just plain weird. He tried to remember details of the conversation he had with him at the airport, but to no avail. His brain cells seemed to be malfunctioning, or were simply dying out rapidly. He was, after all, not a very young man anymore! He wondered whether the higher consciousness experienced in meditation was enough, on its own, to justify the consequent extinction of millions of cerebral cells, or to compensate for their absence. Why were these abstruse questions whirling around in his head? Mary had once become concerned about his 'flight of ideas'. Apparently it was a symptom of a verifiable psychiatric problem, a sort of mania, and she had tried to get him to go into a rest home to receive free medical 'treatment' at the hands of the Firm's very own psychiatrists! He wondered what unknowable consequences might come from Dick Warner knowing about his private thoughts, his fantasies!

At the Jamboree hotel the man was waiting in a seat in the lounge adjacent to the foyer. He had an easy smile on his face. Suspicious, thought Gerry. He decided that most likely underneath the Dutchman was 'extra serious', even though he was the complete opposite of the stereotyped MAFIA representative; he was blonde, ascetic, prim and relaxed rather than the opposite.

"Hi, Gerry. Glad you made it. I heer you people are into a new kind of drug. Something to do weeth the coconut! Maybe we can do a deal. No need for us to be walking on eech other's feet."

"My, the content of my classes certainly seems to be doing the rounds! It is not my problem if what I teach is causing people everywhere to reassess their opinions and activities," replied Gerry;

"and why should I be discussing my pedagogic expositions with you anyway? I don't even know you. Who are you, may I ask?"

It was necessary for him to go through the formality of this 'I never heard of you before' immunity statement in case of any future legal difficulties.

185

"Just say I am a friend. Call me Hans."

"Well, Hans. I am here to help Jaman educate its people and develop its economy. I am trying to get the farmers to concentrate on producing new, lucrative crops to enable them to escape the exploitative economy which sees the growing of low priced commodities for foreign markets. I happen to be a principled American, despite my association with some rather disreputable organisations, and I try to undo a lot of the damage caused by my more enthusiastic colleagues around the world. If I could believe that somehow you, too, were trying to help mankind, I would certainly co-operate with you."

"Gerry, I can assure you that I, also, am a man of conscience. Many times I have double-crossed my bosses eef I thought that in that way I was helping the poor. We have to involve ourselves een all sorts of incorrect things, in order to make this world a better place. Eet ees no good being an armchair general."

McArthur had a sudden intuition that he could work with this man, even trust him. He seemed to be a complicated person, a very devious character, the sort Gerry had become accustomed to in his varied experiences.

McArthur spoke quietly.

"You, Hans, being a man-of-the-world I suspect that you too probably work for ruthless people and that most likely you are a bit single-minded yourself. Now here is an opportunity for you to make amends for anything you have done that has harmed the poor or innocent. Pretty soon there will be a lucrative trade in a new coconut here. Your people, with their experimental co-operative farms that I have heard are doing so much to help rural communities, are going to find their drug-growing lands here becoming extremely uneconomical. The future will be in coconuts. Nothing will stand in their way, I am assured; the aim is to benefit all mankind, or so the scientists tell us. Forget about poppies, hash, cocaine. Take up a legitimate activity."

"This ees the queerest proposal I have heard in a long time, the CIA advising The Family to go into coconut farming in Jaman! We are a serious people. I would not like to theenk that you are, what they say, taking the mickey? Or trying to take me along a tricky trail. My bosses can get very upset. And then you weel no longer have our co-operation in all those different areas and spheres. Theenk what that will do to your career; the man who made an enemy of the CIA's greatest friend!"

"That would be my greatest achievement!"

Hans silently nodded his head.

"That is what I wanted to hear! Congratulations! I was seemply testing you. You are, what they say, a man after my own heart! I can see that principles are still een your soul, even if you no longer practice your Faith."

"What? Don't tell me you are religious, too, Hans!"

"You would be surprised, Gerry. We only allow drug farming in order to eventually eradicate it. It is not something that can be done overnight."

"They tell me, "said Gerry enthusiastically, "that the new coconut is a fast-growing variety which contains all the precious vegetable juices that are becoming scarce commodities around the world with the upsurge in synthetic foods. It will benefit the poor man and the small farmer everywhere, who will make unimaginable amounts of money from its export value. And apparently it has no side-effects."

Here Gerry was testing Han's ability to double-think; also his claimed sense of integrity.

"Who told you all thees rubbish," asked Hans.

"It's in the manufacturer's pamphlet."

"My people, including a certain brilliant lady een America whose name must remain a secret, weeth access to the highest scientific and intelligence centres, tells us that there is a secret weapon coming out to poison all the poor people of the world and eets code name is 'Supercoconut'. Do you know anything about these dangerous effects?"

"No! Look! I am the person in charge of the Supercoconut project. How can the word of some dame in the States count for more than mine?"

Gerry was shocked. This was the biggest put-down in his career; here he was being told by a non-professional that he was teaching rubbish, even lies! He was being questioned on his own subject matter. As if he didn't know already all these facts, or was doing nothing about it.

"What? Are you sure?", he muttered, pretending to be in a muddle over it all, but also taking on board Han's quite good advice.

"It is why we are trying to get control over it. The poor people of the world are our bread and butter. It ees they whom we 'exploit', as you might say. The rich are useless to us. I am very angry with the way you people are being used in all thees educational propaganda to further the interests of Capitalism. We were never capitalists; we believe een the family and society and all that. You should not believe everything you read een a textbook, not even in your own! We must all work together in these small, faraway countries; eet ees the unwritten law."

"What you say about the new coconut explains many things, such as why was Dick Warner so anxious to send me here, when I know that he hates the country. I thought it was just because he hates me! Why would he want to help people in the backwoods? He is a disciple of Hooligan, who is leaving all policy in the hands of the experts and multinationals so he can play golf. Your own network of contacts at all levels of society here in Jaman will be invaluable in my own, new plan that I am formulating right now."

Gerry continued to speak in an assertive, confident way, yet with his own, silent, reflective thoughts: "our people cannot even begin to match the grassroots links you and your Italian-based organisation of international criminals have at all levels of society. Your grip on the lowest and highest rungs of society is a fact of life. Let us work together, Hans. We will soon scupper this coconut idea. I must say I am beginning to see things in a different light, having heard what you have just said. I will have to think more carefully about things, now. I am even going to rewrite my lesson notes yet again. But I will have to make sure that the ambassador, the prime minister, even Jim McCall, don't get to see the new 'curriculum'."

"How deed you know I was in The Family? I deed not show you eeny ID. Or how you know I am not an educational department agent?"

"Aw, come on, Hans, there is nobody else you could be. You know there is only one other body more dangerous than The Family and that is the pernicious Multinational Corporation. But you do not have either the finesse, the extra-snappy suit, or the ruthlessness to be a rep of one of those. You are too honest-looking, in a relative sense. Nor are you a government agent. I have already met Gloria."

"Ha ha ha ha."

"Ha ha ha."

"I see you are a man of this world, too, Gerry. Let me tell you that we value Jaman highly as part of our property, especially with the casinos and tourist business. Too many people are being led astray there, being exploited, they need our help. We want to save thees country. But if you are to be on our side now, there must be no double-crossing by you. We have a terrible retribution for those who give up the chosen path."

"Kidnapping and interrogation are your specialty?"

"It ees so."

"Good," said Gerry, to Han's incomprehension and consternation.

"What do you mean 'good'?"

"Kidnapping is not always a malign activity. The kidnapping of those who are dangerous, or even in danger and their removal to a place of safety; even the assassination of tyrants, have all been approved by history. Torture was legally respectable in the past," said Gerry, trying to equal Han's ability to shock.

Hans was gobsmacked; he looked uneasily at Gerry and a change overcame his features so that he looked for a moment like he wanted to entirely change the discussion. A red flush of shame and embarrassment came on his face. He looked down on the floor.

"Do you fear eenything? Anything at all?," he asked eventually when he had found his voice. He sounded very disappointed, like someone who had had his cover blown, or had something on his conscience.

"Well, I fear airplanes and heights to start with."

Again Hans seemed disappointed with Gerry's words.

"We all fear life when we have put ourselves in too elevated a position. Humility ees the cure for such ailments," he said, sadly.

"I would need to be hard up if I have to go to The Family for spiritual advice," said Gerry harshly.

Hans looked hurt. His lips moved silently as if he wanted to say something but dared not.

"Here ees my telephone number. Call me if you need help, if you ever have something to tell me, or even eef you just want to chat," he said in a kindly voice.

Gerry was still a bit suspicious of this strange, sinister hoodlum. He left Hans in the lounge – the once threatening individual now had a genuinely sympathetic, even soft look in his eyes as he said goodbye and this made Gerry even more uneasy – then he took himself down the street.

He walked briskly and steadily to discourage the entourage of touts, dealers and beggars who tried in vain to make physical or mental contact with him. He headed for the downtown area, perhaps not a wise thing to do as a solitary foreigner but already word had gone round about a trigger-happy American. The touts were cautious, ensuring that they did not come too close to him.

He walked into one of those large, cheaper restaurants one always finds in the centre of downtowns for the benefit of taxidrivers, office clerks and other local folk who can't afford the more expensive joints. There was the sound of loud juke box music (Slangman Stardust singing again), the chatter of noisy patrons and the sight of a few foreign, beatnik types, with their backpacks, eating away and drinking the cheap local beer. Large fans turned on the ceiling and there was the air of a busy, metropolitan meeting spot. Gerry was now dressed like any other local in scrappy shirt and light trousers and had completely taken on the dilettante mannerisms of the Jaman educated class, at least. Nobody noticed him as he entered, walking, again uncharacteristically, with that same limp crawl so distinctive of the ordinary Jaman individual who refuses to be rushed by the 'hurried dogs of destiny'. He felt he could pass himself off now, at the very least, as an expatriate schoolteacher well-immersed in the local culture. He headed for the queue where one waited to place an order for some spiced dish of chicken or goat and paid the three dollars in return for a piece of paper with a number on it. In a society where lining up went against the national grain, and bumping and shoving was a national sport, it was quite comforting to find that they were narrowly confined between reinforced boarding in a regimented line that denied any opportunity for queue jumping. He was beginning to marvel at the practical inventiveness of the Jamanese. There were wonders of creation here, from the toys-with-wheels the children carved out of discarded wood to play with at Christmas time to the automatic, homemade pistols, the broken down, abandoned vehicles now reinvigorated with new leases of noisy life, and the craftily constructed electrical apparatii utilising by means of ingenious wires the free supply of electricity from public utility lines. He did his best to 'blend in' with the line of people, who all seemed to be at once both extremely impatient and agitated as they waited their turn; and yet unusually jolly, with an air about them as though this was the centre of the universe. Gerry always found such groups of people gathered in one place to be quite revelatory of the unconscious preoccupations of the race. Indeed the reason he had chosen this restaurant was that he knew it hosted the 'salt of the country', and by listening in he would be able to gauge the real state of the country.

Already he was intrigued by the talk of the folk in the queue.

"Dem put up de price of chicken here quicker than in Joong's shop. Somet'ing wrong with country w'en chicken so dear. Soon we starve!," said a fat, sweaty and extremely well-replenished gentleman who was hungrily eyeing the different dinners being carried out by serving ladies, twisting on his toes as if his turn would never come.

"Me say as me say before, it de prime minister's fault," said another man; "he cheat the people with dem taxes. An' he no eat chicken. He eat FISH, so me heard!"

"An' he who eats fish not a true Jaman," agreed another person.

There had developed in recent times an unpredictable, subterranean current in social and political affairs that seemed to express itself mainly in what the different groups or political orders ate and drank. The chief controversy was that between fish and chicken. Gerry had not worked out the significance of all this yet.

"Well, de monks say everyone mus' eat fish every day if de island is to be saved. Or else we *stink* like all chicken-eaters. And he who stinks guilty of the First sin, "said the fat man.

"Dey concoct cock an' bull story," said the second man, "of 'bout how Original Father came from faraway land an' fell foul o' who live in old Jaman and come 'snared in peasant agricultural trickery which de Monks' job to work at freeing

Him hup again. But we mus' exchange dem fish for chicken as de price, for dey say if dey no free hup de Original Father soon den de end of world come and we all mus' die. But it tek a long time to work Him free, with chants and music and smoke. It take centuries. Who believe dis story?"

One young man said that he thought he believed it, or parts of it anyway.

"Why dey say we mus' everyone go back to original Homeland in de las' days? So wha' 'appen say everyone leave an' went back a Homeland? Everyt'ing chaos! No one to do de work!," said a third man.

A man behind Gerry spoke.

"Who persuade de youth give hup their school an' house an' go live in de bush? Who encourage de youth boy an' girl not cut hair an' mek dem dress in black an' white? Who hold illegal schools in bush to heducate hignorant people who can't read hor write in Mystery Stories ? De Monks! Who eat FISH all de time? De Monks!"

"Yes man," said the fat man, "though dey say dey stand on their own yet dey sit hup wid de president an' de prime minister wid their little flags at Festival time; an' Eddie and de government 'fraid o' dem."

"An' dey try tell us dat money no good an' is root hof hall hevil," said the first man.

"Everybody tell us money is root of hall evil. Still dey keep dey hown money!", said the second man.

"So many people believe de monks. But me say as me do. De monks? Dey mus' live in secret. Why? Dey mus' hide something," said the fat man.

At that moment a trainee monk joined the queue. He had been sent on the long journey to Kingstown from the Archbishop's palace in the north to learn how to fend for himself, without any money (it was part of his training). He had now become stranded and was using his last dollar (given to him by an American tourist) to buy a piece of fish. They all looked at him with the mild hysteria of unbelievers who wish for conversion. The fat man spoke in a weird, high voice:

"You people say money his evil. True?"

The trainee monk answered, automatically in a sort of mechanical voice, as if the answer came independently from him and was nothing to do with his own way of thinking or particular emotions.

"Money is de invention of de devil. Jahmonks have money, but dey naw use it, dey SAVE hit for return to Homeland."

"An' how yo pay yore dinner? Eh?," asked the portly man sarcastically.

"Why God mek fish? Eh? We use de God-given fish dat de farmers propagandise against and which are the only healthy t'ing t' eat as dey do not come from Babylon land. Only come from clean, natural water! No pollution! No rich people in Homeland. Everybody mus' become monk to enter Homeland!"

"Trickery," shouted the fat man, "price of fish go hup e'ery day too! Nobody afford cod fish now! You ragaloboons. RAGALOBOONS!"

"Cod fish foreign fish. No good," replied the novice monk.

Gerry wondered how much his own presence was affecting the tone of the conversation; which opinions were genuinely held and which were staged. He had now reached his place at the counter and his turn to order:

"Fish, please," he said loudly.

Everybody looked at him with grave displeasure.

"Tek a ticket, three dollar."

He sat down at a vacant table and eventually it came. He spiced it up with hot pepper sauce. He loved hot spices; he poured it on in great quantity. He was suddenly feeling ravishingly hungry; he was well tucked into the fish and rice when he noticed that the novice monk was having trouble finding

194

a spare place to sit. Indeed the only empty chair was at his, Gerry's, table, a fact that the fellow had also already observed and was desperately trying to avoid having to acknowledge.

"Here, sir," shouted Gerry, "a place."

The youth stared at Gerry and was stuck for words. He came over and sat down, looking over his shoulder at nothing in particular, probably trying to tell himself that the American was not there. Gerry saw that he had a tiny scrap of fish on his plate.

"Nice fish. They say it is good for the brain. Still too dear though, for many of the people here."

"Wha ...?," the monk trainee struggled to speak.

"Fish is expensive now. The Conservation movement. Quotas and all that."

"You American?"

"I am a citizen of the world; we all inhabit the same planet. Your Man has got it right. We must all go home one day."

"True. Some of us near home a'ready. But you mus' be monk firs'."

"Do not look upon me as an enemy. I know that I represent, in the Military Industrial Intelligence Complex, in secular materialism, in my job here, all that tends towards demoralising spiritual movements such as your own. Yet I say to you, I am on your side. Your Master is a true leader, a great being."

"Him King of Kings. He love de hEarth, except in Babylon. Hearthquake when he walk. He teach people grow de first crop of all, given hus by de Lord first time. De right fruit grow on de first day an' de las' day. Him do no truck with de foreign misleaders. Anyway, de Great War a come an' dem all dead. Den de Righteous come into their Inheritance."

"Which is the first crop of all?," asked Gerry, keeping his voice level and matter-of-fact.

"De coconut is de first of hall; de cane sugar is Slavery and de banana Worse Thing. De coconut grow in de Homeland, but not de others. Coconut is Freeman food, de others Slave food.

W'o climb a coconut tree best? Not de foreign man, not de Slave master but de Free Man! Is coconut juice madness and confusion-making like cane juice rum? No, it cool, clear like de Knowledge of the hAncient herbs. Down wid de foreign food, hail an' long life to de coconut!"

"The Americans are sending a new coconut to Jaman which they say will finally wipe out all Jaman coconuts. They say it will be the greatest coconut of all," said Gerry softly yet urgently.

"American lie again. No coconut better than de Jaman natural coconut!," shouted the youth, not eating now, his digestion no longer functioning smoothly.

Meanwhile Gerry was tucking happily into his own meal, gaining an unspoken, tactical advantage over the young monk with the knowledge that with this fish eating, a monk-approved activity, he was making more headway at the moment than the indigestion-troubled lad himself, pulling the odd fish bone from between his teeth to assert a certain world-weary dominance. He knew that to depend too much on the niceties of a knife and fork, for instance, he would only be revealing his own priggish, western cultural manners.

"We hear story 'bout dis hAmerican coconut from hour spies. Dey plant somet'ing in de north, it not coconut, where people can naw go on de land and it cause big flash. It boom like Doomsday and spread de hash hall hover. We all know dis in de Monastery. Orbeck know. De hill farmers know. Heaps of Americans wearing white suits and dey clapping an' awhooping when de thing go off and fill de sky wid strange skywriting. Den a wind strong as mighty lion come an' knock us hall down. De hAmericans celebrate as de nuts come outa sky and hit us all on de heads! I t'ink the hEnd hOf World has come! Later, we find all dese open coconut shells and dey empty an' lying all over de ground. Archbishop Orbeck, hour leader brother, say it great Hurricane, but others say it big American Experiment gone wrong. Since dat time all de plants grow giant an' strange in de north. The food hup there taste funny now."

Gerry was silent. He then spoke slowly and gravely.

"Ever since I visited the Trappists in America I have envied the monks their way of life," he said solemnly; "I wish to speak to your brother Archbishop in the confines of his monastery about the truth of things. I know I am a foreigner, but you tell him I may have some information for him. All my life I have searched for spiritual wisdom. Now I think I have found it."

Gerry's eyes were moist.

The youth, whose name was Alan The One Who Keeps Quiet, looked at Gerry with a more relaxed expression. He seemed impressed.

"Me tell Brother Archbishop Orbeck. He very deep."

When Gerry pulled twenty dollars out of his pocket and gave them to Alan to help with his fare back up north that expression became a gentle smile.

Gerry finished his meal and departed well-satisfied. He felt that he was indeed on the verge of a great spiritual experience. Turbo was outside in his taxi and Gerry got in and said that he was returning to his lodgings on the campus.

"Sure, boss. You doing the town well. But dis part get dangerous after dark. When you go up north?"

"Later. I have got to get in some work first," Gerry replied.

Four months later and much had happened. Gerry had become a regular sight around the campus and was even a regular speaker at the local library Debate Evenings, discussing economics and current affairs with other teachers, public works clerks and some drunken malcontents. He had soon become noted as The Brain and had now set out on a deliberate policy to appraise his students and listeners of what was a new economic policy. He argued now that there was *no limit* to what they could have *for nothing*. It was to challenge that old idee fixe of Extreme

Poverty Is Good For You and associated downtrodden attitudes, with a new philosophy of Work And Sow Now For The Soil Is There In The Ground Waiting And It Only Takes Two Months To Produce Something. It enabled them to look forward to a Nirvana Of The Present which would come sooner, rather than later. This was absolute economic heresy, nay blasphemy. Of course there was a very fine distinction between what were also two old, classic, academic theories, but this simple explanation only served to further intrigue the populace and make them think, which was part of Gerry's purpose. It led to both an adversary attitude in people to the arguments of the politicians in the upcoming general election and also to an immediate academic war between Gerry and his followers on the one hand, and the resident academics who represented the Old School with its total emphasis on Poverty on the other. Even when Gerry pointed out that there were many similarities in their doctrines, such as the continued prevalence of dirt-poverty for most people anyway and the need to always rely on the Future in any case, it did not console the old school who took to describing the challengers as The Newcomers and said that they were intent on leading the youth astray. Many teachers at the institute took up a campaign to have Gerry removed from his post and sent off the island. Gerry, resolute now in his policy of destroying government and financial plans to launch the Supercoconut, was happy with the way things were proceeding, the old established 'peace' of academic convention now irredeemably disturbed, with the American contradicting everything the education department asserted. There were calls for the elusive Professor Gomes to come back from the Presidential Palace, where she was advising Eddie, to deal with the crisis.

The gist of reports sent back to Langley by Ambassador Delroy at first was that everything was on line for the introduction of the new supertechnology and the American coconut. The operatives in Jaman were in place and doing their job grandly, under the impression that they were advancing the cause of Third World development. He even refrained from making any mention of Gerry's eccentric behaviour. On the other hand, indeed, even Gerry found it difficult to reconcile the triteness of his tedious economics lessons, to a now-continually disruptive, cynical, argumentative audience, with those grandiose EPM (economic, political, military) plans of the powerful USA. There were moments in his classes when he thought that he was simply dreaming, that this drama was all a mirage; then the drone of his dictation seemed to drive out even the multitudes of lizards and insects from the walls and ceilings of the heat oppressed room, and he could not bring himself to believe that the whole future of the world hinged on the adequate delivery of his (hastily and incompletely written up) lesson notes. Yet it was with such tardy beginnings that great events and discoveries took place, he told himself. He noticed that the students had now changed their attitude as regards the forthcoming general election, beginning to doubt the political validity of *both* political parties and to question whether candidates were still making the mistake of still insisting on that old scared cow: that technical progress was really the way ahead, or that the youth should dedicate themselves to hard work and education for the benefit of their masters.

Now Gerry found himself being accused of 'madness' by a colleague, a fellow American, who always 'kept to the facts' and to the issue of examination passes for his students, a dereliction of duty as far as Gerry was concerned. Then there followed a period when spies were established in his lectures to report back to the Department on matters. Gerry soon had the distinct feeling again that he was being watched, not just on the job but everywhere he went and in everything that he did. He did not let this concern him but continued on his old, determined ways.

He was facing the moment of decision. Soon he would have to make his move.

He knew now of course that the Supercoconut was the great evil which ruthless people wished to impose on an already long-suffering, poverty stricken world. He, in fact, decided now that it was actually meant to destroy the world as we know it. Pilot schemes had already been in place it seemed, in remote corners of the island, for some time. Some of even the more ignorant were beginning to wise-up on the environmental and climatic side effects. Witness the discussion of a 'Bomb' and thermonuclear, radioactive processes, which is how these unsophisticated, superstitious people would describe the lethal, unforeseeable effects of the new technology. They might cry 'wolf' but would official ears be prepared to hear? If even he himself mounted a direct crusade against the Supercoconut or openly criticised the USA he would be discounted as a madman. This was why his methods had to be so subtle. Yet, it was time now to make a stand. It was the moment to unite theory and practice.

And he welcomed all the help that Hans could give.

He decided that he needed a drink. He opened a bottle of rum, a drink that relaxes one and allows the flow of smooth, unaggressive thoughts. He drank and sighed. He thought of his plan. Photographs of incriminating sights and evidence he would completely rule out. Thankfully, of course. This was mainly because there would inevitably have to be included pictures of himself, acting the tourist or visitor bit with friendly locals or colleagues, so as not to give the impression of taking snaps for ulterior purposes. The police would be on to him in an instant in the latter case and deportation would be immediate. But as for the former, he still could not bear to see himself, in an image recorded possibly for posterity, in the pose of someone who was pretending to be somebody he really wasn't. It reminded him too much of . . . *that* photo . . . .

It was, in fact, also time for the old, well-tried ploy of the incriminating diary. This particular trick always seemed to work in these circumstances.

"Ah," he thought as the rum took effect, "now we are really getting down to the basics of what education is really about."

He would be able to boast to Jim McCall in the future about his clever methods, his overcoming of all the odds. Jim would, at last, be impressed with him. Together they might go on to write a book about world-wide counter-counter-counter insurgency.

He took out the diary from his top pocket. Across the front was the word PERSONAL. Inside were some stray observations on weather, state of health, some people met and, perhaps ominously, comments on Jaman politics and personalities. He now took a pen and wrote for the day:

'A feeling of foreboding filled me this morning as I awoke to another sultry day. I felt the sky was going to collapse at any moment. What is causing this dread?'

That would certainly interest any snoopers; it would mean that he knew something that they didn't. He knew, also, that the next sentence would raise eyebrows:

'I am worried that there is a plot to destroy the Jaman government.'

He closed the diary, feeling he had done enough good work for the day. A personal diary could be a great weapon in any propaganda war. Many were the reputations made or ruined by such modest documents. He carefully put it back in its compartment. Soon he would leave it where it might be found. He knew, for instance, that Gloria had for long been especially interested in his trousers (she had even taken to offering to iron them for him).

The next morning he was up early. He was now about to make a career move, by drinking a lot of rum and letting himself go.

He would appear, for the first time in his life, inebriated in a public place, or more correctly, at a public event. There was no surer way for people to write him off and to throw observers off their guard. He went and made himself a cup of coffee and a cheese bun. The 8am news bulletin came out over JBC, the Jaman radio station.

'There are reports coming in from our correspondent in the north of the island concerning the disastrous state of agriculture there. The farmers' crops are rotting in the fields, according to our very reliable man; and the farmers are tearing their hair out in frustration. Pilgrimages are being organised to The Shrine at the monks' monastery, and the monks themselves are being called upon to intervene with the Supreme Being. However, an official government spokesman says this is all rubbish. He says, quite categorically, that no crops are rotting in the countryside and to watch out for rumour mongers who were hell bent on destroying the government's credibility just before the general election. There were jokers in the pack, some of whom were to be found in the academic world and who might not even be native citizens. An investigation was now being instigated.'

"Well, they would say that!", interjected the disk jockey; "Now hear Slangman Stardust a sing 'Cane Juice Sugar Bitter', music cheer hup de whole nation, forget de politics!"

Rat a tat ta, rat a tat ta ... the beat came out and permeated the whole room.

'The juice it come like honey,
wo wo woe woe wo wo woe,
give hup de wealth of de land
to de foreign man-
We de poor mus' fus an' fus
jus' to catch de las' bus,
in his Volvo drive de Boss
on me foot walk me with a cuss-
Me drink de cane juice sugar,
yea oh yea it taste bitter,
Cane juice sugar bitter.'

Gerry tapped his foot in time with the music. The words struck him as a poetic mix of music, politics and satire. In Jaman there was no real fear of the government, nobody was afraid to speak their mind, music, gossip and innuendo were mixed in with politics in a very robust way. Where mocking of the rich and powerful by the poor, and vice versa, was a national sport, music was the great safety valve. Only the police were to be feared, but then only if you were poor, unhoused or were a general layabout.

He checked the notes for his lecture. It was to take place in the presence not only of his students but also some self-invited officials, including the US ambassador, who were 'interested' to observe his teaching methods and hear his controversial views. His ruse now was to make himself as objectionable as possible, thereby, hopefully, setting in motion the kidnapping-and-elimination-of-agent operation that he suspected was already in place anyway. The three hours before the class gave him sufficient time to have a few pure spirit rums. The lesson was entitled 'After Capitalism and Communism, the New Frontier'. He perused the notes again as the already hot sun climbed high like the strident god of judgement: '. . . greatest challenge . . . fundamental failures . . . whither society now . . . dependence on international markets . . . continual fall in prices . . . return of slavery . . . rise of scientificism . . . people the lowest valued commodity on earth . . . the dangers we face from the new coconut . . . education as the opium of the people . . .'.

He looked at these notes with a new feeling, with pride. Why were teachers forced to teach that which they did not believe in? For the first time in his life he was teaching something that he really believed and he was so nervous he could not face it sober! He who had survived Taran! And an arranged marriage to a Washington socialite! Not to mention the training schools of his youth!

But today there was a beginning of a new outlook on life, an end to the suppression of truth. He would speak his mind on a number of matters. He took a deep sip of his drink and swallowed with a loud guttural sound. He would speak out, and confound the diabolical schemings of his 'masters'. It was all coming together now, Family, Faith and Fatherland. The three F's.

Which had plagued him all his life. They had chased him up alleys to an impassable wall. He would have to turn and fight. He could already hear the sounds of battle, the loud clashes of symbols, the explosions of strongly held beliefs, the drum beats of condemnations. The war was on. It felt like fun. He would be playing games with the powers-that-be. Or was it tragedy? Like the time he went forward to accept the All America Award from the Niceman Foundation on behalf of the CIA for services to people and country. The amphitheatre was full of brass and tv cameras and there was a loud ringing in his ears. A voice told him that the medals, the brilliant uniforms, the brazen pride, the long speeches, the champagne glasses, the military band, were all fronts for wrongdoing. He shouted out before the president, the ambassadors of the friendly nations, his friends, his wife:

"Stop. It is all false."

At that moment he came to himself. He realised that he was simply daydreaming! That he had never openly accosted the Establishment. Even his drinking was done in the cause of serving family, faith and fatherland. For instance there was the matter of that Cardinal, who, admittedly, had made smooth his path in a number of situations in the past and who indeed had given him a letter of introduction and a written message for the monks of Jaman, describing him as a 'very religious and holy man' who might be trusted implicitly. The lies! Still, it might help him get in there to achieve his goal. No matter how many times he had informed the eminent church dignitary that he had lost his faith and did not attend church or observe any of the rituals of religion the Cardinal had insisted on praising his 'good faith' and 'well-intentioned motives' and asserting that he was of invaluable worth to the Church Universal. Mary, Fr McCarthy, Cardinal Rice all treated him as if he was still 'one of the flock', working assiduously and self-sacrificially for the good of souls. He laughed. Sure he might as well sign up again and have done with it, for all the worth it was trying to work out his own personal salvation! Well, when they heard that he had joined the Jaman monks they would be extremely surprised!

Why was Jim McCall able to remain free of all those encumbrances and hindrances from the past? How he envied that man! His ideal had always been to be like Jim McCall.

Gerry swore loudly at nothing in particular and then he saw the film actress outside his window. She was walking past in the direction of the main building. For some reason he suddenly felt electrified and his heart began to pound like it never had before. Not even when under fire. Without further ado he rushed from the room in pursuit of Miss Blue. Incredibly, there was no sign of her outside. He began to panic. He felt he was aflame, with what he didn't know. He searched everywhere and for some considerable period of time. He went into the main building and asked the security guard if a certain American lady had just walked in. The reply was negative; she had vanished, just like a mirage.

He returned to his room, like a man with a broken heart. He wanted to confess to her his life, his betrayals, his miseries. His body refused to cool down; there had been a shock to the system and he felt greatly confused. The drink was having a queer effect on him. His hard-gained Intelligence skills were definitely breaking down.

It was time to go to the lecture. He felt well-fortified; he had put on the Kingstown bush jacket which gave him a rather neater appearance; he greeted a passing student with a hearty 'Hi' as he proceeded in the direction of the classroom. He was still breathing heavily, trying to put the actress out of his mind. Sweat continued to pour down his face. It was time for business now and he determined to put on a good show with his new philosophy and resolve to tell the truth. He would begin with the truth about the United Nations, whose officials were proclaiming a universal rise in Adult Literacy figures brought about by the earnest efforts of the various governments, whilst masses of their people still did not even know the inside of a school! And there were the great religious institutes of the world, promising universal peace, whilst major disputes were initiated by such minor infractions of belief as what choice of diet or clothing was made, or who said what in a book. He had these, and many other examples of falsity.

He entered the lecture hall and noticed the heavy smell of smoke hanging in the air. Discipline was in a bad way, had broken down in fact (smoking of any substance in class was strictly forbidden) and he knew he might be in for a rough ride. Even as he came in the door he was discoursing at the top of his voice, pressing unrelentingly on the minds of his hearers and appealing to that which is highest in man, the ability to think. He could not help thinking, even as he declaimed, that this might be his finest hour.

At around the same time there was a high drama in the monastery on the hill. Incense smoke was billowing everywhere and the anti-incense crowd were in a huff. The greatest controversy in the church at that moment was over whether incense should be allowed. Basically, the young monks were against and the older generation for.

Now there was a new development, for Alan, as a member of a new sub-culture within the main group, had smuggled in some of the illegal 'herb' and placed it in the incense burners so that everybody was inhaling this smoke and not what they believed. This was a new sect that held that whilst incense was wrong, marijuana was a holy gift from the Lord. Alan was feeling quite important as he stood up in General Chapter and addressed Dr Orbeck:

"We mus' do something 'bout de Americans. Dey have teachers over here teaching hus rubbish. Dis man Gerry. He tell me 'bout some Supercoconut thing dat will destroy de hEarth. The holy horiginal coconut is our precious inheritance an' we must not let de foreigner tek it away from us. Dis man Gerry want come 'ere and address us. He interested to meet you, Most Reverend. He say he love our culture; find us very interesting and maybe write article on hus for paper or magazine back 'ome. Him say he search for de Holy Spirit. He e'en has letter from de Great Bishop of de Church of Babylon fo' you."

Archbishop Orbeck thought very hard. While it was evident that Alan was trying to impress his listeners with his own importance, consequent upon his meeting up with someone who was obviously a nosy American, at the same time things were in a bit of turmoil lately and pretty soon he would have to take what was a revolutionary decision; the amalgamation of his church with a secret, influential body that promised great practical support and much good advice on the way they managed their affairs as well as economies of scale. Their administration, indeed their whole mission, had been descending into obscurantism lately. Ever since he had been installed as bishop he had never had to think hard; it was just a matter of making easy decisions and the possession of absolute power and knowledge did away with the need for thought; but now some things had been happening which meant that the great certainties of life even here in the castle were no longer to be trusted. For instance the monks in charge of training had reverted to the radical methods of ancient monasticism without his approval. Novices had been sent wandering around the island by some of these idealistic minor clergy, without the protection of Final Vows, as a supposed 'test' of their virtue (common sense should have told them that the experiment would fail); seeping up the influences of the outside world and, probably without realising it, revealing secrets of the Monkish life to anybody and everybody. Then, Prime Minister Stanley had been on the phone, their erstwhile champion over the issue of state recognition of their religion;

now demanding, in return, church support in his private battle with President Eddie. Otherwise, warned Stanley in obvious desperation, he would publicly declare that the First Great Prophet of Jaman Religion, on his official visit to the island, had privately revealed to him (Stanley) that he did not believe in the Great Tenets Of Faith Concerning Himself; and that there was not the slightest possibility of a Homecoming for the followers of the religion in the near or distant future (this was typical, thought Dr Orbeck, of politicians who believed in nobody else's promises but their own); and of course there was that question mark over his (Orbeck's) acquisition of the title 'Doctor'. It was time, Dr Orbeck now decided, to assert himself by enlisting officially the support of that body of people who, whilst being worldly and efficient, yet appeared to be ready at least to give him the benefit of the doubt on his theology.

He spoke solemnly.

"Let no one be disheartened, for there are false prophets everywhere. Our's is the only true religion. We mus' hear 'bout dis Supercoconut plot thing. From de American mouth himself. We can show him de true religion an' he can go back home an' tell the folk 'bout hus. Our Holy Message be known throughout de world soon."

There were loud grunts and murmurs of agreement around the room. Somebody began tapping on a Bongo drum and soon the air was filled with the sound of low chants and music. Archbishop Orbeck reckoned that with the help of American Intelligence he could devise a way out of the crux that Stanley had put him in. But he would have to be careful in his dealings with 'the world' for scandal must not be given to the younger members and novices of the Faith; he must not appear to be outwardly affected in any way by material or worldly concerns. He must show his followers that he was completely above any illegitimate compromises with government, business, politics or any other of the agents of 'Babylon'.

And in the meantime he would have to deal with the sect that revolved around Alan, ensuring that their wayward ways and beliefs did not spread any further. It was time to introduce the time-honoured method of curbing one controversy in religion by instigating another; and no better way to do this than to induct a complete outsider into the higher ranks of the clergy. He now had such a candidate in mind.

Ambassador Delroy, the person who co-ordinated from the embassy all ex-patriate American personnel working on the island, had called an urgent, emergency meeting with his top staff. He was like a man pursued, with calls coming in from Virginia and the White House every five minutes concerning Gerry; there was even a call from the Vatican. Was it true, he was being asked, that McArthur, a completely unknown American teacher whom no one in the CIA or Pentagon would claim to have any knowledge of (normal Security disavowal), had hit the bottle and was threatening, inadvertently by his loose talk and 'theoretical' suppositions, to reveal secrets concerning America's recent top hush-hush plans involving a certain secret project? So as to prevent a major international scandal he must be dealt with immediately, he was ordered.

Ambassador Delroy eventually was able to remember Gerry; he was the one who had had a dossier on him because of a past history of professional misrepresentation and the assuming of false identities in sensitive areas where the CIA was trying to work inconspicuously. He had had a knack, apparently, of walking unawares into tight situations without realising their significance. He had been letting down the American side by revealing previously unsuspected liberal, cantankerous aspects of the American character in parts of the world where the uptight, right wing self-righteous image was essential. He had even been reported of as encouraging local beliefs that he was an important CIA official, and using this ingeniously acquired reputation to influence local politics and even election campaigns. There was one such election upcoming in Jaman now!

Apparently, another report went, an American official was going around the place making all sorts of claims on behalf of the CIA. He was causing alarm and scandal in people and serious questions were being asked by officials such as how is it that one of your secret service guys is going around making an ass of himself with all sorts of preposterous claims and theories and frightening the life out of the local population? Was it a case of nobody having the courage to tell him that he was behaving badly, indeed while often the worse for drink; of facing up to him and discarding the old practice of never interfering directly with an American's democratic rights and freedoms, even in a foreign land; of, if necessary, facing him down in front of the Jamanese people and publicly humiliating him (and also, by inference, the USA) by removing him from his post and putting him off the island in disgrace? There was no other way for it now, thought Mr Delroy; he would have to have this man called in and brought before the proper authorities.

As he sat sipping a delicious glass of rum and coke, Gerry McArthur felt satisfied that he had at last begun to speak the truth as he saw it. He had also, as he now acknowledged to himself, actually seen the real situation regarding his own contribution to the betterment of the world. There was no doubt but that his message was welcome in even the most inhospitable of places; his warnings heard clearly by the most unlikely of hearers. He was beginning to feel spiritual even, as if at long last his mystical yearnings and quests were coming to their parousia. He had begun to experience in himself a desire for a total, soul-felt abandonment of all material and personal possessions. These strange feelings seemed to have followed that disturbing experience when he had chased after Jean Blue on the campus. He now looked forward to the visit to the monastery with the anticipation almost of a homecoming.

He dressed himself carefully in his new Jamanese outfit, a long, colourful caftan and loose slippers. He had not shaved himself for a few days now and the effect of this on his appearance was welcome. He had begun to let his hair grow long also, being tied at the back in a kind of threaded ponytail. It was a far cry from the suited person who had first landed in the island. He noticed that his face had lost some of the lines of anxiety that had once run across it; his eyes were cheerful and even hearty.

Paulo came up to visit him in his room. It was late in the day and might be termed in fact evening as the sun was going down and the whole world felt to Gerry like it was gearing up for the start of some inter-stellar, inter-galactic space trip (which indeed in fact it was, he ruminated) with its aura of brilliantly bright shadows and blinking flashes of lights and strange humming noises, as at the start of some space age Grand Prix. Paulo Costello and Gerry had become intimates of late, each enjoying the other's drinking companionship (Gerry had visited the Costello family; they had been struck dumb by the shock caused by the appearance of this awesome American in their humble home) and Paulo continued being the recipient of much well-chosen advice from Gerry which somehow had, at least for the recipient, the aura of historic fate.

"Make no mistake about it but the political establishment here is on its last legs and you yourself could make a better job of it than all of those in undeserved power. Listen to me and you will save yourself year's of heartbreak. That job you got yourself on my recommendation in the main city post office is not a bad preparation for greater things to come. Lesser mortals than you in history have started off in such lowly occupations, acquiring a sympathy for their oppressed fellow workers and going on to eventually reign supreme over the portals of power! You, I venture to say, will not only be prime minister one day but also president! And, what is more, you will be a cultured leader unlike those philistines who dwell in high offices at present. How is the novel going?"

"That is what I have here in my briefcase," said Paulo Costello proudly; "it is finished."

Gerry studied the continuation of Paulo's text:

'Not even weeks of the most desperate physical and mental torture were enough to weaken Paulo's resolve. Even as the blows rained down he was thinking: Revenge, revenge .... . Why were they so afraid of him? They must have had intuition of his innate strength and power. Revolt was threatening in the streets as word of his arrest was passed around. Patrons at the El Conquistador were furious and were busy arranging a protest march on the prison. Whenever Paulo felt a weakening of his resolve he just brought before his eyes a mental picture of his bloodied, dead sister's face.

Then he could face anything in his determination to see his enemies brought to justice one day.

Justice, justice, wherefore art thou?

There were the sounds of commotion on the streets below his prison window. He could hear shouts of 'Free The Prisoner' and 'Liberty Or Death'. For a moment a pang of happiness went through his heart. Then he felt his wounds again.

For hours the battle raged. The sounds of gun and rocket fire eventually gave way to the sound of prison cell doors being opened and, Fate Behold, his own prison cell door was flung wide open.

"Welcome to Freedom, O Leader, we are at your command."

Paulo recognised Mr Sher, Alfredo The Thug, Idle Pete and Jos in the crowd. It was just like a homecoming to the El Conquistador; smiles were on everyone's faces. A great moment in history had arrived.

Not long afterwards Paulo was at the head of a raggle-taggle army of peasants that made its way to the Presidential Palace.

Inside the holders of power trembled. President Eddie, noted for his corruption and massacres of innocents, especially trembled.

"Let us send out an emissary to sue for peace," said the President gravely to his chief adviser; "the writing is on the wall."

Paulo combined justice with mercy in all that he did, and this moment which might have been considered the summit of his life allowed of no exception. He even felt a tinge of pity at the thought of the elderly, white-haired man becoming powerless all of a sudden, after so many years at the top. Yes, it was not just mercy, it was compassionate brotherliness shown to those who were least deserving.

"Send to President Eddie and tell him we are ready to talk peace. A safe passage will be granted to him to as far as he wants to go, but he must vacate the palace by midday."

Meanwhile the prime minister and all his secretaries of state were rounded up by an enthusiastic police force loyal to no one now except Paulo. Paulo stepped in as the scene got ugly with ill-done-by widows, orphans and unemployed men threatening to lynch the members of the former government.

"Spare them to face Justice Herself in the tribunals of the land. Let no one cast the first stone until the last stone has been put in place. Let them face their peers; it is a worse punishment," he said loudly, waving his arms around.

From that day on this wave was known as the Costello Victory Wave and became a universal symbol of triumph.

But how to bring justice to the dead?

Up in heaven his long-dead, innocent sister looked down on the earth and saw Paulo's victory. A gentle smile went across her face and a few tears of thanksgiving slipped down her cheeks. Retribution was not in her mind but she knew that the full rigour of the law must be applied on earth and that she could not stand in the way. The erring Fitzrobbin clan were all arrested as they tried to make their way to the illegal airstrip at Mobby Bay where a private plane was waiting to whisk them to a new life. That night for the first time in their lives they knew what it was like to sleep on a hard surface. But the bare-faced, brazen attitude of Senor Fitzrobbin knew no bounds and even now he laughed at his jailers:

"Ha ha. This new regime of Costello's will not last a week. The Americans will step in to save us from this pirate of the peasants, this bandit of the barriades. Wait, and you will see!"

Amidst much joyful celebration Paulo was publicly sworn in as President in front of the palace, whereupon he declared a week-long National Holiday. June 10th was declared National Day from that time on. Representatives of the US President called on him and demanded that he release Eddie and call national elections.

"We have no time for elections at the moment as there is much reforming we must do. Tell President Hooligan that any undue interference will bring down upon him the righteous fury of the Jaman people. At once Paulo went to the window and called the envoys to witness to the large crowd of people gathered outside who were shouting their support.

"Go, tell Mr Hooligan that the whole nation stands behind me. Tell him that I, and I alone, speak for Jaman."

Meanwhile Roberto and Rosina, Paulo's parents, had heard rumours of a new government in Kingstown that promised to better the lot of the country folk. Little did they know that The Leader was their very own son, for Paulo no longer called himself Paulo Costello but simply El Senor, as a mark of humility, so lacking in most world leaders.

Fresh downpours of long-awaited rain arrived for the parched countryside and people were heard to remark:

"Even the gods are pleased with us now."

When representatives of the peasantry were called from all over the island to attend a Grand Planning Meeting in Kingstown, Roberto and his oldest son Juan were selected for their own district, as two of the less shy or withdrawn members of the community.

Oh, but they had nothing to wear! Great efforts of thought were employed to solve this problem of finding something suitable to wear to Kingstown, so that the community would not be ashamed before all the nation. At the last moment, just when it seemed that the delegation would have to cancel the journey, salvation came in the form of two lovely black suits donated by the local Jesuit 'landowners'. Neighbours and friends made a money collection which was sufficient to buy two nice white shirts and lo-they were ready.

A proud mama watched them leave on two donkeys with tears of pride in her eyes and the strength of the community around her. The neighbours stood staring until they had gone round the far bend of the track.

"One day we will have a road here," a man was heard to mutter.

Already signs of prosperity were appearing in the countryside. As they rode along they noticed that crops were blooming that extra bit brighter in the fields and happy smiles were on the faces of the populace.

"We have a wonderful leader in Kingstown; one who was born in the countryside and knows intimately of our problems," they were told by various people;

"be sure to give him our thanks when you meet him. Ask him for a road."

"I cannot wait to meet El Senor and see what he looks like," said Juan happily to his father and for once in his life Roberto civilly answered Juan, smiling gently and saying:

"I cannot wait either."

At last they were on the outskirts of Kingstown. They stopped at a bar, the El Conquistador which, if they but knew it, had been the campaign headquarters of El Senor and now boasted a statue in the doorway of the Great Leader (they did not recognise their son and brother there). Here they were given a drink on the house by the owner, Mr Sher, and they all drank to the health of El Senor and the Prosperity of Jaman.

"El Senor has ordered that all representatives coming in from the countryside be given free drinks and that the brewers, the Puerto Rico family, stand the expense," said The Cap merrily; "Long live El Senor!"

In fact the Puerto Rico brewery was in the process of being nationalised and The Cap, Alfredo The Thug, Idle Pete and Jos were on the new board of directors. Nevertheless these latter characters continued to play the same old game of dominos with the same old arguments and vehemence as before, ignoring the arrival of these 'peasants' which only served to complicate life for them; there had been a shortage of beer lately, for instance.

"Who is the American?," Roberto asked The Cap.

"A very good friend of the Revolution," he was told proudly.

"He gave us the benefit of his experience in the Taran War to advise us on the destabilisation of oppressive regimes and the counter-insurgency tactics of our enemies. He taught us to see ourselves in our own image, to sing our pop songs and to wear our native garb with pride. He taught us to believe in our own culture, our own talk, our own drink, our own selves."

It was obvious from this that the American in the bar was some kind of folk hero; he was at that moment jigging with Melanie the barmaid on the floor in a version of the local Lingo dance to the obvious approval of all.

Time should not be awasting so as soon as they had refreshed themselves they took leave of the kindly people at the El Conquistador and continued on their way into the town centre.

"There are hundreds more waiting to see the President. You may have to wait many days," they were told by a presidential aide.

But the waiting did not matter to the humble country folk.

"Those portraits of the President, does he not bear a resemblance to our Paulo, our dead Paulo?," said Juan to his father one evening.

"That he does," said Roberto philosophically.

But they did not make the connection.

Yet.

Gerry put the book down for a moment and flicked through to see how much was left. He moved forward until he came to the penultimate section with its own subheading:

'Reconciliation'

They stood looking agape at one another. They were all speechless.

"Maria's death has been avenged," said Paulo finally, more to break the embarrassing silence than anything.

"What is my son doing here in the Presidential Palace?," asked Roberto not deigning to believe the evidence of his eyes;

"I cannot believe that you are the President. I will never believe it until my final day. Juan. Let us go home. This is some kind of trick."

"Don't be foolish, father. Look, see if he doesn't have his birthmark."

El Senor let down his trousers.

True enough, the tell-tale mark was there on his backside for all to see.

"Your mother will have kittens when she hears about this. Can you fix us up with some grub, for starters?," said Roberto.

"I have promised a corruption-free regime and that means no special privileges for relatives, I'm afraid. You will have to leave the palace and take your place in the queue with all the other people. This does not decrease my filial respect for you; in fact there is an opportunity for Juan to join the Presidential Bodyguard if he cares to fill in an application form. Nevertheless, everything must be kept above board to avoid the day when they might have to get rid of me for the same reasons our old rulers have been deposed. Yes, everything in the country will be fair and square. Long live the Revolution!"

Roberto found the fact that his son was now ruling the country hard to accept . . . .'

It is a great story," said Gerry enthusiastically, adding,

"now let us see about turning fiction into fact," as they both made their way out the door to adjourn to a nearby bar. □

chapter
ten

Gerry and the US ambassador were being chauffeur-driven in the official car (complete with Stars & Stripes and Eastern Star flags) up to the residence of President Eddie. McArthur was doing his best to conceal his more than usual tipsy state and tried to make casual conversation with Mr Delroy about things seen out the car window, such as the crowd of enthusiastic people who appeared to be attempting to make contact with their vehicle. This did not seem to interest Delroy whose face remained fixed with a worried expression. At the same time the ambassador himself was trying to put Gerry at his ease, reflecting that he was, here, possibly, humouring a madman.

"The Top Man wants to meet ya, Gerry. He thinks you are Mr Big Stuff and can help him solve his problems," said the ambassador quietly, fretting that he was saying the right thing and not send Gerry over the deep end; "but there's no comprehending what goes on in the heads of these Third World dictators."

"He's not a dictator, technically," Gerry corrected him.

Delroy continued to sweet-talk Gerry, to let him think that he was still in the good books.

"We want you to put on a good show and not let the American side down. They seem to have a strange respect for you here. You could even help us to remove Eddie from office.

If you could become familiar with him and get a bit of scandalous gossip, that might do the trick, for there is still a puritan mentality in this society. He has served his purpose and his deputy Stanley is ready to take his place. Stanley is more our man. He was never interested in getting the people a 2% pay rise. And he loves everything American."

Delroy thought he could kill two birds with one stone here; humour McArthur and use him at the same time for patriotic purposes.

"Why does Eddie want to see me especially? Surely there are plenty of proper US representatives around?"

"He wants to see the CIA man. He has a thing about the CIA. He thinks you are the greatest thing on earth. He reads all the spy thrillers."

"How did he come to believe that I was in the CIA?", asked Gerry curiously.

"Ah," said Delroy, putting one hand gently on Gerry's shoulder, "I suppose they put two and two together. Whatever you say will go down well with him. Be yourself; he is an understanding man. Just don't get too fraught up about injustice or the underdog. You are leaning too much in that direction these days. By the way, if you don't mind me saying so, they tell me you were drunk whilst giving a lecture."

"I wasn't drunk. Not in the sense you mean, anyway. I was drunk with the truth. You shouldn't pay attention to every little bit of tittle-tattle you hear. There is, in fact, a lot of malicious gossip around these days."

"There is indeed," said Delroy, agreeing with him immediately.

They whisked through the gates of the palace, no attempt at security vetting being made. Perhaps the flags on the car bonnet were enough. They pulled up and the butler accompanied them into the interior meeting room. They knew, as they awaited his entrance, that they were in the presence of history for President Eddie was very old, and a strange quiet went over the ambassador as he sought to put himself into the right frame of mind. In contrast, Gerry was noisy, asking the butler lots of questions about the building and its occupants. Then Eddie came in, hobbling on an ancient walking cane. His grey beard and slight frame accentuated his venerability and Delroy even felt obliged to bow his head before speaking. Gerry, in contrast, was loquacious, greeting Eddie loudly, shaking his free hand and even making a joke at Delroy's expense.

"You needn't pay too much attention to the ambassador here. He is only third rate in the league of ambassadors; too poor to go to a European country. Ha ha. It's just a little joke. No disrespect meant to your little country, I mean!"

"Ho, I know that what you say is true. I have heard that you were a blunt, honest talker. Professor Marie Gomez has been telling me all about you. You are the CIA man. Correct?"

"Marie Gomez! I have been waiting to meet her! Her reputation goes before her, as they say! Yes, I am the CIA man. Commander McCall is officially in charge, but he has gone native, a technical term, here, so he is not of much use. I have, temporarily, taken over, but poor McCall doesn't know it yet. In the CIA we always leave old stagers in high up positions where they have delusions of power. This way they are rendered harmless."

"I suppose the same applies to politics," said the old stager with a smile.

"But ... the Commander IS in charge," the ambassador protested.

"I'm afraid they don't keep you up to date with the latest changes, Mr. Delroy," said Gerry adamantly; "Mr McCall is sidelined now. In any case he is too busy with other things to be bothered by mundane intelligence business."

Mr Delroy listened with sorrow, even some pity, to Gerry's delusion of power, his barely-concealed antipathy to his old colleague and head of department. These were certain signs that the guy had finally 'lost it'.

President Eddie was looking at Gerry with what was almost hero-worship; he gestured to his two visitors to sit down. A door opened and to Gerry's great surprise in walked Professor Maria Gomez attired not in a formal grey business suit as might be expected but dressed up for the kill in a low-cut colourful dress and expensive shoes and jewellery. There was much make-up on her face and she was, as in the vernacular, looking like a million dollars. She was obviously at ease in this place and she greeted them with a smile and a 'hello' and then went over meekly to Eddie and laid her arms around his shoulders.

"Intelligent women are the best," said Eddie by way of explanation.

"Miss Gomez is my assistant," he continued, "but we are also very close and are considering getting married as soon as some legal difficulties are resolved."

At 91 Eddie had had at least fourteen registered marriages. He was held in the highest regard by the nation for his sticking to the legal norms and formalities of the marriage pact.

"Congratulations," said Gerry warmly.

"Our wedding day will be a public holiday. It is time Romance was brought back and given the importance it once held. I'll bet you have many secret exploits to your credit as an international spy?," he said in an excited voice.

"Yes, I have seen how the big operators work. Anyway, how is the plot against you going?"

President Eddie looked at him askance and Delroy went uncontrollably crimson. There was an almost unbearable silence.

"Do you know of a plot against me?," asked Eddie in a sombre voice.

"There are plots being concocted all the time, all around the place. Even the pope has his conspirators. Stanley wants the top job. Surely you know that? I believe he even has designs on having himself made Head of the Church. He is quite a megalomaniac, that guy."

"He is certainly ambitious. He is always talking about those old emperors and tyrants with great approval, but he is my son-in-law. He would not conspire behind my back to have me killed, surely?"

"You live in the past, Eddie. These days they would sacrifice their own mothers to get a share of the spoils."

"I have treated Stanley like a son. Oh yes, on occasions I have teased him with threats of demotion, especially when he gets too big for his shoes. But I have treated him well. Who else is in on this plot?"

"All will be revealed in time," said Gerry quietly.

"Mr Stanley is a fine, responsible leader," said an alarmed ambassador; "and he supports America in all its dealings in this hemisphere. He has the utmost respect for you. I must apologise for Mr McArthur. Don't you see now that he is not a sane man; that he is not all right in the head?"

"As far as I can see, he is the only one with his head screwed on. I treated Stanley like a son," Eddie said into his tears which had begun to flow freely; in fact he IS my son!"

"The worst intrigues take place between close family members," said Gerry authoritatively; "and blood is not thicker than money."

"Call the prime minister up here at once, Maria," said Eddie loudly, "and don't tell him what for. I will soon get to the truth of this matter."

He turned to the two Americans and said, looking at Gerry with apparent fondness and deep sympathy;

"make the most of the hospitality of this place while we are waiting. Sometimes alcohol is the best remedy."

Gerry did not need any persuading to sample some of the luxury liquors Eddie had in the room.

"What dat ol' man waant?," said Stanley angrily and forgetting to speak in Standard English in his surprise; "it not like him to ask for me to come up like dat. I usually have to plead with him for an audience."

There was uncertainty, even fear in his voice. He thought deeply for a moment and then said:

"I hope my policy of inviting American experts and academics into the country to help our development hasn't got me into trouble. There is that recent case of Mr McArthur encouraging his pupils to sing 'Cane Juice Bitter' and write pop songs in their lessons that was well-publicised the other day. He might have got to hear of that."

"That old bugger is not only having an affair with Professor Maria Gomez;" said Erico Mauris, "he is also planning to put her in the highest position of all; the prime ministership."

A period of silence followed as Stanley collected his thoughts.

"How is it that I have not heard all this before?," he asked suspiciously.

"Look, there is sexual intrigue going on all over the island without your knowledge. It's even been going on in your own cabinet, right in front of your eyes, almost. They are all at it," replied Erico disapprovingly and with much distaste.

Stanley's ears began to tingle at this information. He was an extreme puritan who thought that sexual misbehaviour came even before irreverence to superiors in the scale of misdeeds. He also enjoyed hearing of all the intimate failings of his competitors from which he believed himself totally immune; his next question revealed his persistent preoccupation:

"Whose been at it now?"

"Don't say I told you this, but Magnus Rabid is a homosexual. But only in private."

"Whaa ..?", cried Stanley, "my colleague and ... friend? How you know dis true? Surely I have not had one of them in my own cabinet? I ... could ... never ... live ... dat ... down ...."

"He is a homosexual," said Erico slowly, almost spitting the words out; "his girlfriends are a front, only there to conceal the truth. He laughs behind your back all the time."

"Oow," went Stanlie, beginning to think out his revenge.

"And that is not the end of it. He says you are really one of them. He is always telling dirty jokes about you behind your back, or when you are not around."

"This is a can of worms that we can tolerate no longer. Mr Rabid! Eh!"

He could not help himself letting out a groan;

"We will see. Sometimes I feel very alone in the world."

"Shall I accompany you up to the palace?," asked Erico hopefully. As Minister of Information he always tried to make sure he was in the thick of things.

"He hasn't asked for you," said Stanley sharply.

"You need my advice."

"I don't need your's or Magnus's advice. I just let you stay around as it is the done thing to have advisers. Come up with me anyway, just in case he mentions someone I don't know."

They called for the official car and Stanley said to Erico:

"You sit in the front with the driver."

Erico pointedly did not open the rear door for the prime minister and the driver had to get out and come all the way around to do it. They both sat inside, sombrely, like the patrons at a fancy restaurant, immobile, awaiting service. They did not speak to each other, their minds paralysed with conflicting emotions. There was a silence; it was as if their presence in that official car had somehow altered the whole world. They put on suitably serious and self-important expressions and Stanley gave the order:

"To the Presidential Palace."

As they rounded a corner on the way up the hill on which the Presidential Palace stood a stone or missile of some sort hit the car.

"They get so excited whenever I pass," said Stanley happily.

"Yes," replied Erico, "it's probably the driver they don't like."

"Jealous of his job, I suppose," agreed Stanley.

"Let me tell you something," the prime minister continued, expanding his chest;

"jealousy is the greatest enemy a man has."

"Yes," agreed the Minister of Information.

This time Stanley and his car went through the gates without any formalities.

"That would-be corporal has learnt his lesson, I see," said Stanley with one of his deep chuckles.

"There is nobody on the gate," said a puzzled Erico; "how strange."

Stanley looked back. Sure enough, the Presidential residence had no overt or covert security whatever.

They pulled up with a loud screech of brakes.

They were escorted by a somewhat unsteady-on-his-feet butler into the room where the others were comfortably seated. They all looked at each other in surprise at first, and then greeted one another civilly. The new arrivals sat down somewhat nervously despite a continued attempt to look self-important. Eddie stood up slowly and shakily, gripping tightly his stick with both hands. He surveyed all the onlookers before he spoke. His voice was both gravelly and shrill in succession.

"I have called you here to institute an Inquiry. Allegations have been made concerning my prime minister and a reputed ambition to be president he is said to harbour. Never was treason so disgraceful and so unwarranted. Speak up, man, in defence of yourself!"

He stared at Stanley angrily, yet with a trace of a small, wry grin on his face. At his age nothing much really bothered Eddie for very long.

"What are these allegations. Who has made them?," Stanley demanded to know.

"A very reliable espionage network has been working underground for me. Not even you, prime minister, have been aware of its existence. This man Gerry here corroborates the charge I am making. It is he who has made the very serious allegations against you."

Stanley went suddenly pale as he remembered the earlier conversation with Erico concerning suggested sexual transgressions. For a moment he was near to fainting. Eddie's next words came almost as a relief.

"He claims you are plotting a coup d'etat. You is always trying to take my place; shame on you Stanley!"

Eddie was enjoying this showdown and the discomfiture of his son. It was almost as though the content of the plot was the lesser item, and the underhandedness and intrigue of the whole thing the main, enjoyable part. Stanley, however, was still breathing deeply in relief as the colour returned to his face.

"I will see to it that your malicious allegations are challenged in the courts," he said angrily to Gerry; "and your passport will be impounded."

"Is it true that you hope to oust me?", Eddie asked in a severe voice.

"Lies, lies the whole damn thing," said Stanley.

"You are fired, McArthur," said an alarmed Ambassador Delroy; "pay no attention to this man, anybody. He has lost his reason. We have been worried about his mental state and irregular activities for a long time, and now he has gone too far. You are to report to the embassy in the morning."

"You are not my employer. I am only answerable to the CIA.," said Gerry coolly.

Delroy replied in a high voice:

"Listen, Mr McArthur. I have the ear of President Hooligan. All ambassadors have direct access to the White House."

"Well, then, will you tell these people about America's master plan to take over and wreck the whole island of Jaman. Or do I have to do it?"

"This man is a raving lunatic. There exists no such plan. It is all in his mind. America's only wish is to help countries to develop. We are against any type of imperialism," said Delroy adamantly.

"So. That is what old Uncle Sam has been up to all de time," said Eddie loudly; "I must say that I am disappointed, for I have looked up to that country to set standards of honest dealing and democracy. Thanks to the CIA for being so honest! I will deal with you in my own time and my own way, Stanley."

Maria Gomez was nodding her head vigorously at Eddie's words. Normally when she spoke it would have been in academic jargon with numerous difficult, or rarely heard words. Now it was as if she was struggling to find even the small words and phrases expected of somebody who was a politician's moll.

"Yeah, darling," was all she could manage as she stroked his head.

She was clearly finding her new role difficult. Erico Mauris, flummoxed by the whole thing, was waiting to see which way the cards fell. It was a tense situation and only Gerry, arms behind his head, lying back and drinking the sweet Tia Maria liqueur, was at ease.

It was at this point that they all at first heard, and then saw a military convoy coming up the avenue. It was travelling at a great speed. The remembrance of the lack of security brought frowns of concern to Stanley and Erico and President Eddie himself looked surprised.

There were three vehicles in which were armed 'soldiers'. So great was their haste that all the vehicles crashed into one another as they came to a sudden halt outside the main door. The 'soldiers' jumped out, falling over themselves trying to hold on to their rifles; it would strike any experienced observer that these were not particularly well-trained soldiers. Their leader, in fact, despite his camouflage, was in many ways remarkable for his resemblance to The Cap, Mr Sher, whilst Gerry recognised familiar features in some of the other soldiers' faces also; Alfredo, Pete, Jos, Paulo were all there, or else their dopplegangers. He even recognised some others of the bar's hangers-on. They 'marched' into the building, The Cap shouting out continually what, by the evident confusion of his men, were probably contradictory orders. Nevertheless they eventually made it inside.

"Where is our guard?," Stanley wanted to know.

"My guard," Eddie corrected him.

"Looks like they are taking a break," said Gerry calmly, without too much surprise;

"best to let these fellows in and talk to them."

It was here that some confusion ensued as to what had taken place next. Some said it was a straightforward kidnapping and hostage-taking; others that the group went willingly after being told that their lives were at risk from some third party, or that they were being taken away 'in the name of National Security'. The last theory was that they were actually fooled into believing that they were going on a leisure trip to view sights and hold policy seminars in a beautiful, remote location in the interior. The word there was that they had just gone on a working holiday. There were no independent witnesses, except the butler, who had by then become completely 'blotto' by secretly helping himself to the drinks Eddie had been so generous in sharing with his guests.

All, including Maria Gomez, who was still trying to get into the spirit of things, were bundled up on to the leading wagon with a guard at each side and a most irresponsible-looking, hair-locks, sunglasses-wearing lout of a driver sitting at the front. Then the convoy set off for a destination unknown. All they could tell was that they were going up into the hills and they were still driving as darkness fell. There was a mixture of emotions in the group; keen interest on the part of Eddie, fear in Erico Mauris and Delroy, dismay in Stanley, as the night became even darker in the blackness of the forest. Maria was still wordless and clinging to Eddie. Gerry showed no emotion but kept assuring everybody that they would be all right; he was accustomed to such situations.

"I wouldn't be surprised if Magnus Rabid and General Umberto were behind this," said Erico bitterly, "Magnus never liked our politics."

Maria suddenly laughed at the top of her voice and blurted out:

"Ha ha ha. Magnus know something 'bout politics? Dat dope know nothing! Him only talk de dirty talk wi' me."

Professor Gomez evidently had no respect for her Ministry of Economics colleague.

"But," said Erico, "he will take advantage of our absence if he can," clearly believing that he had been outmaneuvered by someone, somehow.

Eddie spoke solemnly.

"Perhaps it will do the country some good for a change, if they make proper use of the advantages presented by this hijacking of the upper echelon of government, take upon themselves the burden of decision-making and thereby experience the weight of responsibility."

He was looking sort of pleased, as if it was all indeed just a day-trip. Their captors had not spoken much to them but as they went up a narrow, twisting track one of the soldiers remarked:

"Not even de devil find dem here."

In the darkness of the tropical night, with the twitchings of the insects, the chirping and croaking of lizards, the bellowing of giant bullfrogs and the rustling noises of the forest in their ears making them feel that they were, indeed, in the most deep backwoods, they were all taken off the wagon and led in silence into a simple-looking house. A crusty old man and woman were sitting down at a rude table and did not speak as everyone came in. This man and woman were relics of an old warrior race that had once lived all over the forested hills and who liked to show their independence from the laws of the country and normal life. The old man called himself Colonel Jones and the woman called herself simply The General.

"Here are your guests," said The Cap with pride, "look after them well."

"They get plenty o' de bush tea up 'ere," said The General, "an' if dey cause fuss dey ged de machete. He he eeee."

"Noooo. Dey de government! Show dem respect," insisted The Cap.

They all settled down in various corners of the house which was an old two-roomed wooden structure on stilts to keep pests and the floods out (it was in an upper valley, liable to flash floods) and through the cracks in the floor Gerry could see the vague outlines of pigs, chickens, goats and dogs all together in their night shelter below. There were no differences in these structures throughout the tropical world and the inconsequential thought occurred to Gerry that most of the world did not have to pay architect fees. The building work was DIY also. Perhaps the best word for this countryside way-of-life was 'anarchic'.

As it looked as if it was going to be a long stay for all of them, Gerry thought he might make it a time that was positive and suggested to the others there, as they tucked into cold plain rice in cheap wooden bowls (so that Stanley, who was fond of his stomach, had to eat with some dismay but dared not make any criticism), that he start a seminar on Political Methods And Democracy. At first they did not seem to understand, or get the idea, but he persisted, pointing out that there was really nothing else for them to do and they would all benefit from it later as his beneficial instruction grew to produce fruit in more ordered and good government all round.

"Me want to learn from de man from Harvard," said Eddie speaking in the parochial now and getting into the mood of things.

"Me too," said Maria Gomez, wanting perhaps to restore some of her image as a learned lady; "me bet he got lots of ideas."

Only Delroy, Stanley and Erico seemed to be still taking the kidnapping badly and were sulking, or even very scared.

"The first lesson, then," said Gerry as they all pulled up at the table, their hosts going out to boil some tea for the party, "is on the meaning of the word POLITICS. Now let us spell 'politics' together. P-o-l-i-t-i-c-s. They all repeated this, paused, then went on to spell it out again. (Later, Gerry would admit in casual conversation that, by using this rote pedagogical method, he was simply demonstrating to critical and conservative authorities that even the most avant garde of educational practitioners like himself were capable of using old, reliable, traditional methodology.)

One of the soldiers obtained some paper and Gerry took out a pen. He started to write his words out in large print, following 'politics' with DEMOCRACY. For the want of anything better to do Stanley and Erico, too, began to take part in these word games. 'Captain' She remarked to the Colonel and The General in quiet tones:

"Long time since tourists come up here. Look after dem well and dey bring up de dollars."

Meanwhile Gerry felt great pride in being able to initiate the first official Adult Literacy scheme in these faraway hills amongst a recalcitrant people. The first lesson seemed to be going well, despite Delroy's non-participation and some tension occurring between Eddie and Stanley over the spelling of 'AntiConstitutionalism'.

There was a strange silence over the city after the kidnapping of the government. It was almost as if nothing had happened. Vehicles went about their various businesses and policemen and policewomen harassed pedestrians and drivers in the usual way. There was no sign of any major military activity or movement of army personnel. Shops were opened and city folk and visitors alike started going into this one, out of that one and on to the other one. The stray dogs and goats were in their usual vicinities. Jaman House and the palace displayed no outward sign of trouble or anxiety, except for the drunk butler in the Presidential residence who was causing some mayhem around the place (a drunk butler in such an establishment still retains status, it should be remembered by those who wish to conduct business with the powers-that-be). The radio station was blaring out the usual music and the biggest event of the day appeared to be the pushing out of No.1 place in the Hit Parade of Cane Juice Bitter by a new song with the title: 'Coconut tree to rass'.

'Coconut tree very pretty,
an' de fruit is very sweet,
but de American coconut
is impossible to h'eat.

Coconut tree is tall an' free,
an' de folk love de juice,
but who dey mash our coconut
an' sell us American excuse?

Lethal Yellowing kill our tree,
an' now dey tell us it is bad,
yet de breeze a blow de disease
give us new American fad.

An' den we all sing together,
away wid de Supercoconut,

tell it loud, strong an' proud
No American coconut!
IT DISEASE DE GROUND!
IT DISEASE DE GROUND!'

Sung by Slangman Stardust it was written by a songwriter whom nobody had ever heard of before, Jim McDan, a middle-aged foreigner wearing an over-the-top 'arty' outfit, his face almost hidden behind a colourful scarf, who rushed into the music studios one morning and handed over the lyrics of two songs; and then disappeared as mysteriously as he had come. The second song, 'The Train To Homeland Ain' Leaving Fo' We All Dead 'Fore Den', also sung by Slangman Stardust, was close behind in No. 2 spot.

It was not until one o'clock the next afternoon that any reference to the disappearance of the rulers was made and then it was played down under the headline of 'Cabinet Changes'. It appeared that there was a crisis in the country, with the unexpected disappearance of most of the government and the requirement for The Honorable Magnus Rabid, M.P., Order Of Merit (automatically bestowed), Phd (Hon.), the former Minister of Economic Affairs, to be appointed as Acting Prime Minister; a mystified General Umberto, Chief Of The Armed Forces, B.A. (Honorary), being persuaded to become a reluctant Acting President; these arrangements pending the return of the missing former occupants to their positions. It was stressed that during the emergency things would carry on as normal.

In the meantime, the new Acting President and Prime Minister, implementing their first joint decision, would be going down to the docks in order to personally supervise the dumping into the sea of the latest cargo of US food aid, which had been sent to Jaman with the purpose of wiping out the whole population, something that they had learnt from a top, highly secret intelligence source. Also, they had decided that the university and Education Ministry were both *very bad places*, and would be immediately shut down. It was about time, they said, that Jamans took their destiny into their own hands!

The Cardinal, bishop and Fr McCarthy were taking umbrage at reports from Langley and the Pentagon that Gerry McArthur had gone over to the other side. He had apparently been spotted chatting amiably to a Jahmonk trainee. He had also instituted his own, ad hoc lessons in Adult Literacy for all-comers, without waiting for the proper course verification or official authorisation.

"Not Gerry, never," said Fr McCarthy; "there is no way he would be seen to convert to a strange religious cult in that animist, spirit-infested backwood's place; not our Gerry."

The other two men did not seem so sure. They had long enough experience of the private lives of all manner of folk to realise that people do unexpected things, inappropriate things, especially as they got older. Yet Gerry, from a family prominent in church and conservative circles, was a person they felt must not be lost to them. For, being of the old school, his name alone still carried the banner of traditional, national values, even if he had forgotten that fact himself. Also, although not important in himself, the name McArthur was still a clarion call to that old, tight-knit east coast American community, to a long line of war heroes and professionally successful relatives, resonant of all the glory the name McArthur had produced in the past.

"This is the Doomsday scenario," said the Cardinal loftily; "I shouldn't have used him to by-pass the Papal Nuncio and deliver a message to the bishop of the Church of Jah. The drinking I don't mind too much about. It's the propaganda value to their heretical religion of his public approval and even perhaps his spiritual involvement that we must worry about. Is our man in Jaman not able to sort him out?"

Fr McCarthy attempted to speak here but the bishop interrupted him before he could say a word:

"The Apostolic Nuncio is at his wits end at the way things are going over there. But Hans is on the spot. He assures me, personally, Your Eminence, that he has got the number on everyone there. Including this Gerry McArthur. He is just biding his time, awaiting the proper time to strike. The boys are holding their hands, until the right moment."

"Aah, those lads! Always ones to go right to the brink," said His Eminence, impressed.

"A bit gone to the dogs these days, though," insisted Fr McCarthy.

"Ah, wait and see now. The popes got it right with them before though, in the distant past, you know," the Cardinal stated happily.

"What do you mean?," asked the bishop, wondering what on earth the cardinal had in mind.

"I mean," said Cardinal Rice, "when he banned them".

"Mary tells me," said Fr McCarthy, "that a lady who she knows found a diary in a secret compartment inside his trousers which, after some comments on the local political situation and remarks about biotechnology, makes ominous references to some more worrying things. The End Of The World, the Second Coming and other apocalyptic events. It sounds ominous."

"A lifetime's effort on the part of many people has gone into trying to get Gerry to return to the Fold, from as far back as his early days in the infantry. I am not prepared to see it all go down the drain at this late stage. I promised his father-in-law that I would turn him into a good Catholic, and on his deathbed he made me repeat that promise under oath, on pain of Hell. He was a demanding man. I will succeed yet," said Cardinal Rice unhappily.

"It is a question," said the bishop, who was the hardest man of all there, "of whose brainwashing methods are the best. He has always been a tempting target for foreign sects, for if they could make a major catch of him then our indoctrination methods would finally be proven to have been weaker. There was that time when we thought he had converted to Islam. He had been investigating North African terror groups on a supposed holiday in Algiers and dressed up in Arab gear in order to attend a political rally. Mary was afraid for a while afterwards that his ravings about the merits of Islam were a genuine belief; it was with great relief that we discovered he was only going through the phase of 'all religions are just a single search for the One True God'. However, it does show that travel carries its own special dangers to the spiritual health of the soul. Sometimes the border between reality and make-believe is very narrow with such characters as Gerry. He may now have stepped over that precious threshold."

"Yes," said Fr McCarthy, who was the only individual there who actually knew Gerry (the others got their information via Mary), "that has always been the trouble with him; he thinks too much and too deeply. I have always said that he has only got to sort out his marital problems . . . ."

He was interrupted brusquely by the bishop.

"It is not as simple as that," he asserted; "it is really the world-wide plot against the Church that we should be considering."

The bishop was on the extreme Conservative wing of the church; his utterances were considered notoriously extreme even by those on the political Far Right. He continued in a high tone:

"Every power and every institution in the world is working to undermine us. What others take for political, or military attacks on the US, we see as elaborate schemes to attack only Mother Church. What looks like a simply vexatious vote in Congress, or a seemingly harmless broad-ranging social scheme of the United Nations in an insignificant spot somewhere is always another turn of the screw by our enemy. Look at Japanese car imports. Quite clearly they are part of the plot against the Roman Catholic motor vehicle, especially those made in Italy and France, two standard bearers of Roman Catholicism in the past. It is no secret that Fiat's contribution to the Lada helped to bring down the Communist Empire. Do you know that even the viruses and bacteria of the most lethal types selectively choose our Catholic people in the Third World to wreak their havoc? I even have my suspicions about climatic and natural events . . .".

The Cardinal and Fr McCarthy were growing more and more restless as the bishop was talking, their eyes rolling up to heaven; they were accustomed to his ravings.

"We do not have to believe that everyone is against us," said the Cardinal, "but only some very powerful people and agencies."

"Correct," said Fr McCarthy.

"If only he hadn't stopped going to church in his younger days then we wouldn't have this problem. He can believe what he likes, what matters is that he is seen to return to the practice of his Faith. I am sure Hans, if he gets his chance, will see that he is received him back into full communion," said the bishop.

"Well, they say he has gone into hiding now; that he has even begun interfering in local politics," said Fr McCarthy; "but of course he may be only on one of his drinking sprees. I am sure that an offer of a good office job back here in Washington will persuade him to come home. Now, the church must not be too didactic, or dogmatic, with him, as he is not the sort of person who, psychologically, can take a high degree of pressure on these matters."

"The church can never be wrong," said the bishop loudly, "you know that we don't accept the findings of modern psychology and science. Even if we find our facts contradicted later as with, say, Copernicus and Galileo, we are still in the right as regards the *meaning* of the whole thing. The sun still orbits the earth and the planets still revolve around us, for all intents and purposes. Any fool can see that!"

President Hooligan was at last having his long-planned interview in the Oval Office with Dick Warner, de facto head of the CIA and other subsumed agencies. Initially Dick was very cool, calm and collected whereas Hooligan was somewhat tense, so severe was the reputation of Warner which had preceded him. Hooligan knew he was under scrutiny as much as Warner was and that Dick's assessment of him would count in the corridors of power. It was with some trepidation that he greeted him.

"You've been here before, haven't you?," said Hooligan with a forced grin.

"I have seen them come and I have seen them go," replied Warner coolly.

"Hopefully we can work together in a positive way, scratch my back and I'll scratch your's and all that," said the President hopefully.

But Warner was disappointed with Hooligan. More to the point was the matter of the presidency under Hooligan. Things had been beginning to slip a little. There had been an absence of decision-making and policy was in the doldrums. There seemed to be no real urgency backing Dick's Grand Plan for taking over the whole world (as distinct from just parts of it). He would mention Jaman now and the Supercoconut and all he would get in return would be a blank look, as if he (Hooligan) did not know what he was talking about. It was the same with all the other offices of state recently; the left hand did not know what the right hand was doing. Things were being left alone, as if whole policies would simply sort themselves out at the end of the day. Worse, the CIA was being treated just like any other government department. It was no longer seen as top dog in the new, practical Washington.

"What's this news I'm getting about some left-wing coup in Jaman? I thought the island was your specialty, Mr Warner?," said Hooligan, feeling quite uneducated about these matters.

"There has been a coup in Jaman. It caught everyone by surprise, even the CIA and government, apparently. The country is under the leadership of a strong left-wing general, just of the type that we hate. He has already banned all American products. Our people there have been kidnapped by left-wing terrorists. We may have to send in the marines in order to facilitate a very public 'rescue' operation and reinstate the previous government. I can assure you and the American people that I have everything under control there. I think I know what is going on."

Hooligan for his part could not help feeling disappointed with Warner. On seeing him enter the office he was astonished to see that he was not wearing the famous, fearful bow tie and insidious silk shirt but was attired instead in khaki and some sort of silly, bemedalled military uniform.

It was then as if all his imaginings and fantasy about Warner had been punctured like a balloon.

This experience was, surprisingly, one of disappointment, of loss. The man was no more than an office creep. There he had been worrying over whether he would be invited to play golf at the Langley links or attend the secret CIA briefings, hoping that he would be let in on the decision-making and the intimate proceedings, when the man was no more impressive than, the doorman. What had he been worrying about for so long? Who possessed the Nuclear button? Not Warner! It was he himself! He could blow up the world if he wanted to, not Warner! It was he who could demonstrate his power by ordering a nuclear strike on Jaman, as Warner had been lately urging him to do, and not Warner himself! He had never realised all this before, the answer to where all the POWER lay. It was he, Hooligan, who had his finger on the nuclear trigger!"

Dick, sensing that something was going badly wrong, pulled his last, desperate card.

"Could you sign this little bit of paper here which gives me joint control over our nuclear arsenal?," he asked in a patronising voice; "it will relieve you of a lot of worry."

Hooligan gave out a loud bellylaugh, such as he had not emitted for years. It was indeed like a big weight off his mind.

"Ha ha ho ho. There is no need for me to sign anything. Why should I listen to you? You are just an office minion, a fledgling tyrant, a nincompoop in some highly privileged office-job-for-life. You are a paper tiger, Warner; a threat only until someone stands up to you. You are a figment of the imagination; you don't really exist."

"You will rue this day," said Warner angrily.

"Oh go away Warner. I am recommending that you be replaced at the CIA, by Mr Gerry McArthur, currently furthering our American interests in Jaman. I hear from a most distinguished Cardinal of the church that he is a very reliable, even religious man. His wife I know well. She has told me all about you and how you played on poor Tom's personal weakness to subvert his position as director. She has always been very useful to me in handling the gossip on the Washington circuit."

Dick Warner did not know what to do or say so he clumsily stood up, feeling self-conscious now and wanting to get out of that room as quickly as possible. He managed to utter one statement through a scarcely-concealed sob:

"What will happen to policy now? It's going to be in the hands of the barbarians."

"It's no concern of your's. Go back to your office and your infantile fantasies and clear up. There is no place for you in the real world any longer."

And so it was that Dick Warner suddenly found himself powerless and inconsequential, sitting back in his office chair for one last time, wondering at what might have been, all his previous power now passing to some measly idealist; the formation of all future curriculum planning under the control of a simple, field operative. □

chapter
eleven

Gerry McArthur was now facing a major crisis in his life. His job had been put in jeopardy by his 'inappropriate attitudes' and abusive behaviour. He had gone to his bosses and insulted them by casting aspersions on their characters. He implicated many others, in the public as well as the private domain, in supposed political crimes.

He had been threatened with having his passport impounded and with the sack. His colleagues became wary of him, of being seen in his presence even, for fear of coming under the dark shadow of disapproval and suspicion themselves.

Gerry's heart and perspiration rates had risen alarmingly to dangerous levels, in what appeared to observers to be a continually bad hangover. His students had begun to notice a further deterioration in his lessons and some of them were expressing their disquietude aloud. They even went so far as to register, one Monday morning, their concern to Gerry's immediate superiors, taking themselves solemnly along to the Head office in a united, determined, petition-bearing delegation.

And to cap it all, he had gone on extended leave somewhere without informing anybody.

Meanwhile Gerry's own personal 'project' up in the hills was going well. He had written in his diary, which seemed now to have become public property, about how he had been fed up with the illusions and woolly thinking of academic circles in

Kingstown, Harvard and elsewhere and preferred to test his own ideas now in a situation remote from modern, artificial amenities, asserting that he was going to conduct a sort of educational experiment never tried or even imagined before, not even by the theoreticians of Harvard University in their most outlandish, champagne and petty rivalry-fuelled chatter at inter-departmental do's. His words exuded enthusiasm and zealotry, the diary being littered with many exclamation marks, vigorous underlinings and ticks on various pages. He had been especially looking forward to his role, as an objective observer, in detailing how the 'subjects' of the experiment reacted to being taken out of their surroundings and placed in an unfamiliar environment. He intended to go up there with 'the lads' in what he felt would be a mixture of educational project and tourist adventure trip, persuading a number of well-connected, powerful Jaman personages to come along also, to partake in the experience of the rustic lifestyle.

The area around their 'cell' was covered in thick forest and patchworks of different crops. The Cap had originally promised to bring samples of some of these plants to Gerry for the purpose of the latter's research, at the time, into a viable Jaman horticulture; for instance there was the marijuana plant on which, although illegal, the rural economy depended so much in certain areas; Gerry had wanted to discover whether there was a future for *Cannabis sativa* in the face of the challenge from the Supercoconut. The Colonel and The General had bundles of this plant drying all over the place. When offered some to sample Eddie and Stanley protested that they could not partake in what was an illegal product without giving scandal to the electorate, and refused to accept. The others lit up and inhaled of the Devil's Smoke, except Gerry, who was careful not to imbibe; (he claimed he never smoked, that he had observed, especially in Taran, cannabis's toxic effect on people with hidden guilt complexes, clouding their judgment and plunging

242

them into existentialist hell whilst their clear-eyed, guilt-free colleagues went more alertly and efficiently about their bloodcurdling military tasks and even in greater apparent safety after smoking the stuff).

The next day began as hot and humid as any other in that tropical montane forest region and McArthur felt privileged to be there taking in the beauty of the land, hearing the rustic sounds of ground and air and the simple wit of the people.

"What do you make of the government?," Gerry asked them a few hours later during one of their seminars. He did not address the question to anyone in particular but threw it out to all.

"There his no government up here. We hare the government," said The General adamantly, her words spouted with great fervour and intensity.

"Dem people in Kingstown dat do try to interfere with us are hignorant. Dey never live in de country. What is his name, President Eddie, Big Eddie, big Fool man," said The General loudly and to emphasize her point she waved her machete in the air.

"Him a big fool altogether," said Eddie loudly, "me know him well. He run de country too long. Only since he long ago paid the workers more money; but he nuah do any good since, only help him relatives."

"True," said Stanley, "him a phony".

"Look at de prime minister," said Eddie interrupting, "him only prime minister because he is relative of de president. He has no talents or sense whatsoever. He is a waster who should be picking fruit for a living."

"True," they all went and even Stanley was forced to agree.

"True," he said quietly, "de prime minister bad too."

It was amazing, thought Gerry, how honest people could be when their backs are up against the wall. Not a month of Question Times in parliament could have elicited such truths.

"When we get rid of the government, then we will see progress," said Erico Mauris joining in, "and I know what I would do if I was prime minister. I would put a stop to all this political in-fighting, backbiting and gossiping that goes on in political circles whilst ignoring the legitimate cries of the poor for justice and equality. If I was in power I would see to it that the country was run by professionals, not by greedy amateurs and egoists as it is now. I would see to it that there was no distinction between town and country. Everybody high and low would receive my considered attention."

"That," said Gerry emphatically, "is what democracy and progress is all about."

They were all fed badly-cooked bush food and no one dared to make any remarks on the quality of the meal. There was an unspoken feeling that they were feeding on some common lizard or snake-like creature and the herbs they were drinking were probably narcotic. Yet they all felt that they were on some mysterious adventure; that they were partaking in some sombre educational experience and that their own futures as well as that of the country would somehow be different after this. They did not resent their imprisonment but instead appreciated their uniquely open surroundings and the opportunity for free speech, away from all the social conventions of the city. They were as one in enjoying the novelty of the situation in which they found themselves; city people in the midst of a rural backdrop, politicians in an educational setting, disillusioned sophisticates in the presence of social illiterates, relatively rich people amongst the poor. They all had a great deal to learn, and the idea that their lives might be in possible danger did not occur to them, at least not immediately. They saw their 'captors' as tour guides, their interrogators (there were a lot of question-and-answer sessions) as educationalists and their judges as friends.

At least for the moment.

Maria Gomez was having, or pretending she was having, trouble with some of the material, especially the big, cumbersome words that always seemed to graft themselves on to these kind of educational topics. Not only was she having difficulty in saying 'comprehension' and 'punctuation' but she was displaying a considerable degree of (pretended?) embarrassment in attempting to do so. She was making a great show of cooperating with Gerry but, it seemed, had still to overcome some difficulty in hiding her high-brow, academic credentials. There was something false about her forced bad pronunciation of the big words. She sat beside Eddie, holding his hands as he helped her with some of the more difficult terms. Gerry almost despaired of Maria ever even getting to Basic Level Stage One, and he wondered about her previous 'career' as a top government economics adviser. But he had known of other talented specialists who were unusually ignorant in some of the more down-to-earth skills of everyday life.

She was clearly involved in an elaborate subterfuge here. It was a clever put-up; she had probably also reasoned that her life now depended on concealment of her real talents. He, nevertheless, still felt irritated by her futile 'learning' efforts, as no matter how many times a word was repeated she never recognised it on any further occasion.

The Cap, Captain Sher came in accompanied by a soldier whom Gerry immediately recognised as Turbo the taxidriver. They had bundles of a vegetable commodity and were highly enthused. They placed the plants at one side and Turbo spoke in the precise manner of a senior army officer:

"It is with great pleasure and also an honour that we have yo all here today as hour guests and to see how we get de t'ing done. For many years we have been in control of hall de herb that come down from de hills. It is a valuable product dat we mus' see does not get into de hands of de wrong people. De simple farmers have no huse for it and dey get good dollars for their hard work; we pass hon to Big Man McCall in Mobby Bay an den he do what he likes wid it. It is jus' a useless, foolish herb dat grow easily. When Mr Gerry come it like de Bigger Man come an' we delighted to show him how we do things an' now he sees for himself all we do up 'ere. Dis is de backbone of de hoperation an' widout The Colonel and The General nobody get nothing. We hare de boss of de whole show. Yo are bound to secrecy hon all dat yo see an' hear in dis place."

Everybody nodded their heads in agreement that they would keep their mouths shut in the future.

Captain Sher spoke next:

"We tell de new government dat we hold you up here as our guests. We say dat we kill you all if dey come find hus. Not true, but dat is what we tell dem! But you not fear, we are your friends! True friends! Here, have a drink of de fine bush tea; it do you insides much good. You can all have a Sing-Song if you wish; show heverybody how happy you are. You mus' stay here some more days, until de new government see sense an' do what we tell dem."

Light applause from those present followed for a few moments. They all felt a little more at ease with these words from the commander; they had been worrying somewhat over the fact that they were not free, for instance to leave, or even to wander where they liked or go searching for fruits further away in the trees. They were enjoined to do their pacing around in the immediate vicinity of the house. They had the impression that they would be tolerated only as long as they stayed put and carried on with their lessons. They were not expected to ask any questions either, except those that related to the seminars that were now becoming almost oppressive in their tedium. Nor did they know how exactly to take Gerry. In one way he was just like them, appearing unwilling and discomfited to be here at the mercy of their 'captors'. In other ways he seemed to be at one with the military people, happily carrying out their orders for the arrangements of each day the various leisure activities such as settling washing times for each in the waters of the river, or employing bamboo pods to try and catch the jack fish, something at which none of them had any success but which Eddie in particular seemed to enjoy; looking at times as if he was getting more out of this adventure than anybody else.

Gerry himself, meanwhile, was deep in thought.

He was, he realised, going through what could only be termed as a religious crisis.

He was watching, with an appreciative audience, Erico bowl at Eddie a small ball which they found somewhere about the place, in an impromptu game of cricket. Bored with the game, he began to reflect that lately he had been feeling compelled to reconsider his thoughts about the Great Issues of life and whether or not there was a God. The last time he had gone through this ordeal, which was quite painful, was in Taran when he had faced death on many occasions. His mind went back now, like a rifle shot, to one memorable scene outside the Happy Bar in Wrong Way City where he had been monitoring guerrilla movements with the help of a female native guide (apparently the Freedom Fighters came to town occasionally to taste the delights that such bars had to offer, and where they would mix happily with American personnel). Suddenly a lorry pulled up with the 'enemy' firing out at them all at once and he and everyone hit the dirt. He was definitely injured, he thought, and probably heading for the next life, if there was one. He would be in serious trouble, soul-wise, he realised, if he was called to eternal account now, as the lady he was in the company of was not a person of chaste virtue and he had been enjoying somewhat her playacting. Was there a God or was there not; was He an Intelligent Being or just an amorphous mass of powerful molecules; did He take an interest in the interminable feuds on earth or was He completely in the dark about human matters? His answer came, or seemed to come, in an amazing stroke of luck, as the shooting suddenly stopped when the military police arrived on the scene and the 'enemy' drove away. Although the place and everything in it had been shot up he was, it transpired, completely unscathed. That 'hit' he imagined he had received had been nothing at all. As he stood up and shook the dust off himself he looked around and saw that everyone else lay dead. It was a remarkable scene, as bodies lay drooped all about the place, hanging out windows and doors and on the pavement; one was even hanging from the ceiling fan, still revolving. He felt guilty, as if it was his own fault that he, too, did not lie dead, or at least badly injured. Somehow or other it all made him into some kind of accomplice with the enemy. He blushed guiltily when the police looked at him. And yet an eternal question had been somehow answered, he had been spared, yet again, by a kindly God.

There was no other answer to account for his many miraculous escapes.

There was no mistaking the attitude to him in the Forces either; it veered between being totally scathing and totally respectful, like the respect one has for a madman, or a shaman. A kind of awe. All the men had it for him, superiors as well as the drafted personnel. It made him stand out, like a freak in some sordid show, this dicing with death. And yet he would have questions for this benevolent God. Why were his more worthy companions not spared? Why did he have to suffer those long periods of fear as the shooting went on around him so he could feel their wounds himself and might even 'die' many times, and yet the ultimate release of real death would always be withheld from him? And he had entered yet again into that dark period of religious scruples when he felt in his innermost being that there was no benevolent God, no Paradise for the slain. Life, it seemed, only ended in unanswered questions, and the body in some inappropriate container. He felt desolate; the ministrations of the padres were a sick joke and there was no comfort to be found in human companionship, for that too, especially with the likes of McCall around, was as dodgy as life. It was a gloomy time. He carried on long, interior, imaginary monologues with the gurus of mankind, from the biblical prophets to the eastern pundits of meditation, conducting long, involved debates with himself. Sometimes he would be heard, whilst alone, talking out loud. When he was sent for a compulsory medical and told that meditation on metaphysical issues was simply a sign of an untreatable, obsessive illness, unacceptable in a military unit, he laughingly dismissed the psychiatrist's ineffectualness with disdain. He had hurled abuse at him and his profession and walked away with a sense of covert victory over the forces of superstition and obscurantism.

These preoccupations now returned to him and he found that he was going through the same tribulations again, up here, just when, paradoxically, his life's greatest achievement was apparently taking place! His major problem was with the question of the validity of a Superior Being (or more correctly, Being Itself or Being As A Supernatural Being). It also seemed that his preoccupation with Being As A Supernatural Being was somehow linked to the precariousness of his present position. But he could not see what the connection was. He felt that if he could crack that one all would be solved.

There was no doubt but that he had hoodwinked these people here into thinking he was something he wasn't. In trying to be true to himself he was being false.

It was time he faced up to the truth about himself. His talk of Tourist Ventures Into The Interior and In-depth Third World Education had led him into a situation which he felt he could no longer completely control. Oh indeed, his general idea had been that with the experience of an alternative government in Kingstown led by Rabid and Umberto, as they began utilising anti-Americanism as a way to ingratiate themselves with the mob, and began making serious mistakes, the people would soon begin to see the good points of the old crowd and invite them back with great joy and celebration. He would have defeated Warner, the Supercoconut and the Anarchic Opposition who had infiltrated the supposed Official Opposition, all in one go. He consoled himself with this scenario now at his moment of self-doubt which, again paradoxically, was growing stronger as rapidly as even his masterplan seemed to be heading for a pre-eminent, worldly success. The thing was:

He was on the verge of having to make a decision about his spiritual future.

He could, if he wished, bring about the total destruction of the Jaman government and all the characters here present. Even up here in the forest it was possible for him to manufacture a satisfactory bomb, thanks to all those useful lessons long ago, he mused! But it was not his way anymore. He had been misled into accepting violent solutions as long ago as his shooting of Lieutenant Colonel O'Hagan. Now he realised that had been a victim of very poor training. In any case they were all just jokers here, each in his or her own way; they had meant no real harm to anybody. No, he would never kill again. He had a very quick word with Paulo ('quick' because he didn't want people to notice he was on familiar terms with any of the captors); and told him that indeed all power was now within his (Paulo's) reach but that he would, if he was not careful, end up being no better than any of them in the long, if not in the short, run.

Even the new government wasn't going to last for long; he had been listening to a transistor radio he had concealed in the roof and their star was dropping already. They were making exactly the mistakes that he thought they would. They had made an open enemy of the USA; a bad thing to do and it didn't say much for their chances of survival. The way ahead now was for him, Paulo, to persuade The Cap and the others to bring back Eddie and Co. to Kingstown at the right moment and have himself made into a national hero. The president and prime minister were changed individuals now anyway, and they had learned some very hard lessons about the country and its down-to-earth inhabitants. He should try and have himself appointed as Professor of Literature at the university; it was the safest and most secure job in the country. Paulo agreed; he said he would never forget Gerry's friendship, and when he was Professor of English Literature he would aim for that grammatical reform of the language that they had often discussed, emphasizing to his future students that such reform was indeed within the power of the masses and they need not bother any more about 'speaking correctly' or worry about failing exams simply because they had not mastered the freemasonry of catch-all, imperialist-imposed grammatical rules.

"I'll have a word with The Cap about bringing our party back down to Kingstown as soon as possible," continued Paulo, "there has been a bit of a problem with Alfredo and the others though; they are wanting to use their guns. But The Cap is happy now that he will certainly be the new Mr Big, having proved his credentials by kidnapping the whole government and taking control of the farms up here. Your Mr McCall had better watch out!"

They were suddenly interrupted by the sound of gunfire, loud cries and shouting. Gerry's heart dropped down to his pants and Paulo looked bemused as they both took cover behind a banyan tree. Apparently, they found out later, the firefight had broken out between Alfredo's happy band of 'soldiers' and gunmen from another, rival farm who had come over to see what they could rob. The interlopers were astonished to meet with such staunch opposition, their terrorizing of that neighbourhood having previously gone unopposed for years. They proved to have a 'yellow streak' however and after losing their leader and his main henchmen, who had made the mistake of flaunting themselves up front, expecting to have to face nothing greater than pathetic pleas for mercy, they fled away into the forest and indeed never showed up in the vicinity again. The Colonel and The General had joined in the attack, and at long last The General had got a chance to use her machete.

Goodbyes when they came were emotional. They had heard the news that large crowds in Kingstown were demanding the return of President Eddie. Umberto and Rabid had gone into exile in China. Paulo was now giving the orders, explaining to everybody what was what and why this and that was happening. Never in his most far-fetched story-telling could he have imagined a more satisfactory, fulfilling and powerful conclusion to all his dreaming.

Erico was behaving very humbly, for as Minister of Information he should have had some inkling of recent events, but he had been more surprised than anyone else by the various twists and turns of fate. He knew now that his information sources had proved pretty useless and even Stanley was looking at him with disdain, still remembering the 'homosexual' slur. Erico wondered if a change of government post for himself would be the solution. Making sure that Eddie and Stanley were within hearing shot, he said to the two patriarchs of the humble cabin as they were leaving:

"I would advise you to put in for a home-improvement grant with the Ministry of Housing. I promise you that when I get back to Kingstown I will personally see to it that your application is successful."

The Colonel and The General stared at him with gratitude; whatever he meant by those words, and they did not understand their meaning, he had proven himself a true friend of the people up here, promising them all manner of things should his life be spared; he could quite understand if they had to kill the others, he had said. It would be wonderful to have a friend in high places, they now thought. Tears flowed down their faces as they waved goodbye, The General still tightly clutching her blood-stained machete.

Turbo came over to Gerry:

"Me ged me taxi so now me tek you up to de monastery. You safe there. Dey tell me dat new man in your teaching job an' they clear out your room. A word in yore ear. De president an' prime minister are grateful for your educational services but dey wan' yo hout of de county now. Dey think it unhealthy for de country dat you stay around. I hear Erico plan at night to kill you. It wrong, but they say you know too much 'bout them. Don't say a word now. Come wid me to the next poncianna tree round hill where de car a hide."

Gerry was not surprised by all of this. He had already heard, via Delroy who had been keeping a very low profile in all of this and was trying now to ingratiate himself with Gerry because he was on such obviously good terms with the guerrillas, of another plot to lure him back to the USA, most likely by the 'inside CIA'. Apparently there was a (possibly phony) offer of a top political post in the pipeline. It was all par for the course. He needed to get away for a while to think about it all.

Sure enough, there was the old reliable Austin Cambridge parked under the tree, but sporting a new, khaki colour which was a good camouflage in that forested region.

"Dat yore Austin, Turbo?," he asked, impressed at how such a vehicle had managed to make its way this far up the mountains, and speaking in the Jaman accent that he had now, it seemed, acquired quite naturally.

"Me giv' it a new lick of paint for dis operation. It run all de supplies hup here. But me think that de hengine need more hoil. Dere no oil so me put in coconut juice. We go now."

Gerry discovered that there were already three women and one man in the car, along with a few chickens, a large canvas sack filled with what looked like marijuana, and a kid goat. He sat between two of the ladies, who were very large. He felt his bones being squeezed between their bones. To his surprise they were pushed to the track by Turbo who then jumped in and they set off down the rough, boulder-strewn mountain track at a good speed, no attempt having being made to start the engine.

"Watch this," said Turbo happily, "we go thirty miles wid no engine."

They cruised silently down the hill, still maintaining top speed.

"The radio says a tropical storm is coming, it's getting very blustery," said Gerry with concern, observing the rain coming down as a darkness fell over the land and the tree tops began to dance drunkenly in the rising wind.

"Yea man," said Turbo with little concern. He was a driver totally identified with his vehicle; once he was behind the wheel he was like a lover bonded to a woman; he was in total control of his universe.

They made three stops in the next twenty minutes, picking up more men and women with their children and their farm produce so that Gerry wondered how they had all managed to squeeze in. But this they did with no effort.

"Hold tight Gerry man," said Turbo, "we have go through forest, river, cliff, swamp, and volcano 'fore we reach de monastery. It a long journey but we speed hup."

He let the car hurtle down the incline without any application of brakes and they gathered speed as the storm, which had now, according to the excited announcer on Gerry's radio, developed into a full hurricane, reached full pitch and they raced into their first overblown river. They got across the swirling waters of the ford by sheer force of speed and weight, Gerry estimated. Up and down valleys they went, the engine being brought into use only whenever it was a matter of going uphill. The storm did not seem to bother anyone in the car and so he did not dwell too much on it; it was the sheer drop at the side of the tracks that troubled him, looking down at a thousand feet of slope face which, at bends, saw the side of the car going right to the edge. At odd moments they came across fallen trees across their path, and then came the landslides. The car seemed to negotiate these without any problem. The noise of the storm now was so loud that it even drowned out the talking and laughing amongst the passengers. Turbo commented that he had been driving his Austin Cambridge through the earthquake when it hit Kingstown twenty years ago in 19 something.

"It was a new car den, only ten years hold. The road crack and we jump hit like a racehorse. Then de houses came crashing down on hus but we got through."

"It's a smashing piece of technology," said Gerry, impressed.

"An' it still have de same tyres from de first day," Turbo boasted.

Through the long night they drove, and the hurricane eventually moved away and Turbo said that it was only the swamp and the hot lava from the erupting volcano left now.

"Soon be there, Gerry," he said with confidence, "and den me tek dese people down to Kingstown. Be there in two days."

As the light of dawn appeared, showing up the storm damaged crops, vegetation and houses on all sides, the strange sight of the long-armed trees and bushes of the mangrove swamp came into view, a mist now beginning to rise from its fetid surface and the local vultures known as John Crow filling the sky, hovering around either looking for something dead or waiting for something to die. They saw a well-dressed Indian gentleman, who looked extremely impatient and business-like, waving them down from the side of the track and Gerry had a bad feeling at once about taking this man on board. The man's face had a very strict, superior expression.

"Get in man, plenty of room," said Turbo, commenting, "we don't pick up too much passengers today; mus' be de hurricane."

They negotiated the swamp, and Gerry noticed that even Turbo was quiet now, concentrating on the task at hand and taking no unnecessary risks. It did not take long for the Indian gentleman to get going, however.

"I am Mr Michel Prayag from Indian Town. I have a very important meeting to attend in Kingstown, for which I must not be late. Can you not drive a bit faster, driver?"

"Me go as fast as me like," said Turbo, annoyed.

"You speak like an ignorant man. I would not be seen in this car if my own wasn't getting its regular service. This vehicle should be off the road!"

"What yore car den? A sick donkey?", was Turbo's reply and he gave a loud, sarcastic laugh.

"It's a Volvo. I am insulted to be in this load of rubbish. I am a humiliated man that I had to take a ride in a broken-down old crock! Get yourself a new door man; this one keeps opening. It's not safe! I will fall out! Lord save me!"

"Yo have de biggest honour in de world to be in me car. I would not exchange dis car for your Volvo, your house, all yore money and yore wife as well; but she is a mad woman who sell herself to hall her neighbours when you are not looking. She at it now."

"Dis car," said Michel Prayag calmly, "smell of dog urine and the madmen come in it at night to shit and sleep. It famous in the island as The Taxi Shit House."

He was still trying to keep his calm, although his more exact English had deteriorated somewhat.

"Yore Volvo," said Turbo, "is Obeah car and next time you an' yore family go in it will be last time when it crash and yo all dead."

"Shad up," said Mr Prayag glumly.

There was silence for a time.

They came out of the swamp and entered the country of Mt Dragon, where smoke and sometimes lava from a continually erupting volcano were the expected hazards. This time they did come across only a small river of lava and Turbo was able to drive straight through it.

"De trick is to go fast in it," he said contentedly.

The ash that settled on their windows obscured the view somewhat but eventually they came to a fork in the track.

"Dis way de Monastery, dat way Kingstown," said Turbo; "de Holy Men only ten kilometres away."

"Look Turbo, let me out. Me walk," then you can get down to Kingstown quicker," said Gerry.

"No, man, it not safe to walk here. Me tek yo."

"No, Turbo, I want to walk. I want time to meself. I want to walk along in peace and quiet. I want to pray."

The car pulled up and Gerry got out. He took all the cash that he possessed out of his pocket and gave Turbo the hundred dollars.

"Bye, Turbo and thanks. That's the last of my worldly wealth."

Turbo gave him a queer look and said:

"Till next time, Mr Gerry, be careful."

The car sped off with Turbo giving five long beeps of the horn. There was a massive amount of smoke coming out of the exhaust. □

chapter
twelve

Some small children followed Gerry along the track begging him 'ten cent' and he sadly informed them, 'no money'. Now he was also a lying, miserly old codger in their eyes, as well as everything else, he ruminated. How difficult to explain to them that not all wealth came in the form of cash. He remembered all his pointless economics lessons, and of how he and his associates had tried to establish new economic fashions in the face of endemic stagnation and exploitation. What did it all mean now; what did theory or politics mean to them here in the backwoods?

"Big road up ahead," he was informed by one of the children; they were still clinging to him in the hope of a miracle that might somehow resemble that of The Feeding Of The Five Thousand. They eventually left him alone to his thoughts, and went off about their affairs not realising that they had just had the extraordinary grace of having accompanied a pilgrim on part of what was the final stage of his spiritual journey to a hopefully provident, eternal destiny.

The heat of the sun in the already drying countryside was like the grace of nature's benediction on his head and he felt himself involuntarily remembering all the religious rituals of his childhood, memories coming incomprehensibly back now in middle age to haunt and remind him that there had been some kind of faith in a better, spiritual world long ago, an innocent, humble attitude on the part of some human beings who were probably not very different from himself. He thought now that their dogmas were not any more ridiculous than all the other strange religions that he had come across in the world; the bloody, sexual and yet saving myths of the teeming masses in other, great foreign cultures and exotic lands, the strangely similar beliefs of other, less technically-advanced masses of humanity who also worked, ate, slept, dreamt and casually justified all that happened around themselves by means of their own inadequate, outlandish, even bizarre creeds. He felt he was a poorer person for being without such a belief. Hadn't he had enough of politics, sociology, politics, armed action, the Power Game and all the rest of it? It led to nowhere.

"Where are you, God?," he asked aloud now in 'prayer', experimenting to see if he would get an answer.

There was no answer, no thundering 'I am here, you blithering idiot', or 'Why have you been hiding from me?,' or even 'Do you know how many serious sins you have committed?.' There was only silence, broken by the bird songs and the wind in the trees of the natural world.

In front of him now was the wider, paved road along which the occasional truck or service vehicle on hurricane clean-up duty came speeding by. He did not feel safe any more for surely the government would have agents out for his arrest, or assassination, for having caused them so much embarrassment? He would certainly not be safe with members of Umberto's armed forces, and the police would probably want to question him about drug movements in various parts of the island. The sooner he was off this road the better and he now, in some fear, said a little prayer that another taxi or bus would come along the road, regardless of its physical or technical condition!

It was the first prayer he had said for at least twenty five years but he felt quite shameless at that moment, for his life, if not his honour, was at stake.

Some workmen passed him by, suspiciously and angrily eyeing him and for a moment he was sure that they were going to stop and harass him. They obviously had a more urgent mission elsewhere, and that had probably saved him. He felt the fear as the hairs rose at the back of his head and his neck muscles tightened.

After all that had happened, he had finally lost his nerve!

He now hid in the bushes every time he heard something, or someone, approaching. He was in fact spending more time in the bushes now than on the road, and progress was minimal; he was waiting for the blessed sanctuary of darkness and by now he must have said a hundred prayers. From his position behind a cherry tree he saw an army lorry, filled with armed soldiers, pass by and they appeared to be searching the vicinity for something or somebody. Later, a police car went past. Night fell and he cautiously took himself out on to the road and continued on his journey. In the clear moonlight it was possible to see ahead and a jump-into-a-ditch occurred whenever anything or anybody approached. At one point he took a detour to avoid what he was certain were some men searching for him in the distance.

He had to walk through a village whose houses had been badly shattered in the storm; people were still out trying to repair the damage as best they could and they paid little notice to the stranger walking cautiously by. He even offered his commiserations to one or two of them and was glad to receive, upon request, a free drink of water. For this small piece of charity he was immensely grateful, and he reflected on how the human virtues were, after all, quite important.

Another lesson in life and virtue he learnt along the way was humility. The humility of being protectionless, without the security of a job or money; having no home or convenient ease of transport; the strange feeling of being without a position of influence in a government agency or in any respectable power stratum of society. All he had was his gun. He now realised that this was more a danger than a source of consolation. By holding on to it he was not only being untrue to himself, but if he were caught with it, it would be used as a sufficient excuse to shoot him on the spot. Such instant justice was a regular occurrence with the police here. Better to trust in providence alone now, he thought, especially as he had no choice. If he threw the gun into the undergrowth and abandoned such weapons forever he would feel better for it. More virtuous. He put his hand in his pocket but there was no gun there.

Strange.

Could he have lost it somewhere along the way? Had it been stolen by his erstwhile companions? He looked at the pen which was what he had actually pulled out of his pocket. It, too, was of little use, especially as he no longer intended to keep a diary. He threw the pen with great force into the bushes. There went another old habit from his former life. He felt more free now. If only he could get to the sanctuary of the religious headquarters of the Jaman Church safely, he would be more happy than he had ever been in all his life.

At long last he came to a roadsign that made sense to him. It showed an arrow pointing straight ahead and said: The Monastery of The Lord 1 kilometre. It also said: Kingstown 1 kilometre with an arrow pointing the opposite way, but he put this down to some metaphysical confusion often found amongst isolated, rural residents. So he had travelled nine kilometres in three days; but in himself he felt he had travelled an incredibly greater distance in that time; an infinite distance in terms of thought and religious faith. God had arranged for him to get this far; he had survived again a treacherous journey.

It was getting towards dawn as he came into view of the huge settlement that made up the religious headquarters. He was astonished at its extent. He took a concealed position, lying down in tall grass overlooking the area. The monastery was a large modern building in the midst of many smaller houses and outhouses. Around the outer perimeter fence were the huts of local people, who probably offered their labour, or in some other way tried to squeeze a living from that impressive, clearly resourceful set-up in their locality. He now sensed that this place might be the key to everything that happened in the island.

He had previously observed that as he had got nearer to this place the wider and better-surfaced the road became. In the vicinity of the camp there was not one, or even two, but four different roads heading off around the vicinity like nobody's business and then leading away, it seemed, into the cul-de-sac of the forest. It had, here, all the self-sufficiency of an old plantation estate, even, from what he could see from his vantage point, with its own shop and hospital; a school too; perhaps it might be compared to a small town in one sense, a military barracks in another. He felt a slight shiver of apprehension. There were vans and cars busy around the monastery, some leaving and others entering along one of the mysterious forest roads. Gerry had read his history and knew of a tradition of advanced farming methods carried out on enclosed, secretive plantations going back to the days of slavery. He knew that these establishments could, in practice, be prisons of exploitation and torture as well as, in at least one or two instances, places of 'enlightenment'. He hoped now that the monastery was like the latter, although he was not feeling too optimistic on seeing a number of armed guards hanging around the entrance gate and along the perimeter fence.

A small aircraft flew low over his head and he buried his face in the weeds. He saw it land on a previously unnoticed airstrip inside the fence. A figure in clerical dress got out, being greeted obsequiously by three other clerics in lesser dress, who then began to chatter and point excitedly at another group of people gathered at the entrance of the monastery. Gerry tried to make

out the words on the large signpost at the entrance of the compound. It read, he decided after much straining of the eyes,
Peace And The Brotherhood Of Man.

This made him feel a little better, especially if those words represented the true philosophy of those behind the fence.

Well, this was it. He would walk in and declare his renewed belief in God. He would preach righteousness to the Nation of Zion. No matter if he was rejected as a false prophet. So had others, even the genuine ones. There was some kind of fuss going on in the grounds but Gerry paid no attention to this now as he slowly walked towards the gate. As he approached it he could see that there was further information inscribed in gold-script on the notice board. He read it with interest and then his mouth dropped open.

The Community of the Nation Of Zion in Association with the Society Of Jesus (Jesuits), making the single United Church Of Jaman. Leader Archbishop Orbeck, 2nd in command, Fr Hans, S.J.

Gerry knew at once, something told him, that this was the same Hans who had met him in Kingstown. He had sensed, even back then, that there was something fishy about the man.

When he turned to the gateman he produced a piece of paper from his pocket.

"This is a letter of introduction from a high church dignitary in America to Archbishop Orbeck. I believe the Archbishop is expecting me. I have sent ahead a message from Kingstown, conveyed by a member of your community, Alan, to His Reverend Excellency giving him notice of my impending visit."

The gateman studied the letter of introduction carefully, taking his time to turn it this way and that, upside down and sideways. He held the paper out in front of him, then high up in the air. He held it to the sunlight. He placed it on a flat stool and scrutinised it from a distance. Finally he held it to his nose and sniffed it.

"OK. You in."

As Gerry walked through the gate he sensed that there was an air of revolution about this place; there was a constant sense of activity. It was not what he had expected; he had imagined that it would be a quiet, meditative sort of institution with perhaps some native jollity and an extravagance of worship and, perhaps, loud speechmaking. He had even been prepared for the prevalent fashion of 'speaking in tongues' and 'being possessed by the Spirit'. But not this factory-style, highly orientated 'bee-hive'. Ahead of him he saw approaching a line of people, marching two abreast towards him and led by someone whom he vaguely knew.

It was Alan The One Who Keeps Quiet.

He appeared to be leading a delegation out of the monastery compound.

Alan recognised Gerry and gave him a wave of the hand, more a salute than a wave.

"Dey have abandoned the Righteous God. Dey have taken hup wid de Other God. An' dey hav' allowed church incense inste'd o' de holy ganga. We leave. Everything change. We go begin again' wid our own God. Our old God is our friend; this God is hour enemy"

There was great anger in his face, and his companions, mainly young though with a few old fogies amongst them, were also outraged. They marched out through the open gate, which was promptly shut after them.

A minor cleric came over to Gerry.

"It is not encouraged for strangers to come into our precincts withour prior invitation," he said curtly.

Such a typical officious type, thought Gerry. You meet them everywhere. He would soon have something to say to them about all that!

"God bless you," was all Gerry replied.

"I am afraid I will have to have you arrested," said the man crossly, "until we see what can be done about you."

"That's fine by me," said McArthur, thinking that it would be better to discuss his business with somebody else anyway. He would be wasting his words on this mini-martinet. Why, wondered Gerry idly, hadn't he rebelled with the others? Of course that sort never do. He had probably been the one who had insisted on forcing the issue.

He was put in a very small room at the side of the actual monastery building itself; it was airless with only a small smoke-glass window through which everything was very hazy. The door, however, was not locked. He waited in here for two hours, and took the opportunity to go down on his knees and say some very long prayers. On one side was a spy hole, through which an eye would occasionally peer in.

At long last someone opened the door and he took this person to be a novice for he was very young; and then he suddenly realised that it was not a male person at all but a young girl, dressed in the livery that appeared to be common to them all here; a black gown with a white inlay and a little round badge on the lapel made up of the colours yellow, black, green and red surrounded by a white circle of peace. He ... she said:

"Come with me, sir," quite respectfully.

"We have separate living quarters and we are called The Sisters Of The New Order", she said on his questioning her about her status.

He wondered if the sending of her to fetch him was some kind of calculated insult; he would have to study the internal work-allocation of the organisation to find an answer to that. They went inside the monastery and he was put in a meeting room, sparsely furnished with only a long table and plain, wooden stools. He waited there alone for another hour. Then Archbishop Orbeck strode in. He greeted Gerry in a formal manner, a weak smile and a limp handshake.

"I believe you have a letter for me?," he said in a gruff voice; the kind that is usually very good at chanting and singing.

"I have here a note of introduction from Cardinal Rice in America. I believe he sends his filial and cordial greetings to you and requests that I be given safe passage."

The Archbishop, who sat at the top of the table, opened the sealed envelope and read out the contents.

'Fraternal Greetings, Dear Brother in the Lord,

I am conveying to you cordial greetings and intimate friendship. I am forwarding in the strictest confidence the offer of a Cardinalature in the Roman Catholic Church, by means of the unofficial channel who presents this letter. He is a man who comes from the best religious background, being descended from an ancient nation that has seen the planting and spreading of the message from the earliest times, and his own family are above reproach. In view of the political amalgamation of the political world and the insidious assault on religion by secular society, it is our aim to unite under the Apostolic Succession the Greek, Coptic, various other Eastern Rites and your good selves. As soon as we sort out an agreement on the nationality of the Lord, which seems to be the main issue that divides us, we will be true brothers in the Faith. It is my suggestion that we establish a joint committee to work on this question. I do realise that any association with us may be interpreted by some of your members as an act of treachery and blasphemy, but if you do take this attitude please do not take it out on the bearer of this letter, by means of cruel ritual murder, burning at the stake, guillotine, removal of the heart, human sacrifice or whatever it is you practice in such situations.

Signed: Cardinal Rice, Overseer of Ecumenical Relations USA. ✸'

"Ah, how times have changed," sighed Archbishop Orbeck; "we have already seen the light and now possess unique wisdom, thanks partially to our Jesuit brothers, that we deeply wish to see spread to our less fortunate brethren in Rome, Constantinople, Canterbury and elsewhere. Soon we will be sending our missionaries over there."

"Have you met Fr Hans?", asked the Archbishop.

"Who?," replied Gerry, pretending that he had not heard the name before.

"He is a most charismatic person. Single-handedly he has curbed heresy within our community and shown us the way to truly practice the word of God as stated in the Bible. By means of his preaching alone he has revitalised all our spiritual lives."

"I think I may owe my life to the Jesuits," thought Gerry to himself.

"How do you practice your faith?," he asked inquisitively.

"We are helping the farmers to plant and market their products in a large co-operative community. We are by-passing the middle men and setting up Direct Trade Outlets around the world. We are establishing a state within a state where only the welfare of the people will matter. At the moment we need to arm and defend ourselves against our enemies, for there are still potential slave drivers in the world. But in time there will be no need for guns, physical force or even cannabis growing, which we are slowing weaning the farmers away from. We have formed an order of sisters, under the leadership of Sister Josephine. It is a revolutionary idea for sisters and brothers to live and work together in one community. The Cardinal's letter is superfluous; we do not need titles or high appointments now, for each individual is a king or a queen here in their own right. My own designation as Archbishop is under re-appraisal at the moment. I have told Fr Hans I want to be known only as Saint Justin Orbeck"

Well, thought Gerry to himself, they said that the Pope had lost control of the Jesuits. What were they really up to here? They would certainly have their job cut out to reform this pompous Orbeck fellow.

"I have wanted to come to the monastery for some time. I humbly request your permission to address your community. I want to speak on the dangers of insidious forces that are manipulating Jaman society. I want to speak of one great danger in particular that is facing your religious community."

"Oh," said the Archbishop, "what is that?"

"You will soon learn of it."

"I will discuss your request with Fr Hans. I must go now; I have another meeting."

"Can I have a drink of water please?"

"Get it in the kitchen. I'm off."

Gerry found the kitchen after enquiring from a helpful sister who was busy about her own affairs washing the clothes and when he went inside he quenched his raging thirst with some cool, crystal clear water. What a relief! As nobody was offering him food or any hospitality he helped himself now to the fare he saw lying around the place. He ate hungrily and somewhat guiltily, hoping nobody would see him. It seemed as if the fact that he was now actually within the compound, and had passed his interview with Orbeck, meant that he had a measure of freedom to walk about the place. He would probably be able to find a little corner with a bed somewhere now, and have a nice sleep.

But it was not to be. A messenger came to him and said that Fr Hans was now ready to see him. He was waiting in his private office and would Mr McArthur come immediately? Gerry followed the man along a pathway at the side of the monastery main building to a small hut in the middle of an empty space, as if it was in the middle of no-man's-land. The monk knocked and gestured to Gerry to go in.

There was the same Hans whom Gerry had met in Kingstown, sitting at a desk in what was really a tidy, efficient-looking office. He left his seat and greeted Gerry with a warm handshake.

"Nice to see you again, Geerry," he said with a smile.

"What are you doing here, Hans?"

"I am a preest of the Roman Catholic Church. Deed you not know that? I never denied eet."

"I thought you were a Mafia member."

"As new style missionaries, we must infiltrate into every activity een society. Eet ees the only way to convert the world. We must earn the respect of the world. But the most important conversion ees that of yourself. I see that you have gone back to saying your prayers."

"I am learning of the unpredictability of life, and the paradoxical possibility that there is a type of Providence after all."

"Providence has brought you here. The choirs are singing in Heaven today. The Church is a stronger Community of Saints for your conversion. I have watched you on your path of progress here in Jaman. It is good that you have given up your old way of life and your unsatisfactory job. Those are material accruements that we can shed without any damage to our immortal souls. Well done."

"It was not all entirely voluntary, Fr Hans."

"Providence."

"Have you heard about my recent exploits? I saved, on one occasion, at least fifty people from being mowed down by the cops in Kingstown. I have undermined much insidious US policy here and have directed a reformation in the Jaman government. I have profoundly influenced the educational system of the country for the better. I have even been hearing a rumour that they want me back in Washington now to take up a post as Director of the CIA. But best of all, I have found that I don't want to be Director of the CIA, a head of department, or anything."

There was an air of desperation about these claims, as if Gerry was frantically clinging to the last remnants of self-respect.

"Ah, Gerry, the truth is, you may theenk that you have done many great things, but in reality you have done nothing. You have achieved nothing. Your imagined, greatest exploits are empty dreams, illusions, perhaps fantasies. You have suffered from the delusion of all straying souls, that of imagined reality. Theese things are useless," said Hans softly.

The words hit Gerry like hammer blows, for he knew that they were true.

Hans looked at Gerry with a sad expression, and then continued to speak, almost as a master to a pupil.

"Those supposed exploits give you a temporary uplift, a fleeting sense of self-eemportance. Then you feel empty again, and more unsatisfied than ever before. As you have found, your heart aches for sometheeng eeternal."

"True enough," agreed Gerry; "but where does all that leave you with your worldly enterprise here, protected by guns and methods that would be familiar to our old friend Machiavelli? And what about your bullying of a simple, harmless Third World cult that is only trying to give some sense of self-worth to downtrodden, brainwashed people?"

"Well, all this paraphernalia of a big business efficiently organising eets membership into a self-sufficient, self-govern-ing enterprise based on fair trade practices, reducing self-interest to a minimum and teaching self-reliance, ees all a facade. Eet ees there purely as a sop to the world; just a little show to eempress people, who at the moment can only be eempressed by childish endeavours. It has nothing to do with our real purpose, the capture of souls for the Lord, including your own good soul."

"Is that what life is really all about then?," asked Gerry in wonder.

"Of course. Eet has always been about that. In history. In culture. In everytheeng. As soon as they are sufficiently enlightened to see the real issues of life this whole thing will be dismantled and forgotten. All these politico-socio-economic innovations and experiments have happened before. We tried it een South America long ago. That too was disbanded. So, too, were the Jesuits, once, for that matter. It is all irrelevant."

"What about your destruction of the Jah religion? Isn't that a repetition of history too?"

"We keep what ees good and discard what ees bad in religions where we find them. The Jah Faith was no worse and no better than many others; in fact eet was much better for eet was at least based on parts of Scripture neglected by the church een the past. The only trouble ees, their Jah ees a False God."

Gerry began to feel that he had walked into a subtle trap. He would have to use all his expertise and mental resources to ensure that he was not only not manipulated here, but that he actually was able to escape should he wish to. He had a slight apprehension, based more on imaginary vistas than any real or obvious threat, that he was becoming a prisoner. He had come to find God; not to partake in some establishment experiment carried out by well-trained, perhaps even well-meaning, experts. There had been something final about his entry into the camp and the closure of the gate behind him. Hans seemed to know alot about him. Did he even know about *that* photograph? Still, he could not be held here forever by a church organisation bound by the vow of chastity, for he had a wife elsewhere.

For the first time in his life, now, he thought of Mary in positive terms.

"I feel privileged to be here," he lied, "and it is my wish to get to know the members of the community and perhaps share a few ideas with them."

"Our person-in-charge, Wilbur Orbeck, told me about your desire to addreess the community. What about?"

"I cannot say. For at that moment the words I need to utter will be given to me," said Gerry, quoting Scripture for the first time in his life and surprising even himself.

"I'm afraid that's not allowed. Some of our novices een particular are still very impressionable," Fr Hans said somewhat coldly, adding, "I want you to begin by teaching the groundwork of Spelling and Grammar to those of our membership who have missed out on a schooling. That would be a veery idealistic vocation for you."

"I can't stay here," said Gerry, beginning to panic and realising that he was now meeting his professional match, for perhaps the first time in his life;

"I'm married. I have a wife back in the States."

Fr Hans seemed to suddenly relax, in relief, as this statement. He leaned back, stretched his arms out wide and smiled as if at a secret, private joke.

"Now that ees another matter, Gerry. Your marriage has been a major source of embarrassment to the church. As you know, your Mary has for long being a member of the Washington circuit and she has always done her best for you and your career. Of late she has been pushing your candidature for a high level job. When informed by Fr McCarthy (I have been on the phone to Washington) of your conversion to the True Faith, though, she has been over the moon. Apparently she has also been shown a photograph of you in Taran. I don't know what was on eet or who brought eet out of a cupboard, but I suspect eet was of some compromising situation, and eet had the effect of her agreeing to you remaining here. She has finally agreed with Cardinal Rice to abjure all legal claims over you, which were canonically dubious een the first instance anyway. She has given her blessing to your staying heer, for she feels now that at last you will be safe and not be exposing yourself to all sorts of dangers een the world, especially heavy drinking."

"Have you any proof of that?," asked Gerry, feeling his links with the outside world becoming even more tenuous.

"She ees going to write to you, and I will let you have the letter when eet arrives," said Fr Hans in a factual voice; and then changing his tone completely to a more intimate, companionable refrain, added:

"You know, as regards that photograph, there ees nothing like full confession for the cleansing of the soul. It ees better than any narcotic, I can guarantee you. You have no more self-respect to hang on to now."

Gerry was gobsmacked.

"Go and wash yourself. You are exceedingly dirty. A brother weell shape up your hair; we are retaining hair locks but washing ees essential. We are, also, banning pork for the moment and there ees strict segregation of male and female living quarters, something that is giving us a beet of a problem at the moment. A General Confession will follow a little later, when you are ready."

"I can confess now," said Gerry humbly, co-operating; "to start with, I killed a man in Kingstown town, breaking the ninth commandment and justifying it as a hypocrite; and long ago I shot a man I shouldn't have ... ."

"No, not now. Examine your conscience first. And it was not the *ninth* commandment."

Gerry had worked out what he was going to do. He would gatecrash the weekly meeting that was due shortly to take place in the outdoor auditorium and take over the proceedings, in the process deliberately making a disgraceful show of himself. He would expose this place to be the hotbed of reaction that it was. He would ask, were they in touch with the true Jah, the true God, or only 'civilised' man's interpretation of Him? He would, hopefully, be thrown out, rejected from the novitiate, sent into the outer darkness.

But he would still have faith in *that* God, the One Who had saved his life many times over the years.

The next twenty four hours were spent by Gerry in a fruitless search for alcohol and cigarettes. He even forgot, or neglected, to say his prayers. He was wild with a deep desire to escape from the place. He slept out in the open, feeling the chill in the early morning hours and wishing, above all things, that he could be alone in the woods again. Then he said another long prayer and felt better again; even a kind of peace.

The weekly meeting was going on in the amphitheatre. He could hear the chanting, the bongo drums, the calling on 'Africa' and the 'Ancient Homeland' to provide Salvation and Repatriation from the dreaded Babylon. Incense was ascending to the skies and there was a most beautiful hymn, '*Jah A Lion*' being sung by a huge choir in the background. The sisters, dressed up in colourful ethnic dresses for the occasion, were part of the choir and their voices gave a sweet empathy to the proceedings that made Gerry hesitate for a moment in his intention to disrupt the show. Somehow these people *were* connected to God, he felt. And, strangely, when he thought about it now, what had originally been the formal chore of delivering an official message to Archbishop Orbeck had eventually ended up as a strange personal adventure; one of those turns of 'Providence' that had now led him into a situation that was, if not satisfactory, at least interesting. But, although he now trusted God, how could he trust those who were His so-called representatives here?

There was nothing for it, but to speak the Truth.

Inside the so-called auditorium there was an enthusiastic mood. The new Spiritual Directors, approved by their very own Archbishop Orbeck, had not turned out as oppressive as they had feared. They were encouraging the chanting, the singing, the playing of drums, the study of Scripture, the spreading of incense (even if it was of a novel, strange-smelling variety), the unique, deep, earthy inter-communal chatter about 'alienation of the barren earth' and the 'the uncanny, insistent permeation of Mother Earth into the unknown, unnamed, abandoned soul', and so on. They were glad for the stricter regulation of their day; but they worried about the now officially-declared delayed prospect of repatriation, as evidenced also by the apparent exodus-disclamatory, down-to-earth-projects that governed their life now, which involved getting up rather earlier in the morning and going to bed before they would wish to. It was hard, but hopefully it would not last for long and they would be able to revert to a more relaxed attitude to everyday life, just as in the old days. At the moment it was all a bit of learn this, learn that, *then* the inheritance of the earth will be your's!

They looked at the Original Human Being Dance Troupe on the stage. It was the prelude to the entrance of Archbishop Orbeck who was now, everyone knew, about to announce his abdication as Head of the Church and hand over to the recently ordained (according to the new rites) Father Sang, and state his own re-dedication to the solitary, selfless pursuit of self-identification, also known as the meditation on the unknown 'I', the mysterious soul, a traditional task beloved of the universal, spiritual Diaspora, in a hermit's hut quite far out in the bush. Orbeck came on stage, bowing down before the young acolyte who was shaking smoke in his face as he walked backwards. The acolyte imagined a scene in which he was fending off a monster with this new incense, which he had not yet got used to; he had been told to strictly look on it as a symbolic cleansing and ascending of prayers to heaven; not as something valuable in its own right, and this he found hard to do. He was, in fact, under trial himself. He had been chosen for this task simply because he had been one of the doubters, one of those who had been tempted to join in the great Walk Out with Alan and the others over the issue of 'smoking'. Orbeck followed, or was led, by the incense-swinging monk to his seat in the centre of the stage. Fr Hans and Fr Sang were standing in the wings and Gerry, observing the scene from some steps further away, was reminded of the high church ceremonies of the pre-Conciliar Roman Catholic Church of his youth.

He strode in with a purposive fixing of his shoulders and head, as he had been taught in military training camp and reminding himself that aggressiveness was always the best policy in situations where one was outnumbered.

"Stop. In the Name of the True God, stop. Before you carry forward these changes, hear me voice. I cry hout in de wilderness. Me words dem heavy, dey weigh me down."

The audience did not know what to make of this middle-aged, hippie type (though his dress and hair style were now more like their own than an American's) speaker who, despite a faint American drawl, spoke just like them, standing there without fear on the stage interrupting the sacred proceedings. Yet they were unaccountably impressed by his words, as also by the manner of his delivery.

"Drive hout de false gods from amongst yo, an' do not listen to de voice of de heretics. De farming his huseless. De church his huseless. De chief priests hand scribes hare huseless. De civilisation rot. Dis place his han habomination hupon de hearth. Look at de Horbeck an' de Sang. Dey fancy dressed hup like birds of feather. Dey say dey de servants bud dey lord hit hover yo. Throw dem hout! hAn' de smoke! hIt smell hup de place! Yo no need smoke! Yo no need fences to keep de good hout an' de bad hin. Guns hare de devil's playtoy. Change de world! De True God his not like me nor yo. He dress like poor man an' harm Himself wid Love han' Peace. Love An' Peace, Brother an' Sister!"

At this Gerry fell down, took a small rock out of his pocket and threw it into the air in the direction of a large bell, which it hit; this was as a protest against idols as well as a gesture of abandonment of all worldly things. He then removed his clothing and knelt, naked, in prayer in the centre of the stage. When he had finished, he thought to himself that this, surely, would be enough to get him thrown out. He also felt a great elation that at long last, after a lifetime of what he now saw was pretense and vain ambition, he was being true to himself and to God. But instead of the expected escort to some private quarters and polite if firm eviction from the compound, he found that he was being applauded by the audience and that there was now a great singing and joy and emotion in the place.

He was given the black gown with a silent respect emitting from the monk who presented it to him. Even as he put it on he was asking himself if he really knew what was going on; was he in control of this situation; or had he finally been outsmarted?

No, he must get rid of these old habits of thought.

At least there was no prospect now of the Supercoconut being unleashed upon an unwitting country. They had triumphed, he and the church together, in what had been a joint effort, it seemed.

He went over to Sr Josephine's office, to discuss lessons for the novice sisters. After knocking he went in and got a shock. It was 'Jean Blue', the film actress he had admired, and chased, from afar. But then, he should be surprised by nothing now.

"I have kept away from you since you arrived," she explained, "as I, and Fr Hans, wanted to be sure about your vocation."

"How did you get involved here?," asked Gerry humbly.

"When I flew in to Jaman with you that day I was under a disguise. There is a great deal of suspicion about foreign missionaries here, as around the world, and as a sister of an American religious order I would have been watched in everything I did. As it was, by bringing in an empty trunk which was a very suspicious thing to do, I was immediately labelled as simply some kind of smuggler, most probably a drug smuggler and not a too bright one at that. It allayed suspicion. Sorry to have misled you. Now we can work together in a spiritual way, as a spiritual sister and brother."

Providence, thought Gerry to himself.

He went back, in the declining light, to his cell and took a sudden interest in who, or what, occupied the cell next door to his. He glanced in through the spyhole. To his now much diminished surprise he saw that the black garbed occupant was Jim McCall, deep in prayer and oblivious to his surroundings.

Gerry thought to himself, as he watched, from his cell door, the dusk-light departing, reminding himself also that tomorrow would be another day when the sun would appear again in all its old, familiar brightness and life would begin again, that at least he wouldn't have to face any dangerous flight out of the island for some time, in some dodgy old aircraft. □